VOYAGE TO THE END OF THE ROOM

FOR MY PARENTS

VOYAGE TO THE END OF THE ROOM

Tibor Fischer

Chatto & Windus
LONDON

Published by Chatto & Windus 2003

2 4 6 8 10 9 7 5 3 1

First published in Great Britain in 2003 by
Chatto & Windus
Random House, 20 Vauxhall Bridge Road,
London SW1V 2SA

Random House Australia (Pty) Limited
20 Alfred Street, Milsons Point, Sydney,
New South Wales 2061, Australia

Random House New Zealand Limited
18 Poland Road, Glenfield,
Auckland 10, New Zealand

Random House (Pty) Limited
Endulini, 5A Jubilee Road, Parktown 2193, South Africa

The Random House Group Limited Reg. No. 954009
www.randomhouse.co.uk

A CIP catalogue record for this book is available from the British Library

ISBN 0 7011 7333 5

Papers used by Random House are natural,
recyclable products made from wood grown in sustainable forests;
the manufacturing processes conform to the environmental
regulations of the country of origin

Printed and bound in Great Britain by
Mackays of Chatham PLC

HERE

THIS IS how I became rich: I was at home at four-thirty on a Friday afternoon.

Rich? Rich for many. Comfortable for some. Comfortably well-off I would say. By most standards. I own a flat which is more than adequate for one person, a space which, in many cities of the world (both the rougher and ritzier ones), would be judged excessive. I have a majestic study. I have two bedrooms, though the second one could be considered a bedroom only by estate agents, since if you were to put a bed in it, there really wouldn't be room for anything else. I have a reasonable lounge, a respectable kitchen and bathroom, and – here's a real extravagance – there's another would-be bathroom, containing a toilet and a tiny basin. The flat's split-level and the generous staircase adds to the sense of expanse. I always find walking up and down its chunky carpeting soothing. Being at the top of the house, the light's always good and the walls are old and solid enough to limit my neighbours' sonic invasions, and, as I'm two storeys up and muffled by trees (thoughtfully planted a hundred years ago and not yet entirely destroyed by the fumes and shenanigans of motorists), the din from the road doesn't reach me either. In the two weeks of sunshine that pass for summer in this country I have the luxury of a roof terrace and the chance to give some of my plants an outing.

I've often wondered why I'm so fond of plants; at first I thought it was a hankering for nature, the reassurance of green. Then I began to suspect plants are pets for those who are unsure about their ability to care for quadrupeds. When a plant expires you have a bout of guilt, but an aspidistra won't give you reproachful looks if you don't take it out, and you can't mourn a cactus. And how else can you get oxygen these days?

So, I have a lot of room. Many families have to make do with less. I have an excess of wardrobe space so all my clothes can be located at a glance. My disc storage is exemplary, and – here comes the embarrassing part – the small bedroom has become a shoe-stack, housing a hundred and nineteen pairs of shoes. This, I confess, is real indulgence, because I'm not a great one for going out and I generally pad around my flat barefoot. In my defence, I would like to point out I amassed them over a ten-year period and they are the way I like to reward myself for good performance. As vices go, fairly harmless.

Although my possessions and I enjoy an uncramped lifestyle, our location is not the most exclusive part of London: the communal garden in front of our block – a game tangle of green in a tundra of construction – attracts few birds (the pollution seems to have exterminated all of the flying fauna apart from the most disgusting pigeons) but many transients. Riots, gunplay, car-jacking, robbery, punch-ups, mattress-dumping, urinations – a quite comprehensive range of unpleasant activities are all observable from the comfort of my rattan armchair.

In the beginning I used to phone the police and it took me quite a while to understand that they didn't want to hear about any of this. Either they wouldn't turn up or they would saunter up forty minutes after the call, giving the most slothful transgressor plenty of time to make himself scarce. The solution to this problem is plain and simple, and it's interesting that the many ministers, politicians, civil servants and various layabouts of various bureaucracies who are well paid to solve these problems don't.

But here's the clincher.

I also own the flat underneath, on the first floor. Although not palatial, it's more than enough for one or two, should I ever decide to rent it out. It came up for sale during my first wave of affluence, and property after all is one of the best investments. No argument over that, as Ethiopian taxi-drivers, Albanian accordionists, Swedish dotcomers and molled-up Russian aluminium barons beat a path to London. Owning the flat underneath also removes the risk of disturbing anyone with late-night music.

There is more. Sickeningly, I also have money in the bank. High-interest account. Not a lot, but enough for a family to live on for a year or two, and of course, I'm still earning. Better ways of investing it exist, but, and I appreciate this sounds terrible, I'm not interested in money. I love spending it, but I can't bear racking my brains over investing it in some clever scheme. Deep down, I simply don't care. I don't enjoy leaving the money in the bank, because principally it rots there, and like everyone else I hate bankers (I love the old joke: What do you call a thousand bankers barbecued alive? A good start).

These days I don't spend much apart from the travel. On the clothes front, I'm ready for anything. Weddings, funerals, parties, interviews, seductions: I've got designer frocks, prepped and in cellophane. Embarrassingly expensive lingerie is untouched in its packaging. My wardrobe doesn't get much wear and tear because as I work at home, my pyjamas and very old tracksuits take the strain.

As for music, I already have more than I can cope with.

My flat isn't enormous, but I have thousands of slaves to do my bidding. I have Lithuanian pianists, Korean violinists, Icelandic tenors, Dutch divas, American harpsichordists, Senegalese cellists, Balinese drummers, slaves living and dead, of almost every nation to play music for me. I can make them play again and again, louder or quieter.

The choice every time I want to listen to some music is almost tiresome. The first stage of choice is easy: up, down or hanging around. Then it's a question, if you want to go up or down, how far up or down you want to go. If you're glum, is it the sort of glumness that you want to ornament with another layer of dejection? Or is it a vexatious misery you want to dispel? Or, if you're elated, do you want to be driven into a frenzy? Guessing what sort of music you want to listen to can be exhausting, but on occasion getting it wrong can be surprisingly pleasant.

Finally, how much music can you listen to? Working at home means I can listen a lot more than the average officenik, but I have over five hundred discs that represent fifteen years of collecting, of birthday presents, of Christmas presents, of I-would-like-to-take-your-clothes-off presents. If you listened for twelve hours a day, every day, that would be six weeks without repetition; and a lot of music, usually the more rewarding, requires half a dozen plays before you begin to get a grip on it. The great pieces you can listen to dozens of times, naturally, with the enjoyment growing and changing all the while. I've concluded it would be profligate to buy any more since I have every field covered, two or three discs to accompany every emotional permutation, though I will doubtless succumb to some new release promising more.

And a great piece by a great composer is an almost undrainable pleasure. I have twenty-five different recordings of a double piano concerto; though it was with the purchase of the twenty-fifth that I worried I might be fiddling with my sanity.

There's something slightly embarrassing about liking a great composer. Of course you do. It looks so obvious, so lazy, so dull. There's always this tension in your tastes; no one wants to fit in with the crowd, to bellow herdishly. This desire is contrasted with the desire to evangelise for a new discovery; we want others to share our pleasure, but only to a certain point. I can't imagine anyone, even those who go for the most obscure and awful music, enjoying something and not wanting to share it with someone. We might not want to share our food or our money, but we do want to share our judgement. We want to be considered of good judgement, knowledgeable. We want others to think we have more fun. But we need meeting-places of the mind. A Kilimanjaro of the spirit that we've all visited so we can say of other things: it's shorter, or taller, or the same height as Kilimanjaro.

Apart from the music, I have my huge film library, and, from the dish, hundreds of television channels. And while their controllers do their best to keep anything intelligent out, they fail periodically. So although my wealth is modest, I defy any dictator, any potentate, anyone richer than me to have better home entertainment. Even those with unspend-able fortunes only have one mind, one mouth, two ears, two eyes and one pleasure station. There's only so much fun you can take. A hundred years ago not even someone with their own country or a shocking fortune could have had it this good, even fifty years ago it was magnates only, and by now the crackheads have more entertainment than they know what to do with.

Richness descends not when you have a choice of yachts, but when you have abundance and freedom. Oh, and you are likely to retain them. I could go out and buy new furniture, new clothes or jet off to any part of the world and loaf for a month in a suite with a mammoth minibar and a barn-sized bathroom.

The financial distance between scraping along and galore is, cruelly enough, quite small if you're single. If you want to raise eight children, that's another matter, but once you can escape the gravity of rent and credit-card payments, things go your way. Few pleasures are greater than knowing you can close your door, ignore the world and create your own.

Moreover, my becoming as-good-as rich wasn't the result of any astuteness or hard work on my part. It was a by-product of my wanting to take some flamenco classes.

Dance is very much like a cult, you get sucked in further and further, and you pay more and more and you rarely get a chance to make any money out of it.

At sixteen, I tormented my father for some extra cash to take up flamenco in addition to the innumerable dance classes I was already attending. Knowing he'd yield, he made a stipulation: 'Owww, you have to sign up for something useful as well.' We understood each other well enough for me to know he had in mind something that might give me a chance of earning a living. I kept my side of the bargain, but I left it late. By the time I got to enrol at the local college all the worthwhile courses, like the one in computer graphics that I had been honestly keen on, were full; even worse, all the tempting courses were full. There was only one course that was presentable and that had vacancies: slightly harder maths. I desperately hunted for slightly easier maths but it didn't exist. So it looked as though my career in graphics was finished in its intentional stage and I gritted my teeth to find out what the maths were slightly harder than.

I didn't find out, because the slightly harder maths tutor sold his car, bought a pneumatic drill and started digging a hole in his basement in an attempt to reach the earth's core in order to prove some theory. So the computer graphics tutor took over, and the course became slightly harder maths meets computer graphics and sits quietly in the corner, though this was at a time when courses in computer graphics consisted of little more than switching on the computer. But my father was right.

When I finally had to knock dancing on the head years later, I evolved into a designer, largely because I could switch on a computer and draw. If I were trying to get into the business now with those qualifications, I wouldn't even get an interview as a receptionist.

So I suppose my contribution to my fortune was not failing as a designer. I had a reputation and a phone and that's why I became rich. It was Friday afternoon and I was locking the door on my way out to buy some peppermint tea when the phone rang. I could have gone off and left it to the answering machine, but I picked up the phone and was offered the job.

I didn't want the job. It was one of those we-need-it-yesterday things you get offered a lot as a freelance. They needed one more character for a computer game. My weekend would have become a sleepless hell, and I wasn't in the mood. My prospective employer, an embittered Japanese project manager, didn't want to give me the job either. He complained venomously about how he had been let down at the last minute by a designer who had decided he wanted to be a ladyboy in Bangkok; how the hundreds of other experienced, well-qualified designers he knew in Japan were busy, on holiday, suffering spiritual crises, having skiing accidents, giving birth or had become contestants on game shows. He seethed as he listed the countries he had scoured for help: America, Germany, France, Spain, Bulgaria, Poland, India.

As he enumerated the implausible events that had pre-vented hundreds of talented designers from taking up his offer, I could smell his bad sweat, the rancid tobacco on his clothes (it took me a while to twig what a long day he must have had because they're nine hours ahead in Tokyo); he was very angry with me, indeed he hated me, and I sensed he wanted an apology from me for all his toiling. Despite his clear and immediate need for a designer, he still chewed over my CV with me before, with incredibly bad grace, offering me the job.

I didn't want it. But as a freelance you can't bring yourself to say no. You are in a constant terror that no one will ever talk to you again let alone employ you. The word 'no' cannot pass your lips. Uttering that word would bring career calamity; it would incur the wrath of the payment gods. However, I wanted this job to vanish.

So what I said was: 'You'll have to talk to my lawyer.' I went off to get my tea, confident that I'd hear no more about the job, since I didn't have a lawyer. On top of which, the lawyer I didn't have would undoubtedly have gone off for the weekend; or even if he hadn't, he would have forgotten about me.

I hadn't forgotten about him. I was getting my coat at a party when this lawyer had walked up to me and said, 'I specialise in intellectual property and I'd like to shag your brains out.' A lame line, but well delivered, and it wasn't accompanied by a slimy leer as if it had been delivered by, say, a human-resources manager. It wasn't one of these offensive propositions where the pleasure lay in being offensive. He was drunk and I was in the mood. He had given me his card afterwards, but I had never taken up his offer of representation because I hadn't needed to and because, as any woman knows, favours are rarely executed after the event.

Funnily enough, I had ripped up and put his card in the bin that morning. I hate clutter and unnecessary things (the shoes are essential for my peace of mind) and I like everything in its place, and I really had no place for a card from a married intellectual-property lawyer. But it would be a suitable way of dodging the work: I rescued the card from the bin and read out the number. I was confident that that was that.

Afterwards, I learned that the lawyer had been locking his office door when the phone rang and had only gone back in because he had been expecting a call from a Syrian lacrosse player. He not only remembered me but by the time I had returned from the shops he had ferociously cut me a deal which gave me a shedload of money and, more significantly, a percentage of the royalties. 'I love it when you can hear them sobbing at the other end of the phone.' I was furious with him, but I couldn't say so.

I had four hours' sleep that weekend, finished the job by Monday afternoon and the rest is a stream of steady payments. It's odd that they paid me, because it would have been easy for them not to. Collecting money from companies two streets away is hard enough.

I've never met anyone who's played the game. I've never even seen the game on sale here (mind you, I haven't looked very hard), but it was, judging by the cheques that have been forwarded to me, successful in Japan. In normal circumstances, the fee would have bought me two or three good pairs of shoes, but I ended up with a half a house and thermal stability.

So my only tip for becoming rich is not to try.

I go down to the hallway. I always think of it as a beach, where debris and wrack get washed up.

There are several letters, face-down – so none of the other residents have appeared yet, or they went off before the postman delivered – but nothing for me. Four envelopes loitering in a corner of the hallway, which I have been tolerating for weeks, I scoop up for disposal. I am slightly disappointed there's nothing for me, because although, like most of us, my mail consists largely of junk, at the heart's core is an irrepressible hope that one day some good news will glide in.

I walk back up the six flights of stairs to my kitchen. I chose a top-floor flat precisely because it forces you, whether you like it or not, to exercise a little. Even a trip to the newsagent's becomes a modest work-out. I prepare breakfast and deal with the unclaimed envelopes. I let the post loaf downstairs for a while even though I know the addressees won't be turning up to collect it. They haven't been here for years so why would they start now? But I feel I have to give correspondence some respect, even if it's clearly flannel, until the pile starts to annoy me or gets to the size where it might be concealing my letters, and thus possible good news.

If I had a forwarding address for any of the previous residents, many of whom I knew (in the loosest sense), I'd probably suffer from enough guilt to forward them, but I don't. Unwanted post waiting for long-gone addressees, clogging up the beach.

While I drink my coffee, I gut the envelopes. Why do I carry on doing this? There is an excitement in opening others' letters, but it wears off when you discover their lives are as monumentally uneventful as yours, and when you can see the letter is from a credit-card company, you know no amusement is in the offing. But I open the letters before I chuck them in the bin just to verify that there are no desperate messages from unfortunates kidnapped and awaiting ransom, and because along with the hope of good news, is the hope for some amusement.

The first envelope is large and manila. It was getting on my nerves because of its size, capable of covering smaller but more important letters to me which might contain some good news. The addressee is one E. Lambert. No E. Lambert has been living here for the ten years I've been here, and this is the first time an E. Lambert letter has turned up here.

The envelope divulges a thick catalogue of sex toys. Millions of these are sold every year, apparently, and it leads to the question whether there can be a man, woman or child in the country without the solace of a butt-plug. The address on the envelope is entirely correct, down to the postcode, so this is no slip or misguess by the postman. Does the company send a catalogue to every building in the country surmising that most of the time, sooner or later, someone will open it?

The next envelope is a press release addressed to a journalist who left here four years ago, correcting an earlier press release I tore up some months ago about a new brand of cotton bud. This was also puzzling because the journalist, Mitch, only reviewed films, and I can't see how you can have a new brand of cotton bud. What can you change, and why should people care? The press release is two pages long and says nothing; one of emptiness's finest flowerings. I have to say I admire that.

On the annoyance scale, Mitch was only very irritating. He kept a pool table leaned up against the wall in the hallway for years. He never helped to clean up the communal area, but would always say 'me next time' every time he spotted me fighting back the filth. I wondered whether it would be equally irritating, more irritating or less irritating if he said nothing. On balance it would have been less irritating, because he wasn't saying it for me, but for himself. He was hypnotising himself into the belief that he wasn't a shit.

He also played salsa music very loud. Once, at three in the morning, I was blasted out of bed by what sounded like a surprise party thrown by the occupants of the flat below. I got dressed to remonstrate but when I got out on the stairway I discovered the music wasn't coming from the first-floor flat (this was before I bought it), it was coming from further down: Mitch's flat. The worst aspect of someone dispensing volume at stadium level is that your fevered pounding on the door can't be heard. He was holed up, gone amok with salsa and drugs.

He did apologise, and offered to lend some videos, he had walls of them. I never took him up on the offer, and I subsequently figured out it was because I preferred disliking him.

A mauve flyer for a club event that took place a month ago emerges from another envelope, sent to a girl who left two years ago. Then there is a credit-card application form for Sylvie. Sylvie left three years ago, but if she had stayed here she could now be the controller of thirty different credit cards. Maybe there was a time when credit-card companies pursued the affluent but now they tend to be more desirous of the have-nots. She used to live in the closet that was described as the flat at the back.

I first met her at a party in North London. It was so far north that I was almost exhausted by the time I got there, and as soon as I walked in I realised it had been a mistake. The guests had already given up on enjoying themselves and it was only ten o'clock. Having a drink before the long journey back, I got talking to Sylvie. Gradually we established that we both lived in South London, in the same area, in the same street and, finally, in the same house. We had been living in the same house for nine months, without catching a glimpse of each other.

At first, Sylvie was a little perturbed about me, suspecting that I was some deranged depraved creature of the city who liked to follow strangers home by pretending to live in the same house, for nefarious reasons.

I'm beginning to suspect that I'm perfect: that may be a problem.

When long-left-alone jungle tribes are dragged into the spokes of civilisation, they get mangled. It's not simple matters that result in their destruction. It's not that they're not as well armed as the interlopers, that they can't manage to adapt, or that they have nothing to sell. They're flattened by the awareness that their beliefs have failed: it's not destructive to learn that there is a better way of hunting a peccary, that synthetic fabrics have their uses, or that you need to master another language to trade. All of us can be extremely adaptable when it's to our advantage to do so. One belief trampled is a nuisance, but to see all your answers as litter on the streets of your conquerors . . . Getting the numbers wrong for a lottery draw, or getting wet because you didn't take an umbrella because you surmised it wouldn't rain is radically different from discovering that your family all hate you and that the bank in which you had your life savings never existed.

Is the loss of the feeling that everything will be all right simply an indication that you've finally grown up or that you're not right in the head? I don't dream any more. Or I do, but not with any conviction. It's like watching a football match when you don't support either team and you don't know any of the players and you don't have any interest in the sport: it passes the time, but you don't care.

When I say perfect I don't mean perfect. It depends how you see the term really. I've done two shameful things, which weren't that shameful, but on the other hand I quite enjoyed them, which you shouldn't do if you're perfect. One involved a football club.

I get annoyed. I get annoyed over small things. Is it better or worse to be annoyed by small things rather than big things? It's more understandable to get annoyed by big things, but on the other hand not getting annoyed by big things must demonstrate some self-control. Surely getting annoyed by small things, if you've restrained yourself from getting annoyed about big things, is allowable? A brief holiday from discipline. On the other hand, since there are only small things to get annoyed about in my life, perhaps it's merely a weakness on my part.

I'm annoyed about the absence of a cheque this morning.

I've been waiting for this cheque for about a year now. It's not a large sum of money. It is a small sum. Bizarrely, that Hit and Run productions haven't paid me this small sum of money is more annoying than if they hadn't paid me a large sum of money. It may be disagreeable and reprehensible, but you can understand the reason for not paying a large sum of money: wanting to hold on to the cash for as long as possible. However Hit and Run is a big, thriving concern. Feeding the goldfish in their reception for one day would cost them more than the sum of money in question.

I'm lucky. I don't need this money. What's more, even if I needed it, there's not much I could do with it, because the amount of money is so small. I'll explain why this is so annoying.

They came to me. I didn't go to them. They phoned me up with a small job. The woman I talked to was desperate. I did it as a favour. It was the design equivalent of doing the washing-up. I sent in an invoice, professionally. Then the waiting began.

First of all we had the period of disappearing invoices. I had to send in three. Matters were complicated by the disappearance of the handlers I was talking to. I started off with a Heather, moved on to a Dawn who rapidly became a Gail and then someone whose name I can't remember, and a Nicola. Each was unaware of the history of my payment, and none of them had much affection for the task of sorting it out.

I would phone up only every three weeks or so, I didn't want to be a nuisance, and I would always have a cheery chat with the girls, asking them how they were, whether they had had good weekends, demonstrating my concern for their well-being. Indeed, with Gail I had quite a lengthy chat about running footwear: I had the chats because I like to be polite. I believe that courtesy costs nothing and we all have to get on in the world and also, imperfectly, I was hoping that cordiality might hasten the arrival of the cheque.

The best subterfuge if you don't want to pay someone is to tell them that you are paying them. If they had started off by saying 'we'd sooner cut our legs off than give you a penny', that at least would have given me the option of considering some legal attack, even though the sum involved wouldn't have bought me the blink of a lawyer's eye.

And the thing that's most annoying is that they're not doing this to annoy me. They're just bungleheads. The phase I seemed to be in now was the 'this Thursday' phase. Whenever I phoned up now I would be greeted with disbelief and annoyance as I explained that I hadn't had the cheque, the implication clearly being that, at some profound level, it was my fault: I was hexing a simple process. My interlocutor would take a deep breath and say, 'I'll look into it.' I'd hang on for ten minutes and then an exasperated voice would announce: 'It'll be issued this Thursday.'

I gird myself up to make a call. Nicola's job is now being done by a Mabarak. The change of gender heartens me. I run through the chronology of events and the non-existence of the cheque. Mabarak doesn't sigh or fidget during my exposition. He says: 'I'll look into it and get back to you.' Normally, I'd protest at this classic kiss-off, but Mabarak's manly attention has given me confidence. I want to believe.

Later that day he does phone me back.

'You've made a mistake: you didn't do any work for us.'

'Sorry?'

'I've checked and you haven't done any work for us.'

'I'm telling you I did.'

'I've checked and you haven't. You must be confusing us with someone else. I'm afraid I can't help you any more.'

I'm at a loss. This has stumped me. Were it deliberate it would be a superb tactic. You hire someone to redecorate your flat and then when it comes to payment time, flatly deny that they have done the work. How would they prove they had painted that wall yellow? I consider giving up the chase. By now, I must have spent the fee on phone calls. I sit for a while and gauge how the prospect of capitulation is digested. A bead of annoyance forms in my stomach and swells steadily. My guts won't go along with it. I wish they would, but they won't. And there's no arguing with your guts.

I recall that although they haven't paid me, and although I did nothing but dust some pixels, for some strange reason, I am credited on their home page.

I talk to Mabarak and refer him to the company's own home page where my name is clearly there amid a host of others who tinkered with it. Mabarak has no comeback to this. This irrefutable proof of my veracity irks him. I hang on for another ten minutes or so. Finally he returns: 'They'll send you a cheque next Thursday.'

I go down to the beach to gather the post. It's nearly a week after next Thursday, and there is no cheque. There are two letters for me and two for Sylvie. In addition to the flotilla of credit-card offers left in her wake, there is regular correspondence from debt-collecting agencies. The first this morning is from a debt-collection agency calling itself The Debt Collection Agency of Great Britain. No marks for imagination here and a rather feeble attempt by a company based in Kidderminster to sound august. Curiously, all the debt-collecting agencies seen to be based in dumps up North. The letters amuse me because for the last three years or so they have been promising month after month the same thing: that they are going to do something.

There is no signature or name on the demand for payment, presumably so aggrieved defaulters can't take it out on anyone. 'You have chosen to persistently ignore our previous letters . . . ' it begins. There's always hot air about solicitors and bailiffs tooling up, but surely no one could take their threats seriously after five letters or so. The most entertaining letter is the one they send out once a year with only a phrase or two in enormous bold letters:

TWENTY FOUR HOUR NOTICE

They're being stubborn, let them have the large lettering. I speculate how much this debt-collecting costs them. The letters are all sent first-class. The paper is reasonable quality, and although the letters are generated from standard text, someone, however lowly paid, must spend some time on them.

The second letter is different. This is from the Dun Waitin agency. They've never written before. The composition is punchy. 'You can't run and you can't hide. Pay. Pay, while you can.' Underneath this is a large colour reproduction of a man in karate gear using an elbow to break three concrete-looking blocks. He is grimacing, no doubt from the effort of smashing the blocks, but the effect is to make him uglier and more threatening in case the smashed blocks weren't enough. The caption reads: 'Our representative, Audley Bennett, loves to call.' The address for the company is given as Sunk Island, a place I've never heard of, doubtless another barrenfest up North.

There is a PS. 'We know the way to London.'

I get the call from Garba.

'Hope you're well, Oceane,' he says. 'Finland is served.'

There can't be many travel agents like Garba: in fact I'd bet he is unique. He doesn't do it for the money. Well, he does, but what I pay him doesn't really reflect the effort he goes to. Money doesn't always have the clout it's reputed to. It may talk but it often does so in a mumble or a language that isn't understood. Try ordering a wedding-cake in a fishmonger's, even if you offer ten times the market rate. Most fishmongers just wouldn't bother to phone up the nearest patisserie; it would be too unusual for most of them.

Instead of welcoming an enrichment opportunity, they'd be confused as to why I didn't go to the bakery. I'm lucky to have Garba for my special needs.

Garba helps me because he likes to think in unconventional ways. Money is, however, a big delight for him. He does do things like soak unfranked stamps off letters so he can use them. He checks his change in shops. He queries every item on a restaurant bill. ('I don't think that cocktail was worth that. That cocktail wasn't worth that. Tell you what, I'll give you a quid.') He has innumerable relatives and he elucidates how incredibly little he spends on them for Christmas and how he plans to reduce this amount even further. Yes, he does keep the wrapping paper from the presents he receives for future instances of wrapping. When he stays in a hotel, he does steal the toilet paper and the light bulbs (replacing them with old ones so he doesn't get charged – similarly if the minibar has a bottle of vodka or gin, he'll drink it, then refill the bottle with water and carefully restore it to the minibar). He eats what is heavily discounted at the supermarket. He's a fan of cold showers and cold baths and claims soap is bad for the skin.

But Garba isn't your old-school skinflint. He does have his fun; if you want to know where in London to buy the cheapest bottle of the most expensive whisky he'll know; if you want to know where to buy the cheapest set of golf clubs he'll know. According to him the most satisfying moment of his life so far was queuing up outside a gayclub, admiring the queuer in front of him and suddenly realising there was no need to wait any more, no need to pay admission, no need to buy a drink and all the rest. He simply invited the guy in front back to his place. From then on, he never went to another gayclub, only the queues outside.

For him, combating the forces of payment is a creative adventure and a love of mathematical truth. He really does care if he is being overcharged seven pence for his electricity, because he adores precision and because it's money that can go into one of his ventures. In addition to his travel agency, Garba has a range of money-making schemes: a moss-statue workshop, a greeting-card company and a scorpion farm.

I get ready for the evening. As I rise from the bathtub, I am faced with the perpetual puzzler of how much elegance I want to carry. I only dress up now when I go abroad, so I let rip.

I stroll downstairs to Finland.

I'm wrestling with the lock when the door suddenly yields and I am warmly greeted by Mika, in his twenties, but not, I guess, in the region of his twenties that he'd like. He wears a bandanna around his forehead, in the manner of a fashion model, rock star, or a teenage soldier in a poorly organised war, something you have a chance of getting away with if you are a fashion model, rock star or a teenage soldier. One should avoid snap judgements, but probably for Mika his bandanna is meant to be a claim to a roguish wanderlust and a warrior disdain; it doesn't sit well with Mika's loss of control over his belly and a ruddy face that could be that of a sixty-year-old alky.

Mika holds a cigarette in one hand and a bottle of Lapin Kulta in the other. The warmth of his greeting is conceivably attributable to the four empty bottles of Lapin Kulta on the cool, minimal furniture. I like the way Garba has done the place up.

The other guests are a couple, Silja and Tuomas, international lawyers who work for a bank and who are visibly uneasy about Mika's thirst for Lapin Kulta. All three speak excellent English, though I wish that Mika didn't have quite the show-off command of idiom. He hijacks the conversation, effortlessly sideswiping Silja's and Tuomas's attempts at subjectshifting.

My enquiry on Helsinki gets as far as: 'And what about Helsinki —'

'Helsinki. Helsinki is not Finland. I will tell you what Finland is. At first sight Finland is forests and lakes. Lakes and forests. Forests and lakes. Lakes and forests. Forests and lakes and lakes.' Mika has a long drag on his cigarette. I can see Silja and Tuomas are tempted to erupt, but don't want a punch-up this early in the evening.

'So,' I say, 'forests and lakes, what else —'

'But no matter how many times you look at Finland it's the same. More lakes and forests than you can envision. Finland is a very misleading name. There are hardly any Finns in Finland. There are no inhabitants. Now I want you to pretend I say forests and lakes for another five minutes, until it gets very irritating, that is Finland. The careful observer will also discern sauna and mobile phones.' He takes another drag. 'We do also have reindeer and mosquitoes. The reindeer smell and the mosquitoes bite. It does your head in, the forests and lakes. That is why I have lived for the last five years in Madrid.'

My guidebook has told me to be prepared, that while Finns are sociable, they enjoy a good silence and like to share it in the way other nationalities share a beer. Patently, Mika was out of town when the book was written. As for living in Madrid, in a small country like Finland one can readily assume Mika is barred from every bar.

Mika unexpectedly slips into a drunken dumbness. Silja and Tuomas quiz me about what they should see in London. They are much better informed than I am about what is going on in terms of the theatre, exhibitions, concerts. I'm not a great one for going out.

Partly because nothing works in London. Nothing. Over two thousand years ago, Julius Caesar built a bridge across the Thames. The Elizabethans built a bridge across the Thames despite being encumbered with beliefs such as decomposing manure produces ducks and that there are countries where the natives only have one large foot, which when lying on their backs could be used as a parasol. Around the world nations build bridges many miles long over turbulent waterways. The Russians and Americans build space stations, we can't even get it up over fifty feet of docile dishwater from St Paul's to the Tate. Late, over budget, useless, laughable – the hallmarks of British endeavour.

Sometimes I wonder what the commuters, who have been standing in the rain for an hour because their train has been cancelled three times in a row for the second day running because the drivers have overspliffed or not bothered to turn up, late for a doctor's appointment they have had to wait ten months for, unable to console themselves with the prospect of a holiday since living in the capital sucks every penny out of them, while the illiterate muggers who have just relieved them of their credit cards go on a spending spree with total impunity, I wonder what those commuters think. I don't reflect on this too often, because it's too depressing, and because I don't have to. London is impossible and soon there will be no one left but investment bankers, asylum seekers and tourists. And me.

But Silja and Tuomas are pleased to be here. Mika implores the chef to stop bringing him bottles of Lapin Kulta individually. He gets the crate, and starts putting it away in a way you'll want to tell your friends about afterwards. I took a look around Helsinki in the afternoon and I was intrigued to see a small area of metal frames by the waterfront. Several people were gathered there with carpets draped over the rungs, beating them, 'Is carpet-beating some sort of sport?' I ask. Apparently not; just an area designated for carpet-beating so the citizens of Helsinki can beat their carpets while chatting with their neighbours. Silja then explains to me why there is a statue of Tsar Alexander II in Senate Square in the centre of town. 'Visitors are often surprised that there is a statue of a Russian in the middle of Helsinki. But we lived

23

well under the tsars. We negotiated a good deal. Negotiation is the Finnish way.'

The history of Finland is in two big chapters, being squashed by the folk on the left-hand side, the Swedes, and then being squashed by the folk on the right-hand side, the Russians. The Swedes left leaving some castles and the Swedish language. The Russians left leaving nothing but a few duff restaurants, but send over their wolves and nuclear waste from time to time.

Silja and Tuomas then argue over who has the better Swedish. Silja ran off to Stockholm one summer when she was sixteen to improve her Swedish and to work as a cleaner in a hospital. 'We were taught a special technique on how to clean properly, because even a small colony of germs hiding under a basin can spread quickly.'

'What is the secret technique of Swedish hospitals?'

'You have to clean everywhere all the time.'

Silja elaborates how she worked all day and then spent the nights in clubs, even kissing the King of Sweden's bodyguard. It sounds as if Silja is in mourning for her previous self, the sixteen-year-old who didn't need sleep and felt safe because there was a home to go back to. She is my age I'd guess, around thirty, but that sixteen-year-old is buried far away with her courage. I understand that. I've done things in the past I wouldn't do now, I would be unable to do now. Things so far from my abilities now, I suspect the memory must be a mistake.

'No, he said he was the King of Sweden's bodyguard,' insists Tuomas. 'I have been the King of Sweden's body-guard too in nightclubs. Furthermore, an outstanding fighter pilot.'

'Your Swedish is too weak for you to be the King of Sweden's bodyguard. You could be the Mayor of Malmo's dog-walker at best. And I did kiss the King of Sweden's bodyguard.'

Our first course arrives: it's bear pâté, and the taste is okay, if a little peppery. The most remarkable thing about it is that it's bear. I find myself a little uneasy about eating bear: I've had no problems with bears.

'The bears are rare, but there are too many of them,' says Tuomas.

'You don't want to meet a bear in the forest,' adds Silja. 'They are no longer afraid of humans, they are urban bears now. Corrupt bears. Not nice bears. Even a bear with a soothed head is not one you would want to meet.'

Neither Silja, Tuomas or Mika has met a Finnish bear. A discussion follows on the etiquette of bear-contact. Playing dead, holding your ground, and singing are all cited as tactics though Mika opines, 'Respect nature and blow the fucking bear away.'

Silja recommends the village museum on Seurasaari island, where I can see eighteenth- and nineteenth-century rustic Finnish houses.

'But you have to be careful. There are many squirrels. Dangerous squirrels.'

Mika splutters out a mouthful of beer. 'Squirrels are not dangerous. They are small and red. You see them coming.'

Silja's not having this. 'Squirrels bite. They climb on to your head. I know someone who was bitten.'

'The squirrels on Seurasaari sit up and beg; you feed them nuts, they go away.'

'My friend was feeding the squirrels when he was bitten; that was the problem, he had no more nuts. The squirrels have expectations.'

The argument bangs on for some time, as we have two more courses, reindeer tartare which is much like regular tartare, but gamey, and then the main course which the chef produces almost apologetically: white fish and potatoes. It's fine, no seasoning or sauce to interfere with the flavour of the white fish or potatoes. 'There is nothing more Finnish,' says the chef. I learn an expression 'to be as stubborn as an

Ostrobothian' and I practise my fifty words of Finnish, which include forest, lake and bear.

Mika has been silent for some time and now explodes: 'Everyone used to love me. When I was twenty I was the best-known poet in Finland and everyone loved me. What's happened to me?' I catch Silja and Tuomas exchanging looks. Best known? Poet? Loved? Compassion forces their lips shut.

Certain professions have ready admittance. You are lying in bed one afternoon, unemployed, unskilled, unwashed in grotty bedding with no friends, no money and no prospects, and miraculously, by one tiny mental adjustment, you're no longer a zero-contributor, a failurist, you're a poet. And finally, there's no need to write much at all. But there are many other easy-to-adopt professions: singer, film producer, property developer, dancer. No one has to pay you.

I'm sure I'm not alone in this. I'm sure most attractive girls, no I don't think you even have to be attractive, I'm sure most girls on a Saturday night out have met a film producer.

The genesis is the same: you are lying in bed one afternoon, encrusted in your bedding, all quiet on the achievement front, the only lifeforms willing to tolerate you are in your kitchen sink, and again by one small mental adjustment, you're no longer a waster, you're someone who can go out Saturday night and ask women to undress or perform intimate acts. Most won't, but some will.

What is the difference between a real film producer and a bogus film producer? None.

It's easy to launch yourself, you mention some moderately successful films that are likely to ring a bell, but no one is likely to own a copy of, so that credits won't be checked. Or if you're lucky enough to have the right name or are willing to change your name, you can pick up someone else's career more easily than stealing their luggage. Putting on a white coat and pretending to be a doctor is much more demanding in that it's much easier to be caught out or at least you have to work much harder to have a chance of success. One afternoon is enough to be a top film producer, and this is why so many actresses and dancers have sighed and slid off their undies. Best of all, to dodge verification, be a film producer in another country. Be a French film producer in England or an American producer in Italy.

That's how it was for me. The setting was convincing: a plush hotel room (easily available with someone else's credit card). The French producer said hello, unzipped his fly, and then pointed at his chopper fixedly with his index finger just in case I had missed the introduction of this crucial element into the interview.

My decision was largely influenced by my hating the man on sight. However, I did pose the question to myself as I walked out. Was I the one being unreasonable? Was it merely standard industry practice to ask for oral hospitality? Was this just tax? A few gulps of unpleasantness for a life of ease?

These exam-like situations turn up all the time, but unlike academic exams you never find out the answers. This was one time when I found out I had got it right, as the film producer was arrested and revealed to be no more than a suit and a stolen credit card. He was unapologetic, claiming that he had 'made untalented women happy for weeks' with promises of work. Mentally, they were professionals. It was, temporarily, a perfect simulation. They had the boasting to their friends, the contemplation of how to spend the windfall, the excitement to come of being interrogated about their diets and their shopping habits.

He may even have been right. A vagrant, outside one of the clubs I used to go to, had fashioned an empty plastic bottle into a replica of a camera, which he would squeeze to give an approximation of a shutter click. As you approached the club, in the hope of a handout he would run around paparazzily pretending to take pictures of you, shouting ecstatically: 'Look who it is! Oh my God, look who it is!' It was alarmingly pleasurable.

Property developers. Another eminently enterable profession. I admit I met one when I was younger and was impressed. I assumed a lot of responsibility, grit and massive amounts of money were required. Not at all. To be developing property, you don't need any. It's the thought that's required. You only have to look at a building and think: that could be developed.

The property developer I met did have some assets: a sports car (very old, decrepit not vintage) but I didn't realise that he lived in the car, having invested his money in a small hole in the ground where a sweetshop had stood in a part of London where no one would ever really want to live. Passing by several years later I noticed that the hole was still there.

There is an awful predictability about the mingling of alcohol and men: hullabaloo, maudlinity and brewer's droop. Tears throng in Mika's eyes. 'My wife!' he interjects. 'My wife,' he repeats more loudly, with a sobbing whose conviction cracks. 'She died.' He makes rapid stabbing gestures into the hollow of his elbow. 'An overdose.'

I have to suppress the desire to laugh. The desire to laugh is almost uncontrollable. It's possible that all this is true, but it is unlikely. In my short acquaintance with Mika, I have discovered he is an attention-seeker with no hidden depths. Mika is all on display, like the ingredients in a pizza. There are no lakes or forests in Mika. Sorrow ten pints earlier might have been a little more convincing. It is an almost invariable rule that those who court sympathy, loudly, are the least deserving of it. There are people who don't have feelings; they just think they do. I can't prove this. Mika may also be limbering up for the I-need-a-good-woman-to-save-me routine when we get to bedtime.

Garba does a good job of rounding up guests. But there's always an arsehole in every party. I can't work out whether this is because there are just so many arseholes, or because arseholes don't like staying at home. They like to spread it about.

The dessert comes; amber-coloured berries with clotted cream. They are, Silja and Tuomas inform me, fighting to ignore the sparking drama of Mika, cloudberries.

Mika comes in with the volume: 'This is why I drink. This is why I cannot write. This is why I am unhappy.'

The words *stop drinking, stop ranting about your problems, get a job and you'll feel so much better* come to mind. But you can't say that because advice, even the best kind, isn't listened to, and because the solution is so obvious it must have already occurred to Mika. One of the lessons you learn in life: it's curious how the solutions to so many problems are obvious and fairly easy, but they are rarely implemented.

Outside my window is a living encyclopaedia of crime. From my window, without expending a lot of time, without any effort, I have witnessed robbery, assault, arson, drug-dealing, burglary, riot and rape. I've not seen a murder yet, though we do have murders galore, both domestic and professional, in the vicinity. It's easier to get killed here than almost anywhere else in London. The solution to this is simple: more police. Granted, crime can never be erased, but more police = less crime. It is more than a little disconcerting when you phone for the police, as I have done after windowside incidents, and they either don't pick up the phone, or turn up forty minutes later, or not at all.

Silja and Tuomas ignore Mika and talk about youths gathering in the evenings on the housing estate where they live and disturbing the communal flowerbeds. I can imagine the youths and I have no doubt even I could stare them out.

I wonder which highlights from the fiesta of fly-tipping, bag-snatching, car-burning, drug-dealing, gun-playing, blow-jobbing that is my neighbourhood (and funnily enough, even with all this, not that cheap a neighbourhood) I should recount to my guests. I list the many international criminal brotherhoods with representation locally: the Russians, the Jamaicans, the Italians, the Turks, the Colombians. Interestingly, you can see they are slightly envious. That's the trouble with civilisation, what do you do with it once you've got it?

Silja and Tuomas are also very fond of the British countryside; it is quaint apparently. I wouldn't even wipe my feet on the British countryside. I have all my memories of shivering in a tent in August, dodging cowpats, thistles and brambles as well as the cows ('surprisingly bolshy' according to our guideleader) and the badgers, riddled with disease and looking for trouble. 'I have read about it in books,' Silja and Tuomas say. That says it all. You read about something and then you want to see it. I suppose my interest in reindeer and their mushroom-tinged urine is the same.

Mika has fallen into himself. We turn to history. I know nothing about history and I certainly know nothing about Finnish history, but as I learn more and more about other countries and their cultures, I realise you can make up anything you want and it will have happened. Somewhere. Sometime.

Someone tying himself to six vultures and jumping off a cliff in an attempt to fly. A goatherd becoming king because of the way he boiled an egg. A nation banning laughter. From Silja, with the eloquence of a prepared lecture, I learn about the Great Wrath and the Lesser Wrath, sticky periods in Finland's past. I wait for the Rather Bulky Annoyance and the Passably Daunting Niggle, but they don't turn up. I'm sure they're out there somewhere. Wars are worst. There are Six-Day Wars, Ten-Day Wars, Thirty Years Wars, Hundred Years Wars, Football War, Phoney War, Mad War. The War of Jenkins' Ear. Choose any name. The No-one-was-looking-so-we-had-a-war War will be out there somewhere.

History, really, is notable killings. As a small country, you're always getting invaded. If you're a big country you're always invading small countries, and if invasion isn't in, you can always have a civil war, or pick on some small group.

I pay the bill and I'm horrified. Eyebrow-raising. This has to be the most expensive meal I've ever eaten. London's prices are a matter of perverse pride for Londoners. It may be perpetually damp and smelly, all the services function as if we were bombed by foreign air forces every day, but we can afford to live here, although most people can't. We're clinging on. We can take the punishment. It's heartening to see that outrageous charges are to be found outside London.

I pay the waitress; she's been polite and efficient, but no more. Certain nations excel at waitering, though not the Finns. Compliment?

Mika suggests we all have a sauna, however I'm not getting my kit off for him. The history of the sauna is rolled out and Mika tells us about the museum of the sauna, which has some rare photographs of bearded men rolling around in the snow in 1890, something that looked as ridiculous then as it does now. I'm not worried about skipping the sauna, it's too touristy. Silja and Tuomas say goodnight, showing their concern about leaving me with Mika. It was enjoyable meeting Silja and Tuomas. It's always reassuring to know that there are sensible and civilised folk out there.

'I am also very depressed because all I own is a small forest with young trees which no one wants to buy because timber prices are very depressed.' Mika slouches over, working himself up to a final vault on to me.

I don't blame Mika too much. It's a technique. He has some front: he knows I don't like him, he's badly dressed, too sozzled to perform, but still he advances. He's so out of condition I doubt if he could wank himself off. The lurching lunge: it's a technique. Men topple on you with a wagging tongue. Women are at fault here, for letting men get away with this. On the other hand, if we weren't fairly forgiving our species would have faltered away by now. Men, I suppose, by the nature of things are unaware of how clumsy lines like 'do you have a boyfriend?' followed by them taking off all their clothes while you are in the kitchen, don't impress.

'I don't know the way home,' says Mika as I push him out.

'A common problem,' I adieu.

I go upstairs and watch some television and exercise my fifty words of Finnish, though I don't get much opportunity since most of the programmes on Finnish television are in English, programmes I've already seen, and the subtitling is minimal, though the word lawyer crops up again and again.

The news is in Finnish and the beauty of news is that you can guess the contents even without recourse to your fifty words of Finnish. News always involves the same easy-to-recognise elements. There is, always, wherever you are, The Top Cheese said today. What he said is nearly always classifiable as we will improve . . . or we have improved. Then if it's a democracy you get some lesser cheeses carping and mud-slinging; if it's not a democracy you don't get the carping just the mud-slinging at various foreigners or minorities.

There's nearly always a lot of political news because there are a lot of political journalists and because, wherever you are, you can count on some shifty politician to be capering around as the flames of scandal lick his soles. Time to toss in a few disasters. Their order in the news is usually dictated by geographical distance. The newsman's pals: famine, flood and fire, ribby urchins, keening biddies who are often there because the journalist wants to flash his compassion, but just make you feel smug because your home hasn't burned down. Then there are the wars, which involve bearded carriers of those guns with banana-shaped magazines. Prices are always good value, because they are either too high or too low, thus causing discomfort. Same with currencies: always too low or too high. I can't remember one item ever announcing prices are exactly right.

And of course, when there is an item you know anything about, you can see it's complete rubbish. The last good riot they had here, the television crews only interviewed the organisers of the riot who explained that the police forced them into burning down shops and looting sportswear emporia. The television crews didn't interview the owners of the burnt shops or looted emporia.

The absurdity of news programmes, or all the news programmes I've seen, is that they are fixed for ten, fifteen, thirty minutes or an hour, whatever's happening. It would be so refreshing if they put up their hands and said nothing to trouble you today, just a few unsold cabbages, so here's a cartoon; but, no, they bring on the something-lookalikes. Nothing impersonating something.

The big question is why do we need the news? People who don't know who's in government still want the news. Is it because listening to the news allows us to have opinions? Is it because it gives us something to talk about, the human weather? Most readers who put down a paper certainly feel qualified to rule the world.

How can there be something? How can there be nothing? Is something merely nothing in disguise? It must be possible to sit in one room and work it out. I've always disliked the diggers, those who proclaimed they were seeking to find the foundations, because in general, they weren't. They made much of being diggers without doing any digging, and were, in my experience, failurists (really contemptible failurists), rich kids with too much time on their hands, mad. How do you know when that's happened to you?

It's like the one sound you'll never notice, the sound of your own snoring.

I could see that Silja and Tuomas liked me, but were a bit

worried about me. Their coming to dinner was a holiday jape; a little crazy thing they did in London. 'We were invited to dinner to provide a typical Finnish evening for someone. It was very good, but strange.'

I like to travel, but I never leave the house. In the last two years I have visited Japan, Ecuador, Jordan, Italy, Nigeria, Indonesia, Brazil and China. I like to immerse myself in a place, learn a bit of the language, read up and observe. The satellite dish up on the roof gets me almost everything, and the net does the rest. I'll soak up stuff for a few months and then have one or two dinners arranged by Garba in my spare flat below. Garba really goes to town on the decor and the trimmings, for which of course he charges princely sums, but he does it well, and he could get away with less effort.

You never say no. When I'm invited out I always say yes. First of all, there's always a good chance the person who wants to meet up with you will have to change plans or cancel. Then, closer to the event, you can always pull out, citing pressure of work or illness, and you can always make the suggestion that you'll be happy to cook up something if they come round to your place. For a good spread most of my friends are willing to trek over. And everyone's busy. How often do you see your close friends, unless you're eighteen or unless they live next door? We all slip into our little cracks in London, though I may have slipped too far.

No one has noticed. I get the odd lament that I haven't been to visit, but the other thing that's convenient but a little sad is that if you don't see your acquaintances they do forget you. To remember you, people have to see you. The invitations get fewer. But I'm not a solitudinarian. That's why I have my travel.

Staying in is always seen as unhealthy, and in some ways it

is. But almost everything is unhealthy. And what is going out? It numbs you, it stuffs you like a turkey with everyday nonsense: hundreds of mundanities clog, fog and then stop your mind.

It was the woman with the wedding-cake that was the end. I was walking down to the underground when I saw this woman teetering along on the pavement with an enormous three-tiered wedding-cake. Baffling, because I knew there weren't any cake shops in the neighbourhood, and there weren't any parked cars or doorways nearby that she could be making for; it looked, implausibly enough, as if she was just taking her wedding-cake out for a walk, with considerable difficulty. As I drew level with her, even more implausibly, she side-kicked me in the stomach. It was very painful, and I doubled up. The woman and cake continued on their way.

It wasn't because of this that I gave up going out. But it was the full stop in a long unpleasant sentence. I had noticed for some time that I'd always return home in a worse mood than I'd left. At the very least I'd be tired, but usually furious about some outrage. Nothing works in London and you're asked for money or intercourse every three yards. My neighbourhood leads in this regard, but it's much the same all over London. The city, according to what I read, used to be for the benefit of the rich. Now it seems to be run for the benefit of vagrants, nutcases, drunks and thugs. If nothing else I have become a connoisseur of begging tricks.

Spare change? The most basic technique. With this you either have to be very persistent and on a loop, or look quite pathetic. A prop is a must, either a blanket to wrap yourself up in (though you look very stupid in August) or the perennial dog on a string, ideally both.

Of course most Londoners become inured to this. If you look like a perfectly healthy twenty-year-old it'll take you time to get your rock of crack. The masters of the art know that the secret is to make eye and mind contact.

Thus: The do-you-know-the-way-to-Twickenham? man. When someone asks the way it's instinctive in most of us to say something, whether yes or no. And that's enough. You're hooked. Then you find it difficult to leave the story of how Twickenham? has only left prison that morning (and doesn't he look it) and has yet to see his newborn son who is in Twickenham, only a generous handout away. There are innumerable variants on this: *Is there a hospital nearby? Have you seen a policeman round here?*

I'm not a thief. This is a line used almost exclusively by large males when they have you on your own in a poorly lit area, the subtext being that he could be beating you to a pulp and taking your money, so some generosity should be shown for this restraint. *Support me in the struggle for honesty.*

I'm an invalid and I've got to get to a hospital appointment. When rocklust sets in a line like this can get upped to militantly unbelievable levels such as *I'm an invalid, looking after an invalid father, and I urgently need to visit my invalid sister in hospital who has two invalid children about to have an operation on their birthdays.*

I've just lent my money to someone to help them out, so now you'll have to lend me some. This is less common now. There was a period when the word *lend* cropped up a lot, rather than *give*. And more than once when I obliged, the coin I gave was viewed with disdain. 'Is that it?' Apparently, once aristocrats believed everything was run for their benefit, now it's the underclass who are unshakable about their right to have everything showered on them. And it's always those who would be last to offer help who are first to ask for it.

My all-time favourite, and one I have to admit I fell for is: *I don't want any money.* Look at the genius of that line. You stop someone in the street and say precisely the last thing they're expecting. *I don't want any money. I just need to talk.* The woman who gave me this one was in a terrible state, as most crackwhores are. She tearfully explained she had just been mugged on her birthday (and showed some wounds which were more like infected fleabites) while going to see her terminally ill mother in hospital in Cirencester (a very generous handout away). Can you help? she asked, I suppose strictly keeping to the bargain, since there was always the possibility of me hopping into a car and driving her a hundred miles.

The gravity of the woman with the wedding-cake was that she wasn't a skinhead with a pitbull. If you can't trust a woman carrying a wedding-cake who can you?

It was the next time I went to the underground that I felt tired. My legs were leaden and my eyelids drooped. As I sat down on the train, I realised I didn't have enough energy to get into the centre of town, let alone back again. I almost passed out. I got off and more or less crawled home, completely drained by my half-hour outing. I didn't have it in me any more to go out.

I discovered I didn't really need to go out. I work from home anyway. Most of my life goes down the broadband. And if nothing else, London is deliverable. Admittedly drivers often spend hours searching for my address, because very few can figure out that number 55 is to be found between numbers 53 and 57, but almost anything you want from groceries to abroad can be delivered. I don't have to go to the world, the world can come to me.

The thing that terrifies me though is the end of enjoyment. I still get a kick out of good food, music, shoes and a good chat. It's terrifying to think that one day the desire for them might vanish like the desire to go out. And then I'll have nothing to keep the terror away.

The evening sky outside is a preposterous blend of purple and brown. The clouds are square. When you look at it all you can think is that doesn't look at all realistic. How can a cloud be square? If I put a sky like that in my work I'd get some stick. But nature can do as it pleases and go back on its word, no matter what we think.

Why is erasing desire seen as so important? If the subjugation of the self is the point of the self what's the point in having a self? It's like someone handing you a leaflet which says throw this leaflet away.

There is a knock at the door. This doesn't happen very often and I'm glad that's so because it can only be one of my neighbours. I don't think I'm hostile by nature, but I hate my neighbours. I hate Gerald most of all because Gerald doesn't live here any more. He rents his flat out to airheads like Jack, the backpacker from New Zealand who is now at my threshold.

'I'm Jack from downstairs,' he says. We've met a number of times, and he's not reintroducing himself to be polite, or because he's afraid I don't recognise him. No, he's introducing himself again because he doesn't have enough reality cells to remember me.

'You wouldn't have a corkscrew about I could borrow? I'll return it straight away.'

'What happened last time you borrowed a corkscrew and said you'd bring it back straight away?'

He applies himself to thinking about it. His face frowns in concentration as if I've asked him a question about the succession of Aztec kings.

'You didn't,' I prompt.

'Oh, yeah,' he says, pleased with himself for remembering. I don't know whether this is how New Zealand is, or whether I'm just unlucky enough to have the five thickest New Zealanders living down the staircase.

'So?'

'No problems. It'll be back in a minute.'

The next day, I go down to the ground floor to reclaim the corkscrew. It's not that I'm overfond of my corkscrew or that it's a valuable corkscrew. It doesn't have any sentimental value at all, it's not been handed down from generation to generation in my family. It's a readily available corkscrew, a very cheap corkscrew. I'm not uneasy about one of my belongings straying from my flat. No, I want the corkscrew back because I'd like to open a bottle of wine.

The smell from Jack's flat assails you from a distance. The flat is a room barely enough for one person, let alone the hordes of New Zealanders who flock here. It's awkward enough complaining about noise, but I can't bring myself to ask them to turn down the stink, much as I'd like to.

'Hi?' says Jack answering the door. He looks at me with puzzlement. He doesn't have a clue who I am. I ask for the corkscrew.

'Love to lend you one, but we haven't got a corkscrew,' he insists. He's not being difficult, he wants to be helpful. I remind him of his activities the previous day. I don't think he believes me, but he and the other New Zealanders move their sleeping bags and empty bottles around for five minutes, until the corkscrew is exhumed. Who dresses Jack in the morning? You can't be very angry with him.

I go down to the beach. There's a wealth of rubbish. I'm sorting out the ones for immediate removal, when I see a figure looming at the door. I hear the buzzer go in the back flat. No one responds. I decide to open the door and be helpful.

There's a tall, thin man. He has a large, long head and no shoulders. He looks like an erect cotton bud or a stroppy sperm on its tail, but not in a bad way.

'Sylvie?' He smiles.

'Sorry. She moved out years ago.'

'Come on, Sylvie, you're not fooling anyone.'

I hadn't recognised him without the karate gear and the grimace. It's the debt collector.

'Why don't you come up? Audley, isn't it?'

Audley enters my flat peering around professionally, looking for evidence that I am Sylvie and estimating my worth by my possessions. He obviously knows expensive curtains when he sees them.

'I'd like to have a chat about a debt,' I say. 'You're good at your job, aren't you?'

I base my snap judgement on Audley's coming to the house: the first debt collector to do so in a decade of attempted debt-collecting. I outline my debt with Hit and Run. Can he help?

'No problem,' he says. 'Anything you want, with a bag of chips.'

'How do you go about . . . you won't use force will you?'

It's quite appealing to think of the staff there getting a kicking, but I know if anything like that happened I'd feel bad about it in reality. Also, it's hard to say whose fault it is. The many dimwits who've fobbed me off are infuriating, but they're not responsible for the running of the company, and the management certainly aren't. The guilt is somewhere in the cracks. I wouldn't mind some humiliation for the employees, but roughing them up would be too much.

'Ever been inside?' he asks.

'Inside?'

'Prison. You need a really good reason to go to prison, unless you're a headcase. You thump people, you go inside. Threatening to thump people can work, but even that's more trouble than its worth. I'm not going inside because someone doesn't want to pay for twelve phone calls he made to his girlfriend when she was in Australia.'

He gestures at my television and sound system. 'I get the feeling you don't need the money?'

'No.'

'You see, most of my clients are like you. It's not the money that aggravates them, it's that someone's had a laugh at their expense. It's not about collecting money, it's about payback. Or for some of my clients, sending out a message. And while I get results, I don't come cheap.' Audley explains that his fee would be in the region of twenty to thirty times my debt, depending on how long it took the company to crack.

'I have a team and, depending on the situation, I'll deploy the right face. A case like yours, poncey big company with flash office, is ideal for Wilf. If I turn up and ask to talk to someone, I spend all day watching the goldfish tank in reception, and even if I talk to someone, they'll just give me the brush-off and if I'm persistent they call the law.

'But if Wilf turns up, it's another kettle of fish. He's this retired luvvie. You take one look at him and you want to call an ambulance. Even when he's not on, he's this tiny, trembling, shrivelled eighty-year-old. You get Wilf to hobble in, painfully slowly, on crutches, in poor stinky pensioner clothing.

'The receptionists have to watch him for half an hour as he crosses reception, wheezing and rolling his eyes. Then he says: "Good morning. Terribly sorry to take up your time, I know how busy you must be, but my granddaughter is owed some money." And you're in business. No matter what the company does now, they're fucked. They can't win. The best thing they can do now is to write a cheque immediately. They leave Wilf in reception, it's a disaster. He'll whimper softly, start crying, in extreme cases, wet himself. If they try to eject Wilf, that's more disaster. Even the police would side with Wilf. "I do apologise. I hate being a nuisance and bothering you. I know how hard you work, but my granddaughter . . ." There was one boss who wouldn't cough up after a week of Wilf's best work: all his employees resigned.'

Audley leaves me his card. I think I'll be using his services. He gives me a smile:

'I hate to do myself out of a job, but you could invoice for work you haven't done.'

'What do you mean?'

'My mate Phil makes a living out of bogus invoices. He sends out invoices to companies and some of them pay up. According to him, you need a big company and an invoice that's big enough to make it worthwhile sending it in, but not so large it'll make the accountants pay attention. You just send an invoice, for services, nothing too specific, to the accounts department. Most companies ignore them, but you only need a few to send the cheque. He makes a good living, but he spends the whole day stuck at home, churning out invoices. I'd be tempted to give it a go, but I like to get out and about.'

Audley's probably talking good sense. I was burgled seven years ago. Not too bad as burglaries go: only a few small items taken, but my front door was trashed and that was pricey. You don't have time to shop around for a new door when you haven't got one. The insurance company trounced me on the claim and I was left badly out of pocket when things were tough for me financially anyway. So two years ago, when I was burgled again, I invented half a dozen items, not to make a profit, but so that when the insurance company cheated me again, I wouldn't be short-changed. After several months of bamboozling, the insurance company paid out for the invented items, but not for the ones that were really stolen.

I don't have insurance now. The stuff that would be taken in a burglary I can easily replace. I'm lucky in that respect, lots of people can't. If I lost everything in a fire, money would be little consolation for losing my favourite shoes and knick-knacks, and let's face it, the insurance company wouldn't pay out anyway. They simply don't do that. The knowledge that they don't have any of my money never fails to make me feel good.

'Thanks for the coffee,' says Audley. He indicates a free pen, designed to induce guilt, sent by a charity to someone who left the house five years ago, that I've dumped in the waste-paper basket. 'You're throwing that out, are you?'

'Yes.'

'I know it's your rubbish. But do you mind if I steal it?'

'Please take it.'

'No. I have to steal it. If that's all right with you?'

'Go wild.'

Audley slips the pen into a pocket. 'When my father died . . . well, he died regularly. A couple of dozen times at least. But when he finally went, he gathered all his sons round him. There are seven of us. And he said, "Lads. It's a jungle out there. You may think you know how bad it is, but you don't. I know many of you will end up stealing from churches, cheating on your loved ones, facing murder charges, committing cannibalism, faking your own deaths,

43

going on the run, doing unspeakable things involving salad cream in prison with other men to pass the time and other inevitable situations in life. I want to say I'm proud of you all, and I'll always be proud of you, wherever I'll be. You're fine lads. Just remember, there are some things no son of mine will ever do. Never work in insurance. Never work in local government. And only ever go to London to beat someone up or steal something." I always take something in memory of him.'

'But no beatings?'

'Not any more.' I walk him down to the beach. Suddenly, he brings up his right heel and kicks himself in the rear. 'Don't mind that,' he says. 'It's a nervous tic.'

He needs advice about footwear, but I'll save that for later.

I get a call about the missing cheque. This time it's a Val who's dealing with me. I had written another letter of protest, but I must say I'm surprised they've taken the trouble to phone me.

'We've been looking into this business of your money,' she says. Why the preamble? Why can't she just say we have sent the cheque. Sorry about the delay. 'The problem is that your payment has gone to a Marcia East.'

'Who's Marcia East?'

'I don't know.'

'I don't know any Marcia East either. I have never heard of a Marcia East. Why would you send my money to someone else?'

'Clearly there's been a mix-up.'

'So you're going to send me the money?'

'Yes. As soon as we get it back from Marcia East.'

'Wait a minute. You send my money to a complete stranger, but I have to wait till you get it back from her?'

'Yes. We'll chase her up. It shouldn't take long.'
I'm at a loss for a reply.

I consider Audley's offer. I decide to hire him. I'm doing it because I can. It's as much for the amusement as for the settling of the debt. I can see Audley's like Garba. He doesn't mind the unusual. He likes to go the extra mile. And he likes to be paid for it. Fair enough.

I ring him and we discuss the job. He's full of ideas.

'Do you want embarrassment, humiliation or total degradation?' he asks. 'I should warn you total degradation takes months, years, and is beyond the budget of most customers, and it comes with a health warning. You have to be careful asking for that one. And I undertake work like that only if I'm completely satisfied the debt is grievous.'

I wonder whom I should target. The director of Hit and Run? Finally it's his responsibility. Or the head accountant? The guilt falls far more heavily on him. On the other hand, the director hired the head accountant. He may well be innocent of denying me money, but he's guilty.

Being a freelance is hard. If you're at the top of your tree, that's fine. But otherwise, it's grim. You have to work hard to get the work, you have to work hard to do a good job in the hope you'll be asked to do more work, and then, inevitably, you have to work hard to get your money.

'So what's embarrassment like?' I ask.

'Let me give you an example. We get Wilf, in his best urined-up apparel, to stagger sobbing into an expensive business lunch, and calling the director by his first name, to say, "Pete, why won't you talk to your own father?" "Why do you pretend I'm not your father?" and more palaver suggesting close personal knowledge. Now, our target can always say Wilf's a lunatic, and maybe he'll be believed; but maybe he won't. I phone up and say: are you paying? And Wilf's never had to turn up for lunch more than twice.'

'How does humiliation differ?'

'Say our target is a married man and is coming out of a club or restaurant on his own. We infiltrate a young beauty into his company, and whether or not he goes along with it, whether it happens in a doorway or back at our operative's flat, she gets him to hold her jacket and, quick as a flash, gets her top off. The stripper I use, Stacey, can get her top off so fast you almost don't notice it. She pushes her top on to the jacket so that, as our other operative takes a photograph, it looks very much as if the target is holding both in a moment of boozy groping. Now, if there weren't a debt to be collected, we'd be on sticky, blackmail-like ground here. I make the call and ask: are you paying? Again, our target can say he's been set up. Maybe he'll be believed, but maybe he won't. It's easier to pay. We say, just send the money and the picture disappears. Ears like to ear what they want to ear.'

'That doesn't sound humiliating.'

'But once he's paid we send the picture to his wife anyway.'

'Okay. And total degradation?'

'Well, normally I don't divulge that, unless we have a contract.'

'Okay.'

'It's heavy stuff.'

'Okay.'

'I don't want people to get the wrong idea.'

'Okay.'

'But maybe you'd understand. I've only run a total degradation twice. I'll tell you about one. It was for a friend. His kid was run over by a drunk driver, who got a piffling six months in jail, which meant he was out after three months of playing Scrabble. You can guess how my friend felt about that. I said . . . I'd *help out*, if you know what I mean. Don't you do anything rash, I said. I said I'd be willing to *help out* in a very decisive way, if you know what I mean. I said once I've *helped out* there won't be any need, as it were, for anyone else to *help out* ever again, if you know what I mean. The problem would be gone. But he said, "Audley, don't kill him. Make him pay."

'Doing this takes a lot of planning. You've got to get it right. It's like a moon shot, you don't get it right, you've just built the world's most expensive firework. We spent weeks on finding the answer.'

'Which was?'

'Bubble-gum. Ask me about the bubble-gum.'

'Tell me about the bubble-gum.'

'Our target loved to drive. Big car. We started to stick bubble-gum in the door locks. Depending on how long the car was parked, the locks would be fucked or really fucked. The first few times something like this happens it's infuriating, but then as it goes on, week after week, month after month, it becomes something else. At first it was easy, but then after our target guessed someone was after him, we had to use counter-surveillance measures to watch for video surveillance or in case he had hired someone to watch his car. He tried everything. He changed cars. He reinforced his garage. But we were patient, we'd wait months sometimes, to be unpredictable. It was a small nuisance, but it fucked him up completely. You see, if we'd done different things, stolen his dog, broken windows, it wouldn't have been so bad. Problems are like anything else, variety helps. It was that he knew it was coming. And we used different gummers so that if someone was spotted, it wouldn't look as if it was a stalker, or a nutcase after him, but the universe. That's the worst thing possible, incontrovertible evidence that the universe is on your case. Someone who didn't like driving would have given up pretty quickly; but he loved it, that's why he became a gibbering wreck.'

I go down to the beach. The junk is thick. There is a
stationery brochure addressed to a Kirpal Singh, who hasn't
been here for at least ten years. The brochures come for him
every three months, with the smiling face of the company
chairman, Mr Lockhart, on the front surrounded by pictures
of his bargain suspension files and manila dividers. Mr
Lockhart is an old man and he is attempting the sunny,
trustworthy grandfather look, but he looks like what he is: a
shark attempting the sunny, trustworthy grandfather look.
The same picture has been on the brochure for all the years
it's been arriving and one glance is enough to tell you that
you wouldn't want to be one of his employees.

In my work, I can never get that much information into a
smile. There is very little difference between a grandfatherly
smile and a false grandfatherly smile. Perhaps it's my
shortcoming that I can't pixel it. It's like the prostitutes who
hang around outside in the garden. They have a style of
waiting that's hard to reproduce. They're not expecting
anything, they're purely waiting. Some of them wear
unambiguous tart regalia, but most don't, probably because
they can't be bothered to make any sort of effort. It's the
waiting that gives them away, and I've never been able to
capture a subtlety like that.

Mr Lockhart is also offering a personal organiser free
(approximate value one cheap sandwich) if you order
immediately. This catalogue has a valuable function. It
reminds me that there are office workers whose sole
occupation is flicking through catalogues like this and
ordering flipchart easels and transparent staplers; there are
workers whose sole occupation is to deliver them, and
workers who have to use them. And there are workers who
will order immediately to get a personal organiser free.

Two new debt-collection agencies are now in lettered

pursuit of Sylvie. There is also a brochure from a mint offering her a series of gold coins commemorating great moments in human history: the taming of fire, the invention of the wheel, the sevensome, the first chat show, etc.

I settle down to my own post. There's a letter for me from Soulstealer asking for payment for some books I ordered. I'm annoyed because I've already paid. I paid a year ago, and again six months later. When I say I paid, I mean I attempted to pay. A correctly filled-out cheque was sent to the correct address. I did so again six months later, and again three weeks ago. The cheques don't seem to penetrate their defences.

It troubles me to think that there are people out there who view me as a welcher, who put me in the same bracket as Sylvie and the other spongers who have drifted through here.

The second letter, I can tell, will be something juicy. The envelope feels as if there's something weighty there. It's oddly addressed though. My details are typed, which gives the letter an official feel, but my surname is absent. Simply *Oceane* and my address. That's why I've saved it for last.

I open it, and am confused, then stunned. The letter comprises one word: *Hello!* There is a signature: *Walter.*

Hello. It can be a very powerful, effective word. There was a black guy who used to stand outside the underground station, leaning on the railings all day, and when attractive, or indeed not-so-attractive, women emerged he would say: 'Hello.' I never saw any woman respond.

He wasn't much of a prospect. He was young and well built but he looked too feckless even to be a drug-dealer; you feared for his hygiene, his dress was straight from bang-up this morning, and you doubted that someone who idled outside the underground all day would have much to offer long-term. But his technique was brilliant. A spider patienting in its lair, he'd only say: 'Hello.' Simple. Direct. No whistling, motioning or eulogising of the passing women and hence no refusal. He could and would stand there all day saying, 'Hello.' Because it was enough, he knew it was enough. If a woman was interested all she had to do was slow and turn her head. Then negotiations could begin. And with the thousands of women in transit, one or two would think, why not? Because if women are interested, a polite accosting is all that's needed.

Walter's hello is simple, direct. It is an extremely powerful hello, the most effective you could ever encounter.

Walter's been dead for ten years.

I phone up Audley.

'I have another job for you. This one's very horizon-broadening, you'll find. You get to go abroad.'

A silence fattens.

'Hello?' I say.

'I don't go abroad.'

'You said you like to get out and about.'

'I do. But not abroad.'

This is unexpected. Audley normally has such swashbuckling energy and aplomb, it's strange to hear him uneasy, even a little afraid.

'Why don't you? Is it the flying you don't like?'

'No. Everything.'

'Oh, well, never mind,' I say. I'm stumped. Audley had seemed the solution.

The next day, Audley phones me.

'I'm a coward,' he says.

'Someone who does karate can't be a coward.'

'Yes they can. I know what I'm talking about. Boxing, karate, being first up at the karaoke, that doesn't matter. I'm a coward, but I don't want to be a coward with no bottle. If your job's interesting, I'll go. But those cash injections had better come thick and fast.'

'Everyone has a fear of something.'

'Not everyone. I've met some hard men.'

'And who was the hardest?'

'I was crossing a road one night with four of my brothers when this car turned in and honked us. It was a fifty-fifty situation, we were arsing around in the road, but he didn't have to honk us. I gave him a well-known gesture, and the car brakes and this guy gets out and walks towards us pulling on a pair of gloves. He's short, and he says, "So?" almost so quietly you can't hear him. That's all, "So?"

'We're thinking there are five of us, he knows there are five of us, he can see that there are one, two, three, four, five of us, and there's only one of him. He's not drunk, he hasn't got a woman to impress. This is Hull, you go down in the street taking on five, you're not getting a couple of black eyes, you're getting a life-support machine. He's either the hardest man in town or a hell of a chancer. The brothers and I are looking at each other, and he says, "I thought so," and walks back to his car. I think about it a lot. I'm annoyed sometimes I didn't have a go, because I'd like to know if he could really back it up. The curiosity. The curiosity's the hard part.'

I start briefing Audley on Walter. Unlike most talkers, he listens well.

'How did you meet him?'

'I met him in Barcelona,' I say.

BARCELONA

POLICEWOMAN. Cavewoman. Schoolteacher. Schoolgirl. French Maid. Nurse. Blushing Bride. Belly Dancer. Soldier. Geisha. Starship Battleaxe. The costumes were an important part of the show because once you removed the costumes and the skimpy choreography you were only left with what Jorge always referred to as the dusting. I did the French Maid and the Nurse, because the costumes fitted me. The other girls were content with the content, except for Marina, who was always trying to introduce supposedly famous women from history and legend that none of us had ever heard of: philosopheresses who had been stoned, queens whose influence on the development of the potato had been underappreciated, ravished politicianesses, fanatic chemistesses.

'No,' Jorge would say. 'The audience knows what it wants.'

'They must get tired of seeing a policewoman taken roughly from behind,' Marina, the policewoman roughly taken from behind, would argue.

'No audience will ever tire of a policewoman taken roughly from behind. Ten years. Not an empty seat.'

'There must be progress, Jorge.'

'Why?'

Jorge was right. Inertia was a blast. Our audience was ordinarily tourists and of those who weren't, hardly anyone could be bothered to see our show more than once. Exceptions did exist. The reviewer from the trade journal (there is a magazine for everything) rolled in from time to time. There were always television producers who would be 'researching'; as soon as they revealed themselves to Jorge he would throw them out. An ancient dermatologist in a bow-tie, Dr Alfonso, could be spotted two or three times a week. He was a true fan, but for him tradition was paramount. You would get sweet notes from him, beautifully handwritten in English: 'I have not seen such a French Maid since Amsterdam ago thirty years' or 'You seemed invaded during the magnificent nurse scene. I hope all is well. Your presence of behind has profited me a memorable evening. Your most umbilical admirer.'

The turnover of performers at the club was high because while the money and conditions were good, once you acclimatised to doing it on stage, it was a very boring job, and the boredom got harder and harder to shoulder. Also it wasn't a job that really got you places; well, it could get you places, but you'd be doing the same thing in those places and it was a career that was destined to be short.

While I was there we had Christiana (Luxembourgeoise, six-foot-one, could take on the bouncers), Nadia (Russian, twenty-two but looked twelve), Severine (French, bust like two suckling infants), Erika (Swedish, bust like a credit card), Lou and Sue (cartwheeling lesbians from Dallas), Marina (Swiss) and amid this foreign legion of hotness, three token Spaniards, Lourdes and the two Patricias (who looked identical, but who would blow up if anyone thought them sisters or confused them, but who could never work the same night because they looked identical. One was referred to as Moany Patricia and the other as Extremely Moany Patricia; Moany Patricia would moan for half an hour about the range of hairdryer attachments on offer; Extremely Moany Patricia would moan for an hour and half; very few of us could take the identification process).

Then, of course, there was the cupola herself . . . Heidi (Belgian–Argentinian cultivar, blonde, perfect, inexhaustibly filthy). Loquacious men would be limited to a grunt and nod in her presence, because of the imaginings. Heidi didn't even have to do anything, just be herself; on a stage full of naked women she was the only one who looked naked. Heidi would come on at the end, when the audience was wearying of colliding flesh, and faint dialogues would be wafting about. Backstage, you could hear the phut of men in flames and lives being one-eightied. I think her secret was her eyebrows, though I did walk past her once in the dressing room and going past her growler was like walking past an open fire. Even the lads who worked with us, a real xenotangle of Americans, Hungarians, Italians, Poles and Brits, who you would think would never want to look at another perfect blonde, were fidgety around Heidi.

Barney

My first reaction at being offered work in a live sex show was to laugh and say no. Or maybe I said no and then laughed when my friend Amber (who had done so the previous year with her boyfriend) suggested we spend one summer working in a club in Barcelona. They preferred to hire couples but Amber said they could fix me up with a partner. I found the prospect of being demonstrated on stage like a kitchen appliance distasteful.

Then I started to think about it. It wasn't as if the world hadn't explored my geography. I'd sunbathed naked more than once to the delight of notable pervos. As a dancer, in one of my few professional engagements I'd taken part in a

German production that had involved me rolling around on a warehouse floor in Darlington, with a shaven haven and only flour for a costume.

I couldn't even pretend that I hadn't had intimacy without much in the way of previous intimacy. Micro-courtships, which consisted of us finding a bedroom, had occurred at parties. I hadn't made a habit of doing that, but it wasn't as if I had never enjoyed the physics without worrying about the metaphysics.

On further reflection, it occurred to me that I had even performed the act for the public. More than once.

It was what one of my boyfriends, David, used to call going for a barney. The first time was at a party. I could say it was the coke and booze and being globally off my face that made me do it, but it wasn't. A barney consisted of upright congress, Dave standing and holding me off the ground and then jogging about, a sort of forward, more pleasure-giving piggy-backing. So, essentially streaking, plus one of your favourite activities. Fun on the run. We barneyed across the dancefloor to fewer cheers, I'd guess, than Dave had been hoping for.

But it didn't end there. David had a van (something I've subsequently learned to be wary of).

Transport

You might as well say no at the very beginning to someone with a van; they're more into powertools than average, or they're simply serial killers. In either case they won't want to go to the ballet.

Don't think I'm a snob. I strongly counsel refusal when a liveried chauffeur rings your doorbell in the middle of the night and explains that a celebrity is waiting for you outside in a stretch limo. All that's going to happen is you'll be pumped full of heroin and your derriere will be asked to perform tasks beyond the call of duty. Stretch limos should be avoided, because anyone who can buy a nightclub, as opposed to visiting it in order to meet company, isn't going to be interested in you and probably won't want to go to the ballet.

Expensive cars are usually a no-no. An expensive car often means someone who is rich, but who wants to hide it (so differently invidious to a stretch-limo user) and who won't marry you because the rich marry the rich unless they are eighty-year-old men in which case they can be forgiving to hard-up young women, but that's not for me. Or the expensive car belongs to someone who is straining to impress, which is never a good sign; or, equally unwelcome, the expensive car is a sign of someone who is obsessed with cars and not you.

Medium-range cars or second-hand cars should be okay, but they can of course be a sign of someone who isn't willing to make any effort, and while they might be willing to go to the ballet, can they pay for you? Motorbikes are predominantly for the cheapskate or the fanatical organ-donor. All in all, I can't say which form of transport is the desirable one.

Barney

One evening David parked around the back of Catford High Street and we had a dash down the high street, past a bemused queue at a cinema and some bemused diners in a burger bar, before piling into the van and taking off. It was a prank that's better in the telling than the doing, like those things you feel you have to do when you're young with handcuffs and whipped cream, which finally are cumbersome and hard to clean up. It was David's initiative, but you have to have a bit of give and take in any relationship, and you don't choose dancing as an occupation if you don't like to be looked at.

My barneying came to an end at David's athletics club one autumn night (he ran the four hundred metres). Anyone can barney for a few metres but to keep going for any distance requires major power, David's most attractive feature, indeed almost his entire stock of attractiveness.

We had to clamber over the fence to get in, so I was in a bad mood to start with, as my clothes got wet and dirty. As we set off round the track, I didn't find it remotely pleasant or amusing; David's energy was remarkable, admirable really, but it was cold, damp, dark and it wasn't much of an athletics club to boot, in a very unfashionable part of London. There are reasons why unfashionable parts of a city are unfashionable. It's not a question of not being fashionable, which can be completely different from unfashionable. Not being fashionable can simply mean that your fashionability has expired, or that you're in the queue to get the certificate, or that it's an area unconcerned with fashionability. Unfashionability is never an accident. As David and I bumped away, I wished we could at least be in a fashionable part of London, then suddenly thought of Tina. And then I thought why am I thinking of Tina?

We were close to the finish when I heard some feet slapping behind us and for a moment I was terrified, fearing the forces of order and non-public fornication were upon us, when we were overtaken by a huge black guy at such speed David might as well have stopped running. The huge black guy was barneying a huge redhead who cast me a 'men, eh?' smirk as she whizzed past.

'Not again,' was David's comment. I should have known that if something has a name, there's a need for it. David fessed up: his coach had suggested barneying as a supplementary form of training that he, for insurance reasons, couldn't condone.

No

Your initial derision at being invited to Barcelona to raunch up its nightlife softens into curiosity: what's it like? Amber had done a tour the summer before and the more I heard about it, the better it sounded. Everything from your impactor to your accommodation was arranged. The job was quite alluring when lined up with my other possibilities of employment, which were barely in sight: escorting ten-year-old Danes around Stonehenge or watching fourteen-year-old shoppers unfold piles of sweaters you spent hours folding: all for the price of a good lip gloss. The hope of dancing work never completely faded but for some reason the dance market had collapsed and I was aware that better and better-connected dancers than me were mowing lawns. Amber talked warmly of Barcelona and how friendly every aspect of the city and club was.

Then you think: who would know? Unlike some branches of genital commerce, there's no evidence. Making films is different. Amber had made films and her wisdom on the subject was: 'Think of the five acquaintances, whether family, friends or enemies, you'd least want to see you being spit-roasted. They'll be the first five to see the film.' And it wasn't like going on the game. I wouldn't be subjected to the wheezes of old fat company directors and the damage. Other dancers I knew had tried that and even though they had been working the flash hotels, they had been too enthusiastic about it for my liking; just as smackheads always offer you a needle. That sort of fucking for money fucks you up. Don't ask me why, but it's so.

That's one of the drawbacks of dancing. It's part of that actress-model-dancer enclosure that anyone with a body under twenty-four can enter if they have no problem with closing their eyes and opening their mouths. If you have any background in dance it's infuriating to see lumpy oxen transmuted into dancers by saying 'yes, I'm a dancer' and bringing the profession into disrepute by all sorts of non-dance activity.

Amber told me to sleep on it, but the next morning I said no to Barcelona.

I'd got a message offering me a try-out with a dance company in Norwich. Five of us bounced out two days later in a church hall to learn the ropes. When you are fighting for one place, you have to think about strategy. It's not easy: first of all when a man is in charge he's likely to be gay, dance after all being the boyz' stronghold, and of course those who aren't have such a smorgasbord of pussy on offer, lending them a good moisturiser is more likely to curry favour than a blow job. You have to size up your opposition: are they going to drop to their knees and open their mouths? I was still young and good-willed enough to keep these thoughts cordoned off at the back, and one morning the other four aspirants vanished. I assumed the plodders had been given their marching orders and that I was on final probation before being given a contract.

I spent another two weeks working out with the company and eating small pieces of fruit and yoghurt, not because I liked eating small pieces of fruit and yoghurt but because I couldn't afford anything else. A growing coolness towards me rather than a proffered contract became tangible. Finally I caught the director on his own and blurted out the question:

'Do I get the job?'

'There's no job to be got. Didn't anyone tell you?'

I was now stuck in a bed and breakfast with no money. What was annoying about this was that I'd stayed in so many bed and breakfasts where scarpering with an unpaid bill would have been a real joy, but the old lady who ran this one was great. She could see I was hungry and would do the 'I've just made myself a sandwich and I thought you'd like one too' ruse as if she weren't giving me a free meal. Not like the sausage-deniers I've stayed with in the past.

Sausage-deniers

For example, the bed and breakfast in Blackpool where they claimed to include a full breakfast in the price. When you went into the dining-room you'd be greeted by a very small bowl with a cluster of cornflakes in it. The proprietors would then ask you whether you wanted sausages or bacon with your eggs, and that would be the last you'd see of them. I was there for a week and I didn't get my sausages nor did I see anyone else get a fry-up. The proprietors' guile lay in the knowledge that most of their guests were in a rush and would give up waiting after ten minutes, and make do with large helpings of soggy toast. One morning I went hunting for the proprietors. I went all the way back into the kitchen and through into the garden: no sign of them, nor a sausage, cooked or uncooked. There must have been some secret passage for them to hide in.

The next morning they were back saying, 'Where did you get to? We kept your breakfast hot for you for ages.' They did it because they could. There was a large jar of strawberry jam on display, always full, because no one could manage to open it; I'm sure the jam was rendered unobtainable by a glued lid. You knew that every light bulb and sheet of toilet paper on the premises had been pilfered. The twist in bed and breakfasts is that they are generally managed by managers who shouldn't be managing bed and breakfasts. People who hate people. People for whom a small rasher of bacon is a tundra-like vastness. Granted, for all of us the smallest thing can store unimaginable magnitudes.

Feats

Curiously, one of the most satisfying items I own is a T-shirt I got free in a bar some ten years ago. A brewery was dishing out promotional T-shirts and I was lucky enough to get one.

The quality of the cotton is poor and the design isn't much, but even now it gives me a feeling of satisfaction to know it's neatly folded in the wardrobe. I have designer gear there, but I worked for that, I earned that. The T-shirt is a source of elation because I diddled life out of a few quid. There were a lot of other customers in the bar, but I bagged the T-shirt for free. It's ridiculous, but something that cost little more than a sandwich gives me a kick, because I got it for free, without doing anything, just being lucky.

No

I cheated by borrowing some money from my parents to pay for the bed and breakfast. But by this point I had never been so desperate for employment. Usually, if you make the effort, something awful, humiliating and menial is waiting for you, but this time I couldn't find anything. Finally, after tramping round for days, I saw a bar job advertised on a card in a newsagent's.

'Good morning, I'm phoning about the job.'

'What job?'

'Bar work?'

'How do you know about the job?'

'It was in your ad.'

'What ad?'

'The one in the newsagent's.'

'How did you get this number?'

'It was in your ad. Is that Marco?'

'How do you know my name?'

'It was in your ad.'

'I'm too busy to talk now. Phone back later.'

The bar was nearby and I was majorly desperate, otherwise I wouldn't have bothered. After several bizarre conversations, Marco agreed to an appointment. I turned up, buzzed, waited, buzzed, waited, buzzed, waited and hammered on the shutters. No one. I went off angry, but another day of unemployment calmed me and disabled my dignity. I arranged another appointment. Again no Marco. The third time, Marco opened the door angrily. 'I'm too busy to see you now.' This was lunchtime. The bar was closed, empty and silent as only an empty bar can be. Marco was on some proprietorial high, hoisted by his own imagination.

The next day, to my own amazement, as arranged, I came back only to be told: 'I'm too busy. I've got some restaurant reviewers coming.' This was odd as well as annoying since the only food they served at the bar was garlic bread. I was shoved out as two Norwegians appeared. I spent the next twenty-four hours cursing Marco and cackling at the idea of me going back, but by the time the next unemployed afternoon rolled round I was knocking on Marco's door, using my best smile. One of the great advantages of being female is that you can get revenge by smiling; if I'd been male I would have been obliged to punch Marco very hard.

I was now conducted into Marco's office where he plonked himself in his executive armchair, and whipped out his organ, sighing: 'Be quick. I'm very busy.'

It was so multitudinously outrageous that I'm ashamed to say I didn't have a cutting retort available. If Marco had been offering me a managerial position, well, but expecting a climactic treat for a job rubbing garlic on bread and uncapping beer bottles, a wage something in the region of nothing?

There is a style for demanding sexual favours for employment and Marco didn't have it. He was, and I'm reaching for the understatement here, not the sort of man women dream about: he had the weirdness but not the gumption to be a serial killer.

The one with the crumb will use it mercilessly. I knew that I didn't need to be in debt in a grotty back room studying what looked like a dead lizard, with rainclouds in the background. I could be in Barcelona.

I left resolving to make two phone calls. One to Amber, another to a motorcycle gang who had suggested I call them if ever needed anyone beaten up. I couldn't find their number.

Barcelona

At the age of twenty-one I'd never been abroad.

It wasn't a desire to stay in Britain, or a desire not to travel.

My childhood holidays had always been fun. Full of expectation we would all jump into the car. My father would be getting settled in the driver's seat, my mother would be inspecting me and my sister in the back. Julia always sat on the left, I always sat on the right. We would be laden with our holiday amusements (comics, music, nibbles, new clothes), often purchased months before and issued only on departure. We would be fiddling with these as our parents made the final checks (newspaper delivery deactivated and so on). Seat-belts would be meticulously adjusted.

'Ready?' my father would ask the back seat as if our participation in family decisions was vital.

'Ready,' Julia, as older sister, would report first. 'Ready,' I would confirm. The car would then gently trundle backwards down the drive. Julia and I had an important job keeping an eye out for approaching traffic.

My father would wait for the all-clear before reversing the car out to the far kerb; the engine would subside as he manhandled the steering wheel and then a jolt as he hit the accelerator aggressively to signal that the time for adventure had come and we were on our way.

These departures were deeply primeval: the family together, moving off nomadically, supplied for any eventuality (hunger, thirst, injury, boredom).

Second gear, however, was as far as my father got, since it

was only three hundred yards to the Travellers' Rest Hotel, where we spent all our family holidays. When Julia and I were very young we didn't go on holiday because we didn't have any money, but when Dad became a departmental head we went away once a year, but we never went anywhere but the Travellers' Rest.

My mother wasn't very happy about this (that the hotel was in the same street as our house was the hardest part for her to bear) but Julia and I didn't mind and my father wouldn't consider anything else.

The arguments my father mustered in favour of this destination were, in retrospect, not unreasonable if not entirely convincing: why waste time and money travelling? Did anyone enjoy being stuck in a car for three or more hours at a time, worrying about bodily functions and screaming about the right turning? At the Travellers' Rest you could read the menu and converse with the staff with few linguistic hurdles. Above all, the advantage of the Travellers' Rest was that if you forgot something or wanted to check the post, you could simply stroll home, something you couldn't do if you were on the coast or abroad. We could go on holiday but still see our friends.

Holidays, my father asserted, were for shedding responsibility. For Mum not to cook, for him to sleep in. For me and Julia not to have to make our beds. For all of us to indulge in liberties. The Travellers' Rest was a grand old family house, so the facilities weren't earth-shattering, but there were two arcade machines, a mini-golf course, a badminton court (albeit heavily involved with nature), and a bird-bath sort of swimming pool; but when you're twelve these are exciting. As were the boys.

The talent wasn't much at the hotel, because it was small and the regular customers were unimportant businessmen and husbands with surprise divorces. But there was some action. One summer, for example, I met an Egyptian called

Mohammed. 'Everyone in Egypt is called Mohammed,' he had sulked. Mohammed was two years older than me and more interested in Julia, and Julia was interested in him, but because of that she relentlessly ignored him, and so Mohammed and I spent a lot of time together, which made Julia hop around in rage, out of sight.

At Mohammed's instigation we ended up playing strip-chess, which, with hindsight, I suppose he chose because it eliminated the element of chance that strip-poker contains. Mohammed was confident he'd win as he was older and I was a girlie. I'd hardly ever played chess but I beat Mohammed five times in a row; he was so furious he pulled a basin off the wall in the gents' and stopped talking to me.

My mother didn't give up on foreign travel. She took evening classes in Spanish for a couple of years in the hope of using her need to practise the language as a blackmail tool. My father agreed to go to Spain if she could hold a conversation with a waiter in a local Spanish restaurant. She failed the test. Many years later my father confessed to me. 'It wasn't surprising the waiter didn't understand your mother's Spanish. He was Turkish.'

He didn't see the point of travel. He went abroad only once. Mum's parents gave them some ferry tickets to go to France. The ferry docked in Boulogne and Mum was forced to check into the nearest hotel to the port where they spent the weekend, eating at the nearest restaurant, drinking in the nearest bar and shopping in the nearest shop. On the crossing over, it had been foggy and choppy and, looking around from the deck, my father could only see disquieting waves in every direction. 'It's a bloody ocean,' he said. 'No, it's not the ocean,' reproved one of the French crew. 'I know an ocean when I see one,' insisted my father.

Nine months later I was christened Oceane. So I was abroad, in France, at a very tender age, but I didn't see anything and I don't have any memories to speak of.

Yes

When I say I hadn't been abroad before my job in Barcelona, I had.

There was one failed attempt. I had always found my father's insularity comical, but it occurred to me one day I was eighteen and I hadn't left Britain. I swiftly took the ferry to Boulogne to visit some friends who were camping in the Dordogne. Whether or not I reached France is open to discussion. The ferry docked in Boulogne, but I didn't disembark. I was in a lifeboat with a charming guy from the duty-free shop, and then I returned to Folkestone to spend a week at his bedsit.

Then a boyfriend, Ganesh, offered to take me to Bombay. But whether this trip really counts as going abroad is also open to discussion. We landed at night and I didn't see much from the taxi taking us from the airport to the hotel as it was too dark and I had to spend most of my time fighting Ganesh off (it was early in our relationship).

Once we got to the hotel we found it habit-forming. Our goings-on kept us room-bound. We slept in late, did it (lengthily), had room-service lunch (leisurely), did it (lengthily), had room-service supper (leisurely), watched some television (leisurely), did it (lengthily) and slept (lengthily).

Ganesh was a bit of fat farm, the last known address of thousands of samosas, but he had freakish energy, and it's always flattering to inspire such rampancy. Whatever men like to put about regarding their appetites, many like to get it over with promptly so they can go off down the pub with their mates or fiddle with their cars. Not Ganesh. I did want to go out – the view from our room was a brick wall – but Ganesh had paid for the trip and who was I to suppress his ardour? The third day I tried to conscience him out of bed.

'Shouldn't you see your relatives?'

Ganesh weighed up his duties for a few seconds: 'No. They're all shits.'

We would have got out of the room by the end of the week if we hadn't contracted upset stomachs. Ganesh would only expend his diminished vigour in one way.

We drove back out to the airport in the dark.

Barcelona

I told Amber to sign me up. She had worked at the club, so her say-so got me a place unseen and unauditioned. We were due to travel out together, but in the end I went alone as Amber's thrust-supplier had a severe outbreak of boils. I was a little down and nervous about jetting off on my own to be shafted by persons unknown, but I consoled myself with the thought that that's what most holidaymakers do.

On the plane I sat next to a chatty couple, Paul and Priscilla, in their sixties. I was glad to natter and take my mind off how things would be in Barcelona. Paul was extremely talkative, showed me pictures of their grand-children and was delighted to hear I would be working in Barcelona, although I didn't reveal the exact nature of my employment. 'We have a place a short drive from Barcelona now that we're retired. I used to work for Lambeth Council. But we spend most of our time in Spain. We've got a great place, five bedrooms, swimming pool. Of course, just because I used to work for Lambeth you mustn't think I embezzled the money –'

'– of course not.'

'Good. When you say you worked for Lambeth Council the assumption is you're a lying, cheating deadbeat. It's true that whole departments were on the fiddle, and one of my colleagues did spend twenty years building model battleships out of matches during office hours, and there was that scandal in the paper the other week, but that's not the whole story. You must come and visit our place. No one in your family works for the tax people, do they?'

'No.'

'Yes, you could stay for a weekend, and who knows, perhaps you'd like a threesome with me and the wife?'

'Oh, Paul,' Priscilla snapped. I left them at the carousel waiting for their luggage. Perhaps group sex is the new cucumber sandwiches, and it's possible to retain your looks into your sixties, but you have to have looks to retain. Paul looked like a dead walrus that had been floating too long in the Atlantic. 'You should live every day as if it's your last,' Paul shouted after me.

'That's good advice.'

As I walked away I could just make out Priscilla reproaching Paul: 'I've told you, you have to drug them first.'

It was too dark to see much as the taxi drove me to the club, Babylon. With my heavy suitcase I leaned my way up to the main entrance. It was Sunday, so it was closed and lifeless. After a ludicrously long time of suitcase-dragging I found the side entrance, which was opened by a woman with pink hair.

'Hello, I'm Oceane.'

'No, you're not.'

'I've got a job here.'

'No, you haven't.'

By now, I was angry. My debts were growing like some parallel universe. I had sold the one item of any worth I had, my computer, to get the air ticket. I had been outraged by sexagenarian swingers. I was in some foreign darkness with a suitcase that was making my arms and shoulders ache. I shoved past the gate-keeper and went to look for the boss.

In an office, behind a desk, I found a tubby guy with an immaculately groomed beard.

'Are you Jorge?' I asked.

'There is no Jorge,' said the pink-haired woman behind me.

Jorge got up and peered into the corridor. 'Ah.'

Jorge didn't look like a nightclub owner. For a start, he was only a year or two older than me, and there was something unusual about him. It took me years to work out what it was. It wasn't his superlative calm – he would always pause before saying anything in Spanish or English, he rather resembled a tortoise on some high-grade narcotics. It wasn't the two-tone teal suit he was wearing – the one nightclubby thing about him. He was happy. He wasn't happy because he had banked some money, or because he had heard some good news or because he had ingested some high-grade narcotics. He was . . . happy. Simply thinking about him puts me in a good mood.

'You must be hungry,' he said opening a dull door at the side of his office to reveal a dazzling, cavernous kitchen packed with white-clad figures dashing about who gave Jorge hurried deference as we walked through. An enormous restaurant was next to the club and whenever Jorge was peckish he could use his personal entrance. He explained that the two establishments cross-fertilised each other marvellously. Customers going to the club would be lured into the restaurant after a show and customers going to the restaurant would be lured into a show after their meal.

The restaurant was the best I'd ever eaten in and Jorge didn't spare the wine list. Within half an hour of meeting him I had no doubt he was the best boss who had ever lived and was hoping to marry him. It was too much of a toomuchness: why does Here pass over the caviar when you still have the taste of turd in your mouth?

I asked about my work because I was still nervous about that, but Jorge waved away the question. 'It's all very easy. There's only one warning I give to newcomers. Watch out for the slaves.' All sorts of restraint-seeking men had come to the club to grovel before the Big Lux, to the point where the establishment had been clogged up by chained, gagged and suspended men nominally carrying out chores, most of them supremely pointless. Jorge had to order a clearout after one of his favourite turns, a Polish girl, broke a leg after stumbling over a hogtied slave licking a corridor floor clean (although Jorge admitted her routine with a plaster cast proved to be a winner).

'We have about twenty performers here, in the end we had nearly thirty bondagists lying about the club. They came from all over Europe, politicians, human-resource managers . . . local government. What is it with local government? Particularly from your country. They book a year in advance. It used to be golf. Now it's chains. They steal so much, the people from local government, and they come here to spend it in the most disgusting ways. No one's underthings were safe. We had to adopt a strict admissions policy for slaves. Only members of parliament and newspaper editors, because you never know when you might need friends. I always recommend the brothel down the road, but you wouldn't believe our waiting list.'

The slaves were a menace. They rarely did anything useful and they got in the way. Only three were permitted when I was at the club. One grandfatherly figure in a pair of nappies did the latrine duties; he was always in the toilet when you wanted to use it, and perhaps I'm overfinickety on this, but I don't believe that a toilet bowl that is licked clean is really clean. And while we all have our peccadilloes and weird entertainments I'm not sure I want someone like that in charge of Europe's well-being.

And how much dusting can you do when you're trapped inside a giant inflatable rubber ball, with only your head protruding and a duster clenched between your teeth? At least with the Ball, you could roll him out of the way. The least inconvenient of the three was the naked skinny man who was pegged out face-down in the main entrance as a human doormat who would urge 'please tread on me' and 'you degrade me beautifully' but he wasn't much use for cleaning your shoes.

'Oh,' added Jorge, 'there is more advice. If someone called

Rutger says I told you to do sick stuff with him, I didn't. Take everything Rutger says as a lie.'

Performers were given the option of renting a room in a vast residential space above the club at a very friendly rate. My room was small, but fresh and cheery. I went to the window and with some difficulty beat back the blinds, hoping to see how Barcelona's light was at night. Two feet away from my window was a brick wall which went up as far as I could see.

I went to bed with contentment. All you need is a good room and hope.

Breakfast

Had I brought enough self-mockery to the party?

The restaurant also acted as the staff canteen in the mornings. I went in to have a coffee and croissant and sat next to Hamish, who was the stage manager.

'I wanted to be an astronaut,' he said. Space exploration had been his mania from childhood. To be the perfect candidate, Hamish had assiduously pursued both athletic and scientific activities from an early age. He won a scholarship to university and had completed the first year of an electrical-engineering degree when he won a weekend in Barcelona as a prize in a design competition. One of the girls from the club had met him at the beach, and the evening he visited the club, the stage manager had electrocuted himself. Hamish had stepped in, put the electricity back in its place, and found himself a new career.

'That was six years ago,' he said looking at his croissant as if it were his mother's liver. 'I never got home. Why bother? You have the most beautiful city in the world with the friendliest people in the world, the best food in the world, and you can guess with my job meeting beautiful women isn't a problem. Responsibilities? Flicking a few switches and telling the girls to get their nipples ready. Suddenly Edinburgh never existed. The future of the human race? A load of old bollocks. Why should the advancement of civilisation be my problem?'

'You must be very happy here.'

'I'm not. I'm miserable as fuck.'

Although I tend to be very elastic in new situations, I was wondering whether I should sit somewhere else, but I didn't move fast enough.

'I'm in love,' he continued.

'That's wonderful.'

'No. You hear there's no such thing as love. Unfortunately there is.'

The woman in question was the one he had met on the beach, that career-altering day six years ago. Whom he had slept with once. Six years ago.

'She's jobless. She's penniless. She's homeless. She's friendless. She's seriously ill with cancer. She still won't have anything to do with me. Whatever happened to using a man for his money? Use me. Despise me. Cheat on me, but why not live with me?'

'Have you tried seeing someone else?'

'I've slept with over fifty women since then. Wonderful women, generous women, not just women whose pelvis could break your arm, women who would buy you carefully considered birthday presents and want to discuss interplanetary travel. I was married for two years. You think you're happy but then you notice you aren't. There are always the mistake-makers who make the same mistake again and again and their friends say: why don't they learn from their mistakes? But you can learn and learn and learn and it doesn't do you any good. You might as well be an errorsmith. I'm not a weak man. I can run the marathon in three fifty-two. I went over two years without seeing her, or even thinking about her. Then I saw her again and it might as well have been two minutes.'

'Would you have been happy if you'd managed to marry her instead?'

'Probably not.'

'Why did you split up?'

'No idea.'

'A row?'

'No. That's what's so annoying. If I'd done something wrong or done something that had upset her, then my regret could have an altar.'

I was thinking that I wouldn't sit next to Hamish at any future breakfasts. Lou and Sue came up. 'We're Lou and Sue. We're in room eighteen. Anytime,' they said *en route* for the muesli.

'Perhaps I'm not in love,' said Hamish.

'What's made you change your mind?'

'A good cup of coffee is a dangerous thing. I grew up drinking instant coffee. I was happy drinking it, then one day I went to a café and had an espresso. You only have to have one and you can never enjoy drinking instant again. So if you can't afford to get espresso, or getting to an espresso outlet is difficult, it's better never to have drunk it and to have stayed with the instant.'

'You've lost me.'

'The pleasure. I'm not bragging but I've been around, and it could be that's what I can't get out of my mind. When you've had the best, you don't want the rest. All you can think is, this is not as good, this is not as good. You try everything, but you just think this isn't as good. Pleasure's the payoff, what else do we work for? No god but pleasure. I don't know what it was between us . . . but it really dragged my rhino. Do you want another croissant?'

I believed him. Men, even if they aren't lining you up for imminent boarding, put you on the waiting-list, make a small advance payment of compliment or attention for future transactions. I didn't exist as a woman for Hamish, just receptacle for his musings.

'I've never told anyone this,' he said.

Jorge appeared. I was glad. You always feel the temptation to toss some advice on to a pile of someone's problems, but I didn't quite know what to do with an admission like that. Hamish reminded me of someone bashing a vending machine in a furious attempt to retrieve unretrievable change.

Dusting

'I'm going to introduce you to your partner,' said Jorge. I was immediately nervous again about the demands of wetwork, which must have shown. It was silly really. How could you fuck up fucking? But I was convinced somehow I would mess it up.

'Your job is easy, really, Oceane. Be ecstatic. The men have the hardest part . . . but it's a line of work for them where, I warn you, intelligence and imagination are a tumbling-stone. Come and meet Rhino. He's upstairs I think.'

We started walking up flights of stairs. There were boxes everywhere. In one which was open I noticed some strange glass objects. 'I thought about putting in an elevator,' said Jorge, 'but it's good exercise going up to the roof. And everyone wants to go up to the roof.' There was a very old lady struggling precariously on a chair to wash some windows; it looked incredibly cruel, letting her do something so obviously difficult and dangerous for her. Jorge exchanged a few words of concern with her, but she waved him away. I suppose she was some old retainer being allowed the dignity of labour. We carried on up the stairs. It was the happiest staircase I've ever walked up. 'Rhino's been away. A Hollywood crew was in town and the leading lady has a big problem sticking needles in her arm, so they hired Rhino to lively up the trailer.'

We reached the roof, which was covered by an enormous terrace. There was a satisfactory swimming pool and a border of lovingly cultivated mimosas and laurel bushes defying the withering sunshine. Lying on a recliner, naked apart from a zipped rubber bondage mask, was an enormous, muscular, wall-wide man. Truly, bondage and fetishism are the new cucumber sandwiches. Is there a bank manager who doesn't own a leg-spreader or a ball-gag?

'*Que pasa*, Rhino?' Jorge enquired

Let me bring the words enormous and muscular in again for another appearance. Rhino was a wall of muscle, and okay, I couldn't help checking, it was like an award-winning marrow. Everything was perfect. Perfect formations of muscle, perfect amount of hair, perfect tan, even his pedicure was better than mine, nails rounded like church windows. He was so perfect he didn't look real. I studied the mimosas closely as if I were a mimosa authority so I wouldn't sink to my knees in reverence.

'He has a great false dream,' Jorge said. 'The trouble with any great false dream is persuading the world to go along with it.'

Often you make a decision and nothing happens. Sometimes you make a decision and it's disappointing. Occasionally, you make a decision and you jackpot instantly. And sometimes you make a decision and you discover it's the best thing you've ever done in your life. I had crawled out of a long, long tunnel with wattling of darkness, rain, errorsmiths, pests, lowlifes, into paradise which measured approximately thirty by forty metres.

Was I important? This question came back to my mind. Was the world finally mine? This had been one of the questions perplexing me. I had had a lot of shit. Was that just teasing on the part of Here, or was I right in thinking I was important and better than everyone else? You don't go into dance unless you believe you're the best, but unfortunately there had been a lot of evidence lately that I wasn't.

Rhino offered me his hand. I was relieved he shook gently: it was like putting my hand into a machine.

Two thoughts were uppermost in my mind. First I wanted to marry Rhino. No matter how incompatible we were, no matter how bad his dress sense, no matter if the marriage only lasted half an hour, no matter if he had some ghastly skin complaint or askew teeth under his mask, no matter if he had no more conversation than a wardrobe, no matter how many women would chide 'she was so stupid', it would be worth it because I could point to him as my ex-husband for the rest of my life and women everywhere would contort with jealousy.

I wanted to take a photograph of Rhino and send it to everyone I knew with the inscription: This is my job. I felt ridiculously grateful to him for condescending to shake my hand. I couldn't believe anyone this good-looking would be working in a club in Barcelona. Why hadn't the film crew put him in the film? He was a walking magazine cover. He was also a little daunting because he was so big. I wondered, as I stroked a mimosa, if I could actually fit it into my mouth.

Jorge smiled. 'And it's claimed money can't buy you happiness. What a lie put about by the poor.'

The roof terrace was higher up than any of the neighbouring buildings, but there was a high wall around it nevertheless to prevent anyone in the distance with binoculars being exposed to bare bits. I had been hoping to have a panorama of the city, but I was a foot too short to have access to it. I wasn't much interested in the view now.

'I'll get changed and join you,' I said. Jorge walked down with me and I asked what was going on with the mask. I assumed that Rhino was an obvious nickname referring to his fire-hose, but Jorge explained that Rhino often wore a mask because of plastic surgery and chiefly his addiction to nose-jobs. "'Only rhinoplasty can save me, Jorge,' he always says. "I don't want to be ashamed of my early films.'"

'Will he be in some films?'

'He gets an offer every week.'

Jorge doubted he would ever star in one. Rhino was the longest-serving employee of the club. He had worked at Babylon for five years after bolting from some village in Andalucia and had been in constant demand by the skintraders and other film-makers. He hadn't made any films because he felt he hadn't readied his appearance enough and he hadn't made any money, or rather hadn't kept any because he had blown it all on the knife, his nose being the main target. It was shortened, lengthened, narrowed and widened every four months or so (not to mention the cheekbones, lips, dentistry).

I rushed back downstairs and was faced with the how-much-of-what-to-wear dilemma. Obviously birthday suits were acceptable on the roof and I liked the idea of an all-over tan, but you don't want to play all your cards at once, so I wanted something winning for the lower half. I then took a while adjusting the hair so it didn't look adjusted and making general final checks, so it was half an hour later that I made my return.

Rhino was gone. In his place was a curly-haired scruff in a worn T-shirt who looked worried to see me.

'You hate me, don't you?' he said Englishly.

'Why do you say that?'

'I don't know.'

I was taken aback, but for once it didn't take me a day to think of an appropriate response. Maybe once in your life, you're allotted a swift repartee.

'Give me a chance to dislike you first.' Which I thought was friendly and reassuring in the face of nuttiness.

'You do hate me, don't you?'

I spread out my towel hoping I would only be meeting Spaniards in the future.

'I haven't a clue who you are.'

'All right I'll confess everything.' I had the feeling some powerful pharmaceuticals were trooping across his mind. I hoped so for his sake. I wanted to get some rays and was trying to figure out how much time I could take without getting lobsters. I just wanted some rays without lobsters, without confessions. He reminded me of a man I sat in front of once in a cinema who told me to stop moving my head in the middle of a film.

'How did you find me, Sandrine?'

'I'm not Sandrine.'

'Sandrine, why are you doing this?'

'My name is Oceane.'

He considered this.

'You're not Oceane.'

'If you say so.'

'You act like Sandrine.'

I was thinking about going back to my room.

'My name is Oceane and I'd like to sunbathe in peace.'

When I was first told to stop moving my head that time in the cinema I immediately had the polite reaction of immobilising my head because I assumed that someone would only speak out in public, disturbing all the others in the audience, if there were good cause. Then I realised that my head wasn't jiving around; it was shifting around minutely in a respiring manner and it's not as if I'm tall in the first place. In other words it was like asking me to stop breathing: impossible and outrageous. I ignored the remark, if for no other reason than how could I stop moving my head if I wasn't moving it? The demand came back again louder. It was a difficult situation, because if I started arguing with him, it could only be more disruptive for the others in the cinema. On the other hand, keeping quiet would let everyone think I was some guilty head-twister scorning pleas of reason. I couldn't get up to leave either. I was in the middle of a full row so it would have forced half a dozen people on either side of me to get up. I opted for the rather weak tactic of concentrating on completely immobilising my head, which of course prevented me from enjoying the film, in fact I didn't take in a word of it, just the denunciations from behind me regarding inconsiderate people who disrupted the views of honest cinema-goers. All I could think was why doesn't this happen when you're escorted by of one of those good old-fashioned thuggish boyfriends with an inclination to violence towards cheekers.

The problem I perceived later is that many human beings aren't human beings. The ones who aren't are physically impossible to distinguish from the ones who are. The detail of the counterfeiting is flawless: the ducting of the skin, the split ends of hairs, the pruneness of moles, the guttering of teeth, you can work right down to the carbon and it's spot-on, but they're not human beings. The likeness is so good you really have to be a specialist to tell the difference. They sound like us. They tell jokes like us. They are indistinguishable from us glance after glance.

They're empties. What was going on in the cinema was nothing to do with me. It was the follow-on of a faked childhood. A tap is left running and the water cascades into the flats below, and non-tap-turners have to mop up. Because after a certain age you can't learn to be a human being; you can try, but you're not going to make it. We have to be taught to say thank you. That's one of the most important lessons you can learn. We can all say thank you, but you have to learn. We can all grow, but we have to learn how to. Some might make it on their own, but very, very few.

And how do you test? Difficult. I can't think of a better test than waiting. If someone will wait on a corner for you in the cold, in the rain, even in the sunshine, for half an hour, for an hour because you said you were coming.

Advice

Useless. Information can be useful. *There is a gap in the fence over there and you can escape* is useful. *You can buy oranges half-price round the corner.* That's useful. But *here are some tips on escaping or orange-buying*, they're useless.

'Why do you keep on saying you're Oceane?' said the scruff.

'Because I keep on being Oceane.' I was so close to paradise. The sun was sinking into my skin It was merely a question of blanking out the scruff. Some silence shuffled through.

'Shall I tell you what the best thing in the world is?' he asked. He was waiting for me to say tell me. I didn't.

'A trip to the cinema.' He was certain I was going to ask why. I didn't.

'If you can enjoy it, it's the best thing in the world.'

'You don't ask for much.' Why hadn't I kept my mouth shut?

'No. I do. Because if you can enjoy a trip to the cinema, you can enjoy anything, because if you can enjoy a trip to the cinema, you have peace.'

I closed my eyes loudly. More silence shuffled through.

'Shall I tell you what's sorrowful? Do you want to know what's sorrowful?' he asked

I chose a more direct approach: 'No.'

'In stories sorrow is two pilots in an unsound ground-bound plane with only one parachute. The true load of sorrow is two pilots in a ground-bound unsound plane with five parachutes, but no one jumps in time because they're arguing with each other.'

'Why are they arguing?'

'As many reasons as you want. "You picked the best parachute." "You keep the plane steady while I jump." "I've always hated you." "You were supposed to get the fuel." I can go on. That's sorrow. And when I say peace, I'm not talking about post-dragging-my-rhino calm.'

I am getting a tan, I thought. Memories of lectures on the importance of getting on with others drifted in.

'Now, I'm going to confess to you.' He was waiting for me to say confess what. I didn't.

'My girlfriend was an *au pair*. I was working in a warehouse. Ever worked in a warehouse? You walk ten feet, pick something up. Carry it ten feet to the packing table. You pack it, label it and off it goes. Then you walk twelve feet, pick something up, carry it to the packing table, pack it and off it goes. Sometimes you walk as far as thirty feet. Some of the packers had been working there for seven years. The bad jokes are the highlight of the day. Half an hour after starting the job I was almost passing out from the boredom. I was barely earning enough to feed myself.

'Same for my girlfriend who was *au-pairing* for this rich woman. She did the housework and was a human burglar alarm. The house outfortressed any fortress I know, grilles, alarm systems galore, anti-tank walls. And the dogs, where did they get the dogs from? I've seen smaller and better-tempered lions. I wouldn't fancy my chances with one of these dogs even if I had a gun, you could see yourself shooting one of these dogs and the dog just not giving a woof about it . . . '

'Hard dog,' I commented to move things on.

'None harder. Perhaps you haven't had much to do with the rich, but there's a simple formula. The richer they are, the more you hate them. There are two ways to have big money. To be born into it, or to steal it. Do you know how many really unfortunate people there are in the world?'

'Depends how you define unfortunate.'

'No it doesn't. I'll tell you how many unfortunate people there are. One. There's one bugger out there globally fucked. Because everyone else gets a chance to shit on someone else. It doesn't matter how low-down you are, there's always someone lower. The toilet cleaner in the shittiest toilet in the shittiest country has the assistant cleaner who has the assistant assistant cleaner and so on down the chain, but eventually there has to be one person who hasn't got anyone to shit on and that, that's rough.'

'That's rather cynical.'

'Yes, that's the response when you've outargued someone and they don't like it. Where was I?'

'Hating the rich?'

'Oh yes.'

'What about Jorge, he's nice.'

'Jorge is nice. Because he isn't rich. Jorge has good money, don't get me wrong, but he doesn't have big money. You can tell because he's generous; if he were rich he wouldn't be generous, or rather because he is generous he can never be rich. No pauper ever held on to a coin like a rich fucker. We decided to rob Artemis's employers, not for the money, but because they were disgusting. They only hired her because she didn't have a work permit, so they could pay her nothing and threaten to have her kicked out of the country.

'It was Artemis's idea. She was left on her own a lot, so I pretended to make a delivery one day. She let me in along this steel-mesh walkway with these dogs throwing themselves at the mesh. I grabbed a stamp collection, then since Artemis would come under suspicion, I gave her a classy tying-up and gagging. The owners were due back an hour later. Our plan was to have no contact for a week. The police jump when the rich complain, might be checking the phones, following her and so on.

'The week goes by and I wait for news. I had already flogged off the stuff before the owners had returned home. I waited and waited. Then I went on to the worrying. Was Artemis playing safe? Or had we banana-skinned?

'I went back. With a pair of binoculars, up a big tree opposite the house, I could look into the front room. Artemis was still tied up on the chair, on the ground.'

He was very upset. It was natural and decent of him to be upset about such a discovery. It would only be natural and decent of me to sympathise with him. But it was like little old ladies tumbling in the street. Of course, you'll help them back to their feet but you can't help wishing they had waited until you were out of eyeshot. I wanted him to be upset somewhere else; it was spoiling my sunbathing.

'I phoned for an ambulance straight away, but I knew . . . Obviously the owners hadn't come back for some reason. I totally lost it and left the country. Bummed around working as a diving instructor but there . . . there are a lot of banana skins in the water. It was so unfair. After a few years I went back to England and confessed. I've never told anyone that.'

We sat in the sunshine for a bit. His eyebrows were extremely short and angular; they looked like two accents that had been stuck on his brow.

'Did you go to prison?'

'No.'

He was waiting for me to ask him why not. I didn't. He was very down though, so reluctantly I offered some support.

'But it's not your fault.'

'No. I suppose not. I mean it was her idea. But I still pound on asylum doors at three in the morning every now and then.'

Kindness is an art few understand. A skimpy-thonged figure bounded up.

'Hello, Sandrine. My name is Rutger.'

He was good-looking in that pretty-boy way that lots of girls like. He wasn't fat, he wasn't hairy, he wasn't strong enough to beat you up badly and his face hadn't been subjected to a baseball bat. He was wearing wraparound sunglasses, and thin sideburns, which, and perhaps I will stand corrected on this, have not been desirable on this planet for the last hundred years.

'I'm not Sandrine, Rutger. I'm Oceane.'

'I'm looking for the new girl, Sandrine.'

'Sorry, don't know her.'

'Are you joking with me, Sandrine? Are you a joking, Sandrine?'

'No, I'm not joking and I'm not Sandrine.'

'But you are a new girl?'

'Yes.'

'I am the human-rights director here and there are some educational measures that are necessary for me to take with you. Hello, Richard.'

'Drop dead, Rutger,' said the scruff.

'Your negativity is cheap,' said Rutger.

'Your disappearance is jewellery,' said another arriving pool-goer, who an hour ago I would have considered more than I could ever need. At first I thought he was Rhino, suddenly shrunken. Whereas Rhino looked as if he was the brainchild of a beefcake-crazed gay, the new arrival was menacingly powerful, but he was more the boy next door, provided that the boy next door was into eating and violent sports, rugby, ice hockey, boxing. His was a body and a smile of rule-breaking that would set feminine hearts aflutter. A good bad boy. I was never going to leave this place.

'You are trimming my freedom, Janos,' said Rutger to the newcomer.

'If you want sick,' said Janos, 'pay for sick.'

'Osshan,' Rutger said turning to me, 'Jorge told me to give you some education.'

'No, he didn't,' said Janos.

'He didn't,' said Richard.

'No, he didn't,' I said.

'This is because I have a political edge to my fucking, isn't it?'

'Disappearance is jewellery,' repeated Janos. Rutger huffed off.

'Okay, Richard, a good downing story please?' asked Janos. Richard huffed off too.

Having introduced himself, Janos stripped off, while I

stared somewhere else. Then he took a pipe from a pocket and lit up. This wasn't a bong, but an old-fashioned pipe. With old-fashioned tobacco. As used by elderly, uninteresting uncles when you were small. Smoking a pipe has been mortally unhip for a hundred years, and although Janos's excessively manly figure and rumbustious character counted for a lot, it still looked odd. Does being hip matter? Well, yes, it does. If we aren't here to be admired what are we here for? Life gives you the chance to choose between the cool frock and the frumpy frock, between the music made by an intelligent, demanding musician and the music made by the wazzock with tired, stolen notes, and those of us who make the right choice should be applauded. Surely life is about racking up the right choices and being applauded by the right people? What else are we here for? I considered whether Janos was about to rehip pipe-smoking but I couldn't convince myself. But then who is perfect?

Janos puffed deep and exhaled a twisted rag of smoke. 'The jojo is good here,' he pronounced. I had no idea what he was saying, but I knew what he meant.

I looked up at the heavenly blue sky. Somewhere out there six billion humans were treading on each other's faces. But I was happy. With all the fuss getting work and travelling out to Barcelona I hadn't had time for men-searching. What I needed was company. I was in the right place.

'I sorry for good people,' mused Janos.

'Why?'

'Because soon or late they get well fucked.'

Bearing in mind nearly every one of my previous employers had tried it on, I was surprised, and even disappointed, that Jorge wasn't asking for the odd climactic favour. But he was that rare thing: happily married. 'The greatest invention in history is not the wheel or writing, but the wife,' he remarked.

'Not many men think like you,' I replied.

'Hardly anyone can love. I hope you can, Oceane.'

'Everyone can love.'

'No. They can't. They think they can.'

'But if you think you can, can't you? How do you know if you can love or if you just think you can?'

'I'll tell you.'

'What attracted you to your wife?'

'She doesn't ask questions.'

Jorge took me down to the stage and went through my routine.

'Here is the scenario. You have Rhino, the master of the house, who is sinking into bondage and weirdness; you discover him in his study, rubbered up, like some sad member of parliament or employee of local government.' Here Jorge made an expression of extreme disgust. 'He has an orange in his mouth and his gerbil, Santos, is in danger of having his trusting nature abused and making a dark, lonely journey he would rather not make, when you, the French Maid, enter with your duster and are horrified to see your master in the grip of bad practices. Your heart of gold makes you use your feminine wiles to save him from these disgraceful adorations, and he takes you around the clock and everyone is happy.'

Unquestionably, wetwork in front of a paying audience isn't for everyone, but I would recommend it for blowing away the cobwebs. The first time is a bit odd, like the first time you do anything, whether it's driving a car or making a speech: you've seen it done, but doing it yourself you have to shake off the strangeness.

I was half expecting someone from the audience to shout out, 'You can't do that here' or 'She isn't good-looking enough to be doing it with him', but they didn't.

I was staring into nothing. Loud music ketchups a

multitude of activities. Rhino was as reliable as the sun, rising on time. Two shows a night with me, three on Saturdays, and he was buffeting Marina too. Was he in the right job or what?

The applause was always pleasing, though the gerbil regularly got the biggest hand. After the first few nights it became like any other job; those who seem competent and knowledgeable because they know everyone's names and know where the paper-clips are, aren't competent and knowledgeable, they've just been there three weeks longer than you and that's why they know the names and the paper-clip places.

You become preoccupied with how much your knees hurt and the carpet-burn but after acclimatisation you have time to contemplate the audience and spot the profession: the yobs (invariably English), the couples (the women wearing either a 'you're going to pay for this' expression or a 'how can we get the whole cast back to our hotel room?' frown), bored businessmen who would fold every receipt into their wallets, the arms dealers from a former Soviet republic who would give Jorge an attaché case full of money and say, 'Let us know when it runs out', the local-government employees on a holiday paid for by someone else. And, inevitably, the gaggle of television producers doing 'research'. Jorge always told them no.

'Once you've let a television crew in you never do it again. They lie. They cheat. They steal. Badly. Worst of all, they're boring. The local-government types, they're thieves and scum, but at least they know it. The television producers, they don't. I considered putting up a sign outside, 'No local government, no television', but where do you draw the line? No one who enjoys cruelty to animals? No one who likes golf? This is a business. This is the adventure of venture. Otherwise you'd have two friends in the audience.'

Performance is a lie

Working at the Babylon brought it home, with its regular servings of happiness on a plate. The transition from the well-lit climactic abundance of the stage, where events were wish-sensitive, to the congestion of the dressing-rooms, where one girl with a runny nose would be sniffling into a handkerchief while on the phone to a builder screaming to get her roof repaired, another would be on to the insurance company about the innumerable forms she had sent in after being burgled (while simultaneously seeking a babysitter for her three-year-old), as a third struggles to demountain a vast pimple on her buttock before going out on stage for the harder-faster, and a fourth would be lamenting that despite being double-penetrated twice every night (three times on Saturdays) she hadn't had a boyfriend for over a year, was dramatic. During all this a pension salesman roams up and down telling anyone who'll listen that they'll end up toothless, friendless, penniless and globally hopeless unless all funds are handed over to him.

Eventually Jorge shoos out the pension salesman. 'My brother-in-law. I let him in once a year. You're doing well, Oceane. You're nearly as popular as the gerbil.'

'Yes,' I replied. 'I feel I belong.' I said that because it was true. I was ridiculously comfortable.

'No. You don't. If you say I belong, it's because you've asked yourself: do I feel as if I belong? If you've asked the question, you don't.'

Enjoying a few thoughts in bed before sleep, it occurred to me I was happy. I was contented. One of the peculiarities of happiness is that, at a very deep level, we expect it, as our stomachs expect food.

A play about waiting for a bus not turning up for an hour is never going to be as grinding as waiting for a bus that doesn't turn up for an hour. Reality has no competitor; what it does, it does best. Here is here, and you can't store it or prepare it any other way.

Despite her initial icy indifference to me, Christiana was now forced to ask me to beautician her pimple. I wondered why we had to pretend that the pimple wasn't there. Christiana sighed: 'Why aren't I as brilliant as I'd like to be?' Her too. I wondered why we want to be brilliant. I wondered why I wondered.

Writing about in ecstasy is harder work than you would credit. I'd stay in bed till late and then head up to the roof for some sun. Jorge would always be up early, pottering about. One morning I caught him with a box of those glass objects I'd seen on the stairs.

'What are those?'

'Wasp traps.'

I thought this was a nickname or misunderstanding. 'What do they do?'

'They trap those yellow insects, bzzz bzzz.'

'What are you doing with them?'

'Taking them downstairs. They sell. A Pole who worked here left a box of them and I wanted to throw them out, but I left them by the kiosk where they sell the programmes. A customer asks me, "How much for one?" I say, "They're not for sale." He says, "You're going to sell me one," and I say, "No, I'm not, we're not a hardware store," and then he switches on his wallet and I say, "You're not going to pay that much," and he says, "Yes, I am," and I ask, "Do you work in local government?"

'I thought, well, I'm never going to sell another one, when the next customer in the queue says, "I want one too." We sold the whole box that evening. The mark-up is four thousand per cent.'

A reverent glow came to Jorge's eyes: 'It is the great game. It is the ultimate adventure because you never know what will get customers to switch on their wallets. You never know. It is the greatest art to persuade a stranger to give you money. Selling is the pinnacle of humanity.' He showed me a well-lacquered box made out of walnut which was meant to be for wasp-trap storage. 'When you thought no one could think up anything more useless, here we have exciting new wasp fragrances for your wasp trap and a guidebook to the wasps of Europe, if you want to be more informed about what you kill.'

Richard appeared next. 'The sunshine's fantastic,' I said.

'S'all right.'

'Don't you like it?'

'I prefer not to enjoy it. It won't last.'

I wouldn't bother with lunch but used to take up some fruit to bask with. We'd nearly always say meet at noon. When I say I'll be there at noon, I'm there at noon. I'd always be the first there. Being punctual means you do a lot of waiting.

One by one, the team would straggle up to get the sunbathing going. Richard would be one of the first. Then Vlan, who would start laying out the paraphernalia.

Jorge would show up occasionally to liaise with his cast, issue a few reprimands, or to participate in the lolling around. His favourite reading was a scrapbook with cuttings from newspapers dating back a decade, detailing incidents of aggrieved citizens around the world attacking local-government employees with fists, bottles, knives, automatic weapons and bombs. With enormous satisfaction he would read aloud tales of lunatics taking out entire departments in Switzerland.

Those of us who lived in rarely went out because, well, entertainment and everything else was brought in. After the show, we often fired up the sound system and had some frantic dancing until the early hours. Friends, acquaintances and complete strangers were frequently brought up to the roof to add to the mix.

'My knot is sincere,' Janos greeted Richard. Janos was full of gnomic utterances, but all you had to do was nod and smile.

Richard was reading and translating for our benefit a pamphlet he had been given in the street.

'Adam and Eve were not created, as is commonly believed, in the Garden of Eden. Recent textual studies have shown that Adam and Eve were, indisputably, created in Barcelona.'

'Yeah?'

'It's great. According to this, we know the exact spot they were created. Vila i Vila, 35, the third floor apparently.'

By now I couldn't believe that I would ever leave Babylon. Then Rutger turned up with a group of Brits he had found at the beach. It was baffling that they were on holiday in Spain, because after listening to them for five minutes you'd judge them incapable of carrying out any one of the following acts, let alone all of them in succession: getting a holiday brochure, booking a holiday, getting to the airport. After a few minutes of their company you also wanted to stop speaking English and apply for a German passport.

There were two couples both from Hull, Jan and Ron, Bazza and Toni. God knows what's going on in the North of England.

In their fifties, Jan and Ron's behaviour would have been bad for someone half their age. They were a roadshow of outrage. Ron introduced himself by sucking vigorously on my big toe. This is a high-risk tactic even if you are possessed of stupendous desirability and money, but some girls will go for it. If you are an elderly, unemployed man with a number of skin complaints on display and breath that can be smelt by the suckee, don't bother. I had to use my other foot to prise off Ron, who turned on the two Patricias.

'Twins!'

As one, the two Patricias gathered up their stuff and left. I enjoy my enjoyment as much as anyone, but Jan and Ron obviously wanted sex with anyone. It may be futile having standards, but I couldn't understand why Rutger was being friendly to them, because even if you were planning the most perverse and sickening activities in the world, they would be unthinkable with Jan and Ron. That we learn something as we go through time is an appealing, but untrue idea.

Toni was your everyday mid-forties slapper with piercing galore and only small parts of her body undestroyed, who had figured out that there are only so many climactic opportunities left before death; you knew it was inevitable that she would be showing off her labial rings, heavy enough to moor a barge. You could only surmise she was with Bazza because he was twenty years younger and capable of raising cane more often than a man her own age: he had nothing else to recommend him. They were very proud of having smuggled vast quantities of booze into the country so they could sneak it into bars and get hammered without having to pay. I understand not having money, but not that.

Bazza had a moustache, not in the I-reckon-a-moustache-would-be-stylish but in a this-facial-hair-fucking-proves-I'm-a-man way. Like many small, skinny, unintimidating men he had no notion of how easily beat-uppable he was. Janos could have throttled him with his thumb and one finger, and I found myself wishing he would. Having been in so many situations where I had strained to stop men swinging at each other, I was flabbergasted as Bazza spilled beer on Janos after Janos had warned him to be careful with his beer, knocked Janos's pipe into the swimming pool after Janos had again warned him to be careful and then sat and crushed Janos's sunglasses, after Janos had told him to be careful about his sunglasses, while Janos was recovering his pipe. 'Your sunglasses are crap,' Bazza said by way of contrition. It seemed certain now Janos would give him a taste of Hungarian fist, but instead Janos folded up his towel and walked off.

Bazza's showstopper was shitting on to one of the laurel bushes. Even Toni had to censure here. 'You can't do that,' she said. 'No one'll notice,' replied Bazza.

Jorge appeared meanwhile. 'Local government?'

'No,' I replied. Jan worked as a greeter at a job centre, Toni was a childminder and Ron and Bazza were full-time sperm producers.

'Ah, it's the post-brain society.' He turned and walked off, disappointingly failing to use his authority to turf out the pests.

I was only minutes from the tan that would enable me to lead the world, but I had to leave. As I was folding up my towel, Bazza dived into the pool. If I hadn't seen it I wouldn't have believed it. He jumped into the pool but almost missed it – he flew back slightly and caught his head on the edge. A distinct crack preceded the splash, but the others chatted on. I waited for Bazza to surface. He didn't. One of the disadvantages of not getting drunk and splitting your skull and drowning in a swimming pool, is that you have to go in and pull out the person who has got drunk and split his skull and nearly drowned in the pool.

Bazza looked extremely serene in the water. Blood was colonising the pool at a fantastic rate. I was annoyed with myself as I waded in. If I'd just pretended not to notice for a minute or two that would have been enough. It was a terrible mistake, surely, that I was on the same planet as Bazza? I dragged him out while the others watched with puzzlement. I suppose Bazza was always pulling stunts like this.

Richard stepped up to do the mouth-to-mouth, which was a relief since I had no training in how to do it nor any inclination for it. Bazza was soon spluttering, retching and bleeding everywhere. 'He should go to a hospital,' I said.

'He'll be fine,' said Toni. 'I need to go to hospital,' snivelled Bazza, the hard-man persona rejected. 'Go and find one,' said Toni.

This wasn't going to work. Bazza couldn't have found a hospital if he'd been standing in front of one in England. In his prime, Bazza couldn't have found his dick in the dark. I was about to compare them to animals, but I realised, for instance, that animals have skills, often charm, and that pack animals have concern for each other. I would have thought that their common hobby of worthlessness would have engendered camaraderie. While some apes were inventing invention, others were rolling around pulling faces at each other. Richard led the groggy Bazza away and I reflected that the only success Bazza could look forward to would be being an unconventional fertiliser in a rosebed. I was ashamed of the thought. Who was I to judge anyone? But the thought was there begging to be thought.

'You almost got another one,' Rutger yelled after Richard.

I was too young to figure out why Rutger had invited the white shite up. Because it gave him an opportunity to be important. It was entourage for beginners. Popularity has to start somewhere, and the easiest way to be a giant is to stand among pygmies. Doubtless when they got back to Hull they'd refer to Rutger, if they referred to him at all, as 'the German tosser' or 'that Rutger cunt', but for the moment he was a radiant figure: Rutger was showbiz glamour.

I didn't get to see much of Barcelona. I wanted to but, truth be told, I didn't see any of it apart from the block around the club. I spent most of my free time up on the roof or eating in the restaurant and I only went out once to the shop next door to buy a pair of shoes. Postcards were on sale in the club. Once I did decide that I should go and tour the city centre. The bus stop was right by the club, but I missed one bus by seconds and then, after waiting another fifteen minutes for the next, concluded that the city centre could wait.

There were two other occasions when I nearly escaped the club:

I thought I should go to a dance class, asked Jorge for a recommendation, lost the piece of paper with the address on it, and realised that I wasn't that keen on going to a dance class (there comes a stage when no one can help you). There was a small rehearsal room at the club with mirrors and a barre where I could work out.

One evening I attempted to step out with Rhino. Rhino knew Barcelona and it's always more fun to be shown around. In addition to which I rather fancied the womenfolk of Barcelona seeing me on Rhino's arm (how were they to know that he had the conversational riches of a lamppost and that our relationship was purely physical?). Rhino had dispensed with his mask at this point and his face looked odd, because I wasn't used to it and because it was so striking – you couldn't believe it somehow. He agreed to go out with me not out of any desire to be with me, I suspect, but because he wanted to practise his English in order to ready himself for his Hollywood career. He spoke English haltingly, uninterestingly, but mostly correctly. It was a Sunday, our day off. I had proposed the date at lunchtime and it was agreed that we'd saunter out at seven for exploration and food.

Now, I'm no amateur when it comes to hair-conditioning and I was guilty of severe bathroom abuse, and long deliberations about which outfit to wear. Perhaps this only happens to you once, but I looked in the mirror and thought: who's the beauty? Normally when you look in the mirror you can always find something lacking, some detail missing, or you want a newer dress, a more expensive dress or a redder dress, a little more tan, a little less weight, a new strap for your wristwatch. But my reflection just grinned at me and wished me a goodnight. It wasn't just that I looked perfect, I looked happy, on top.

At five past seven I settled down on my bed and waited for Rhino to knock, but after ten minutes' waiting I couldn't delay the evening any longer and sashayed to his room to hurry him along. It was just then that Rhino emerged from the bathroom, towel-waisted, with outriders of steam; I had heard him going into the bathroom four hours earlier.

'I am worried about my pronator teres,' he said.

'It's darling.'

'You are just saying that.'

'No.'

'This muscle here,' he said pressing it. 'It looks kinda faint to me.'

He went into his room. I'd never seen inside; a quick glimpse revealed more cosmetics and lotions than most cosmetics and lotions shops have. It was the world history of toiletries with a bed. An anatomy of the human body was hanging on the wall, all the muscle groups identified. Women bewail men's failures in grooming, but I could now see that a man who does nothing but preen is as bad, if not worse. I could see it would be some time before Rhino would be ready because, with the best will in the world, choosing an aftershave and a moisturiser from the hundreds on offer wouldn't be easy. I returned to my room.

By the time Rhino had satisfied himself about his divinity, two hours later, I was very hungry and sorely bored from hanging around. Hanging around doing nothing can be very enjoyable, but hanging around waiting for someone is quite serrating. Rhino's emergence, however, swept my ill-humour away instantly.

He was wearing an expensive suit straight from the shop, which fit him like skin, a lush leather belt straight from the shop, a blindingly white shirt straight from the shop and a pair of handmade Italian shoes with a shine that would have made the stroppiest sergeant-major whoop. I almost wanted to have sex with his clothes. And Rhino had a suitable level of danger; we all want a man who behaves as if he is on the verge of rashness or violence, or is at least capable of it, but not, generally, one who indulges in those activities, unless you like sitting around police stations for hours or cutting yourself on broken glass. The marriage was on.

We walked out over the Doormat. The problem with the Doormat, a leading Italian member of the European parliament, was that he tried to dispense extempore wisdom and wit pithily in several languages, something he couldn't do. If he'd stuck to delivering, with gusto, stock lines like 'cheer up, it might never happen' or 'it's a great night for it' he'd have created a certain charm, but he had to go for it and fail: 'Every kiss is like a xylophone's greatest mating.' The Doormat was also causing Jorge a headache because he had turned gloomy, and taken to enquiring whether his users had checked for cancer recently.

'Good evening, young lovers,' the Doormat said as we walked out. 'The pleasure's not guaranteed, the pain is.'

Nevertheless, my heart was screaming at me that this was one of the most momentous moments of my life. This wouldn't be an immemorable night that would slip away. A warm summer's night, a whole foreign city at my feet, the world beyond it just a suburb of Barcelona, in the company of God's better-looking younger brother. I would be on a diet of pure triumph from now on.

I wanted to have a good meal, get completely off my face, have an all-nighter, and astonish Rhino and the citizens of Barcelona with my moves. My life was catching up with my dreams.

Rhino shook his head. 'It's no use. I can't go on.'

The bleakness that had sprouted on his face worried me. Crippling debts? Was there a terrible disease he had picked up? Had his entire family met a ghastly end?

'I've got to work that pronator teres.' We went back in with the Doormat observing, 'Everyone is a tragedy.'

Rhino said he'd only need twenty minutes for the tone-up session and then a quick shower, but I don't know how long he took and I don't know whether he did knock on my door afterwards, because I'd had enough. I went out and stood on the pavement for five minutes. I couldn't make my mind up where to go. There was too much choice. Our restaurant seemed the easiest and best course of action.

Chasing the snail

It may sound a trifle ridiculous, but the need to go out wasn't that great. The first few weeks I was nervous about performing and performing well. The routines weren't difficult but they had to be practised and although I'd been taking off my clothes all my life, there were a few tricks I had to absorb about doing it professionally.

All the expected indulgences of leisure time were available up on the roof.

If you've ever thought about buying a tyrant-size hookah and loading it up with skunk, or if you've never thought about buying a tyrant-sized hookah and loading it up with skunk, my recommendation is: don't. It's the point of no return of dope-smoking. Smoke, I discovered, is acrid for a good reason: to discourage you from taking too much into your lungs for too long, a characteristic that a colossal water-bong suppresses.

Smoking sessions that would have qualified all of us as environmental hazards were held on the roof. The hookah was the size of an armchair, and Vlan, the chief of the wrecking crew, highpriested around it, with specially imported charcoal and specially treated skunk. He discoursed eloquently on how the hookah (which he called a nargill) had been made by someone whose family had been in the hookah-fashioning business for over three hundred years, who lived on a mountain-top in Lebanon which could only be reached by mule (yeah right, as Richard remarked). But it was probably a good thing the hookah's marketing was so poor, because if I'd got one back home it would have been the end of me. This hookah removed your life like a surgeon. Whole days would be shaved off. Beer was also served to mop up any remaining ambition. The great consolation of apathy, of course, is that you don't worry about it.

Vlan was a fusspot, but he did all the hard work and footed the bill for most of the combustibles. He was like those gatecrashers who turn up at your party and commandeer the sound system; as long as they do it right, no one minds. Give us what we want and we don't mind who you are.

I've never been a keen smoker because, in dance, you can't afford to give anything away, but with the hookah you really didn't want to pass the mouthpiece along.

'Drugs aren't the problem, life is,' said Richard before he tumbled over a recliner.

'It's not what you smoke, it's who you smoke with,' countered Vlan.

'Drug lore, drug bore,' muttered Richard once Vlan was out of earshot.

There were discussions aplenty on the roof. But a lot of the time there weren't. Time was elsewhere. I asked myself if I would ever leave this place. There was only the sound of sunning. Marina fiddling with a tube of sunscreen as if she weren't betraying me.

'Who were the famous locksmiths of seventeenth-century Bohemia?' Vlan asked.

'I don't know,' said Richard.

'I don't know their names either; but I can tell you who they were,' Vlan said. 'They were locksmiths who knew each other. At any time, in any country, the successful band together. The famous bakers of fourteenth-century Italy knew each other. The famous horse-breeders of eighth-century Mongolia knew each other. There's always an inner circle. Always a velvet rope.'

'They must have known unknowns.'

'Sorry?'

'They did know nobodies and disastros. Famous entrepreneurs might know each other but they also know bankrupts and botchers. The biographers don't bother with them, that's all. Look at Jorge, he knows lots of bigwigs in Barcelona, but I bet he knows plenty of non-starters right up nowhere creek.'

Vlan was a one-time geologist who had not made the progress he would have liked. Buying drinks for celebrated geologists at geology conferences had been his strength, but he had failed to be asked on holiday with them, the key test of acceptability. 'I should have bought them more drinks. Bigger drinks,' was his verdict. Although, he added, one elderly guy, who had worked in local government, with a fat wife had offered him a threesome.

I would watch the snail a lot. A huge white water snail was inside the hookah and even if you hadn't been smoking, it was captivating to watch it patrol its space with twitching antennae. My belief was it was trying to tell me something. If it was, it should have tried harder. Around the sides of the pool, a dome-shaped pool-cleaner would be humming, which was also irresponsibly relaxing, but I didn't think it was trying to tell me something.

Not everyone supported the hookah. The Poles, Ewa and Piotr, who were married, presided over the serious corner of the roof. They started shortly after I did and differed from the rest of us in the energy of their off-duty hours. While most of us chased the snail, they would be shipping denture glue, solar-powered battery chargers or lengths of copper piping back to their massive families; or they would have enormous textbooks open, studying. Ewa was doing a doctorate in animal husbandry and Piotr in counterfeiting the yankee dollar. We knew this because they told us all about it. 'The problem is not the paper or the plate, it's the ink,' Piotr explained. Ewa had almost completed her doctorate but had developed a violent allergy to farmyard animals. She was also the originator of a lot of the rooftop friction as she made no secret of her disdain for wasters who flopped around in the sun all day smoking skunk and debating its finer points. She might have been right.

She was a pill-popper though. I have no medical qualifications, but I doubt that loudly saying 'I'm taking my medicine' in front of your colleagues makes it more effective. If it was a play for sympathy or to solicit enquiries about her health, it bombed.

'A downing story, Richard!' urged Janos.

'Did I tell you the Japanese one?' Richard had worked all around the world as a diving instructor and had a large repertoire of drowning stories. They ranged from the horrific to the wildly amusing. The drownings were never Richard's fault – I had no doubt he wasn't bending the facts – rather they happened in spite of his efforts. The grim ones were about nineteen-year-old honeymooners or children, the funny ones were about greedy Americans or smartarse Japanese. They had all broken the rules. 'Don't break the rules, they don't break you,' Richard insisted. Many of the stories involved divers forgetting about their weight belts and being dragged down to Davy Jones's locker. There was a Japanese guy who had weighted himself too heavily. Richard had warned him he was putting on too much, but you can only argue with customers so much.

'He wanted to get down there quickly. He got down there quickly. We never found the body.'

The American however had gone down to a wreck site

despite repeated admonitions, Richard suspected, for plunder. They found him sitting on the wreck. 'We never did work out what went wrong.'

'We've heard all that,' said Piotr.

'What about the shark attacks?'

'You've got shark attacks?'

'They're exceptionally rare. Sharks are cowards and if you stick to the rules, they stick to the rules. Largely.' Despite their being exceptionally rare, Richard had managed to witness half the world's fatal shark attacks. 'This young Kiwi was having her first lesson. We were in ten feet of water, about twenty feet maybe from the beach, in an area where sharks are almost unknown. We weren't bleeding or thrashing about, we were doing some goggle-clearing, when a lemon shark, a species not rated for its aggression, a small one, bit off her right leg.'

'Did she survive?'

'She got back to the beach. We found out afterwards that some little snot had been throwing chum off the jetty every day to see if he could attract sharks. So we were goggle-clearing in the shark's dining-room. You can't blame the shark. Imagine going into a hamburger joint, ordering a hamburger and then as you bite into the hamburger it screams, "I come in peace."'

'Richard, you're just fatal.'

Rutger now joined us for some high-visibility imbecility. He was carrying a tortoiseshell cat under his arm, which he lobbed into the swimming pool. The cat bounced off the water, and then, yowling, sprang over the edge of the roof.

'What are you doing?' asked Janos.

'Teaching the cat to surf.'

'You're not a good surf-teacher, are you?' said Richard.

'You're right. I'll train the next cat in the shower.'

'Why do you want a cat to surf? Are you entering it in the cat world surfing championships?'

'No, but my vision is I should diversify into management and a surfing cat could be a winner.'

Hamish and I were sitting in the far corner watching this exchange.

'Do you think we get what we deserve?' he asked me.

'I haven't been alive long enough to answer that question.' I was very pleased with this answer.

'The trouble with crossroads', Hamish continued, 'is that they don't look like crossroads.' Everyone else now chased Rutger downstairs, presumably to expose him to some water torture.

'What do they look like?'

'They look like they're not crossroads.' Hamish had been quite cheerful lately, and in the sunshine he was looking *muy* shaggable. 'Crossroads should look like crossroads, so you know you're at one when you're at one.'

'You're not going to confess something to me are you?'

'Now you mention it, there is something I'd like to get off my chest. The winter. Winter was very severe that year . . . '

Why is it that when someone wants to tell you something, they can't tell you? After Hamish had explained how bitter January had been, we finally got to the meat. 'I had a whiny girlfriend who was very unfortunate. She really was. She'd go out to buy doughnuts and the doughnut shop would be closed, it would start raining and by the time she got home she'd have been burgled and caught pneumonia. But, you know, even the suffering of friends gets very boring. You're sympathetic once. Twice. Many times. You do the full sympathy routine. When it's someone close you can go much longer. But when it's someone who was only good for half a dozen rattles, your courtesy droops. She's unemployed, staying at home, going mad and contracting strange maladies by the dozen.

'Friday evening I come home to find a message from her on the answering machine asking me to ring back. I'm tired, do I want to listen to her go on about her headache which has baffled all the doctors of the nation? No. Heard it, heard it several times before, and the helpful suggestions I gave on the lines of: get some fresh air, get a life, have been consigned to a black hole. Next morning I wake up and think do I want to listen to her banging on about her headache and some problem with her knee? No, I'm going to the football. When I come back in the afternoon, there's another message. Do I want to hear about her headache and the galactic conspiracy which prevents her from reaching the job centre? No. I've discovered a much better use of my time: doing something else. I go out for the night and when I come back there's one short message. "I need to talk to you." Three days later I get a call from the police telling me . . . '

'Suicide?'

'I was her last call.'

We heard some distant screams which sounded like they belonged to Rutger. The others drifted back and reported that Janos had dangled Rutger by his feet out of a third-floor window for a while. Morale was good after the entertainment. I was very much at ease. How long would these friendships last? Were they retractable?

The hookah ran out. Vlan phoned his dealer, but he was busy. We all had asterisks for eyes but everyone wanted to smoke some more; yet no one wanted to trudge out and score. Rutger was volunteered to get the wholesale delivery for the roof. I was rather surprised that he allowed himself to be volunteered.

'Fast,' Janos said, holding up imaginary ankles. He really liked to smoke. I did as well, but I managed to keep the desire under control. Was there really any point in that?

Rutger wasn't fast. Vlan cleaned bits of the hookah, philosophically. He gazed up at the sun. 'What's the most frightening? If we are alone, a cosmic slip-up, or if we're not alone, one of a billion civilisations, too insignificant to even be on the waiting-list for insignificance?' He loved that stuff.

It occurred to me that, really not very far away from our rooftop, an hour or two on a plane, good-hearted men were being tortured, women were stoned to death on someone's say-so, countries were starving. It was far enough away for me to put it out of my mind, but close enough for me to walk there in a few weeks or a few months.

Piotr replied: 'It depends on whether you're more frightened of being alone or being in a crowd.'

Janos said he'd be willing to have sex with aliens as long as they were good-looking. Vlan wanted to discuss what good-looking was, but he was ignored. Rutger didn't come back at all and the grumpiness was reflected in the show that night.

Night

Rutger really did wear his sunglasses all the time. He did his turn with them. He ate with them on and he turned up in my room at three in the morning wearing them and nothing else.

'Oceane, I have this massive erection.'

'Rutger, that's not a massive erection.' I was a little alarmed that he had got into my room so easily, but finally Rutger wasn't that alarming, and Janos was in the next room, I knew, very eager to have a chat with Rutger about his disappearance and the non-appearance of the smokeables.

'This whopper is for you,' he said. Honestly, I have enormous admiration for the German education system.

'Go away, Rutger.'

'You don't mean that.'

'I'm better qualified to judge my meaning than you are.'

'I don't want to hurt you.'

'Come here, Rutger.' I slapped him so hard it stung my

palm. I was very grateful to Rutger then, because all my life I've had the ambition to slap a man, in highest dudgeon, in a totally justifiable manner. Rutger slumped to the floor.

'Would money help?' he wailed.

'No.'

Rutger burst into tears.

'Would you say I slept with you if I paid you?'

'No.' I had to drag him out of the room by his ear. If you want to act the lad at least put some effort into it.

I went to see Jorge in his office. Rutger was the turd in our swimming pool. Surely something could be done.

'Have you got a minute, Jorge?'

'You're late, but yes.'

'Late?'

'Yes. This is the Rutger conversation isn't it? The new girls usually come in after their first week.'

I outlined some Rutgeriana. 'He gets on everyone's nerves. You should fire him.'

'I did fire him. Six months ago.'

'Why's he still here?'

'Because he won't leave.'

'He works for nothing?'

'No. He pays me. This is a business.'

Ewa walked in. 'Could I talk to you alone, Jorge?'

Jorge put his fingers to his forehead and closed his eyes. 'I'm reading . . . Rutger.'

'Jorge, I can't work with him. He's an arsehole.'

'Let me see: working with an arsehole. Is this not what we mean by a job?'

'Jorge, he's turding over our swimming pool.'

I was uneasy at finding myself on the same side as Ewa. Jorge sighed.

'Perhaps it is time to give Rutger a chance to use his talents somewhere else.'

Ewa and I went up to the roof, hating Rutger. About an hour later I was worried that she was going to be my best friend. She then agitated me by saying, 'I've got to confess something.'

'Don't,' I said.

'I think I've ruined my marriage.'

'What have you done?'

'I made Piotr say thank you. My mother made a special cake for us before we left, to eat on the journey here, but I was so busy getting ready I forgot to bring it. But I knew my mother would want some praise for it, so I asked Piotr to write a card saying how much he enjoyed the cake. He said no, I don't want to lie, tell your mother you forgot the cake. But my mother spent two days making it, I said, you have to write a card. So he wrote a card.'

'What's the problem?'

'He lied so well. He lied so easily. He wrote the card in one go, telling my mother how he liked the crunchy bits best. He was so convincing I had to phone my sister to check that the cake was still in our apartment. I've never seen him lie. It upsets me, because I can never trust him again.'

'You asked him.'

'But he didn't have to do it that well.'

Merv was one of the barmen. He wasn't one of those barmen who were waiting to be something else; he had achieved triumphancy. He would always be a barman and he would always look like a keg with a wig thrown on top. He went to the gym regularly but whether he spent the whole day there or idling in a hammock, he was going to be a keg. He was hardly any taller than me, but you could have fitted four of me, comfortably, into his trousers. Merv's speciality was vodka. Three or four vodkas weren't enough. He had over fifty brands on display and would talk about them rather more than most customers wanted to hear. 'I'm not sure I should sell you this. This can only be described as an evil vodka that is aching to ruin your life. You don't look up to it, you know.' (Jorge confided to me once, 'You'd think it would be easy to hire barmen wouldn't you? They only have to open bottles.')

Piotr had tipped Merv off that a Polish contact was in Barcelona with stock of rare, mostly unofficial and harmful vodkas. Medlar flavour, bubble-gum flavour, whisky flavour and the one that most excited Merv called soulstealer. Merv had been in Barcelona for ten years so he agreed to show me around one Sunday morning on his way to the meeting. We sat inside the foyer, waiting for the bus to come, and chatted.

'I love Wales of course,' he said. 'But eventually you get tired of the incest and violence. Barcelona is my city and being a barman is all I want to do. I did try something else once.'

'What?'

'I was a war correspondent. But it didn't work out.'

'Really? How did you manage that?'

'I used an ancient druidic mind-control technique handed down from father to son over the centuries, often referred to by non-initiates as lying. "Do you have any experience as a war correspondent?" "Yes." "Do you speak fluent Arabic?" "Yes." "Do you have good contacts in Beirut?" "Yes."

'It wasn't a bad job, but it wasn't me. I got tired of making things up. This was when Beirut was wild. I left after the psychic-dog story.'

'Did you say pyschic dog?'

'One of the militias had this psychic dog that was giving them stock-market tips. They were making a fortune and buying all sorts of flash weaponry. I was sitting in a taxi in some awful suburb waiting for the driver who had gone to fix an interview with the dog, when this passer-by stops and talks to me in English. I was wearing my Cardiff jersey.

'Women say to me when I wear my Cardiff jersey, "You can't go out dressed like that." They say, "Please for the love of God wear anything but that, I'll do anything for you, even the really sick stuff," and I say, "I'm wearing this jersey because it saved my life." Turns out this character was in Cardiff for five years studying hotel management in horrible poverty. He was quite bitter: the hotel trade in Beirut having taken a bit of a knock, he was living in a hole in the ground in horrible poverty and as he put it he might as well have spent those five years sticking carrots up his arse. Then he says, "It's none of my business but you do know that your driver is auctioning you to a militia."

'I was furious. I was paying the driver big bucks. I don't mind being ripped off, because we're all in on the rip. You rip me off, you're a better man than me, but I don't like being traded like a stolen microwave to a bunch of sixteen-year-olds and kept in a box for ten years. I then had to make one of the most difficult decisions of my life. Should I wait for the driver to come back so I could smack him in the mouth? The need to put my fist through his face was intense, but when he came back he might well be accompanied by the box-merchants. So I had to settle for driving his taxi to my hotel, setting it on fire and then, before packing my bags, spreading several rumours about the driver which would probably get him killed. But it haunts me. His face comes to me at night sometimes and it's one of my few regrets that I didn't jump up and down on his throat. You never know whether you made the right decision, do you? And we all have our taxi-driver stories, eh?'

'Shame you never met the psychic dog.'

'No, but the whole episode was my fault for attempting some journalism. I was in Beirut for years inventing stories or copying down stuff, living in its best bar and doing my bit for the Lebanese by demonstrating how to make proper vodka martinis and the one time I had a real scoop I nearly came to grief. But at least I knew what was going on. No journalist ever wrote a word about the dog. And it wasn't one of these dogs that barked once for yes or twice for no. No rubbish like that. No, it gave detailed instructions in writing about what price to buy and sell.

'You get these experts who say the Lebanese Civil War was a diplohedron of Levantine evil, welded to a buckyball of international intrigue; but I say look at the dates of the Civil War. Fifteen years. Curiously, exactly the age a well-cherished dog would live. Need I say more? What do you think the Israelis and the Syrians were doing there? They all wanted the dog. You can understand why they kept quiet about it. Who would want to have a press conference to announce we're invading this country because we're after a dog that will give us a hundredfold return on our investments in a year? A ghastly business. I really shouldn't have gone. There are many things on my conscience.'

'You're not going to tell me something awful are you?'

'I don't know. I don't know whether it's awful. Right before my aborted interview with the dog I was invited over by one of the militias. The hospitality was admirable; coffee and *taj el malek*. You see if I were to say to a stranger: "Hello, my name's Mervyn, why don't you buy me a drink and tell me how you shag your wife?" I'd get a hell of a kicking. If I say: "I'm Mervyn, I'm a journalist, why don't you buy me a drink and tell me how you shag your wife?" the stranger will at least give it serious consideration. Most of the public, especially those who've never had anything to do with journalists, will do just about anything for them. They think their importance has been noticed at last. There I am enjoying the hospitality and they proudly offer to show me their new artillery in action. I think, well, I've never actually seen an artillery gun fired, in life, up close. So I say: "Why not?" They fire off a few rounds and I even get to let one off. Hell of a din and you can actually see the shell shoot out into the wide blue yonder.

'Then more coffee, more nibbles, a good smoke: we're all great mates now having a laugh. Only now does the thought cross my mind about those shells that had crumped in the distance. "Where did those shells end up?" "Oh, the local Druse village.""

'That must have been awful.'

'No. I didn't know anyone in the village. I didn't know that anyone had been injured. They might even have been joking when they told me that. And if it had been a local village they must have known they were in range and would have taken, one assumes, protective measures. No, what I feel bad about is that we got chatting about dance music and the work of a moderately successful black American band who eccentrically fused dance rhythms with power chords and psychedelia, repeatedly paying homage to the topoi of sci-fi, whose work has lately become highly collectible. That's probably the secret of becoming highly collectible, you don't want to be too successful first time out. Hardly anybody had heard of them when they were going, and hardly anybody has heard of them now. Hardly anybody knowing about you when you want to be famous is disastrous, hardly anybody knowing about you twenty years after you've finished is great for a cult and the application of gargantuan mark-ups. My host lent me his three favourite bootleg albums by aforementioned artists.

'"You are the only journalist who has come to talk to us," he said, kissing me. I didn't have the heart to tell him I wasn't a journalist, I can't even spell (I told my employers I was dyslexic) and I had no intention of writing anything about him, not even pure fiction. If you ever have that alone-in-a-public-toilet-with-former-interviewee-and-their-three-most-indispensable-bodyguards moment afterwards, and it nearly always happens, you insist that you wrote a magnificent piece saying exactly what the interviewee wanted, but the editor pulled it or tweaked it. If I had been a real journalist it would have been quite moving.

'But, apres-dog, when I had to skedaddle, I couldn't return the albums. I've always been very guilty about those bootlegs. Because we all love a bootleg, no one wants to be out in the rain with the plebs, we all want to be backstage with the band.'

'Lucky you were wearing your Cardiff jersey, you'd still be in Beirut otherwise.'

'We all need help, but it has to be at the right time; there's no point buying a drowned man a drink, is there?'

Jorge was haranguing the Doormat as we walked out:

'You can't behave like this. You're too much already without telling our customers that they will die soon in a train crash.'

'She must have misheard.'

'You're going to die soon in a train crash. What does that sound like? You're going to fly in a brain mash? You're going to why in a main gash? You're sowing to buy soon in a sane bash?'

The bus pulled up outside. As we got up, Merv slapped his forehead in the classic gesture of having forgotten something because he had. 'I've got to phone my son. It's his birthday.' I didn't waste time waiting for Merv. I knew I wasn't getting out. I went up to the roof.

I'd noticed that Vlan had been reading a browning, crumpled newspaper day after day. Finally, I fell into his trap. 'That paper must be fascinating,' I said. 'You've been reading it for weeks.'

'I always read the same newspaper, to remind myself that nothing happens,' he said, explaining that he didn't see why he should buy the same news every day. 'Buying a newspaper every day is a pretension. It's not about wanting to know anything because you won't learn anything from a newspaper; what you are saying when you buy a newspaper is: I am a person who buys a newspaper.' Similarly, I thought, when you read the same newspaper on and off for two years, what you are saying, when you can find listeners, is that you've been reading the same newspaper for two years. 'But I'm always uncovering new things,' Vlan added. 'The newspaper may stay the same, but I change. Or it could be that I stay the same but the paper changes? Or that I have penetrated a new level of text. Furthermore, buying newspapers is dangerous.'

'How?'

'Come on. You know how many tragic stories start with "He went out to buy a newspaper"?'

'I'm having a bad day,' announced Rutger, carrying what looked like a defibrillator.

'Excellent,' said Richard.

'I need to hear about someone else's misery,' insisted Rutger.

'I've got a report here about miners, trapped in the dark, in a small airpocket, in freezing conditions, up to their necks in icy water, tapping away, hoping to be saved, but rescued too late,' offered Vlan.

'That's a start.'

'Naturally,' resumed Vlan, 'we are all trapped in a small, dark airpocket, up to our necks in icy water, hoping to be saved, but rescued too late.' We laughed.

Heidi turned up. It was rare for her to be on the roof. She had her own palatial villa nearby. It was unclear, precisely, why she continued to work at the club. Gifts of immense value were regularly delivered to her backstage, and she didn't have to do anything for them. It was merely speculative spending on the part of her suitors. She didn't send any of the gifts back.

She stripped naked, and the roof seemed to tilt. An aircraft-carrier of lust had come into a fishing village. A lot of the girls were lost without their make-up. Marina, for instance, looked terminally ill, and Ewa like a bewildered nocturnal mammal. Heidi could do it in all conditions, four-wheel drive. Her loins had such traction that even though I had never had any interest in that, I couldn't help thinking about going down on her.

She was with Walter. Her thruster was rotated, and currently Walter, the new boy, was working with her. We all liked Walter, me especially. He was loose-muscled and to the casual observer was flirting with slobdom, nearly chubby and always wearing terrible clothes. But he was implausibly strong, as I discovered once when I asked him to pull me out of the pool and he almost launched me into orbit with one hand, and as Rhino discovered when he lost to him in a blink, five times, at arm-wrestling. 'Why doesn't he look strong?' moaned Rhino. 'It's not right.'

He was also quiet, and paid no attention to me, which is a devastating technique when applied close-up. It's no use being quiet and paying no attention to me in a bathroom two blocks away. He had the rare gift of being friendly to everyone, but keeping to himself.

You knew Walter had been involved in some dodgy goings-on. There wouldn't be any 'What are you looking at?' or 'Do you want some?' with Walter. He'd thump you without warning and forget you before you hit the ground. But he wouldn't talk about it; it was unbearably exciting. Despite being, with the possible exception of Janos, the hard nut of the set-up, being incurably male and doubtless staying up all night playing poker, eating food out of cans, going ludicrous distances for football matches and stealing high-performance cars, he'd phone his mother regularly and remember his sister's birthday.

'Here's some freakish bad luck. Hard-working window-cleaner in the North of England does twelve-hour days, six days a week for ten years to save up for his dream car, a Rolls-Royce.' Vlan's tone darkened. 'The first morning he had the Rolls, *he went out to buy a newspaper*, bought the paper and as he left was run over by his own car which he hadn't handbraked properly.'

'Ha-ha,' went Rutger.

'Call that freakish bad luck?' intervened Richard. 'I'll give you freakish bad luck.' Richard did indeed have some good anecdotes, but he'd always tell them. You knew with Walter you'd have to live with him for years before you'd get a hint of what was going on.

'Racont away,' said Vlan.

'How about being killed by a whale?'

'Run out of shark stories?'

'Whales are so big, they're bound to kill people. We're bored with your bad-luck diving stories.'

'This isn't a diving story. How about being killed by a whale in an exclusive restaurant.'

'Food poisoning isn't very freakish.'

'I'm not talking about eating a whale. I'm talking about being violently killed by a whale in an exclusive restaurant, a quarter of a mile from any water of significance. I'm talking about a whale, coming for you, singling you out, as you're agonising over the wine list.'

'Whales aren't supposed to be aggressive.'

'I'm talking about being violently killed by the most unaggressive whale imaginable. This is back in Thailand, my mate Suwat – rich bastard – had built this luxury hotel – the cost of the bed linen alone was terrifying – and restaurant-cum-diving school next to this fantastic beach.'

'How many of your pupils drown?'

'Not one. The diving school was only open for three days. We had this lavish opening ceremony, with local bigwigs. The next morning the first guests are due, when we look out on this gorgeous beach and see this whale. A dead one. An enormous dead whale hogging the beach. Now whales don't smell great at the best of times, but this was gut-wrenching. This whale is shafting Suwat's business bigtime. So he gets his boys to drag it back out. Won't budge. Right, we'll bury it, says Suwat, and phones up his builder to get a bulldozer. As always, when you need a bulldozer you can't get one. Suwat's furious, but he's made the mistake of paying his builder, so he hasn't got much leverage. You can't have the bulldozer, says the builder, but I can do you a favour, I can send someone round with a few sticks of dynamite. Suwat's not crazy about the plan, but he wants to get rid of the whale.

'Now there's been some banana-skinning by this point.'

'Banana-skinning?'

'One of the guests in the restaurant had died. She swallowed a wasp and must have been hypersensitive to its sting and choked. Suwat is getting a shade jumpy. He's heard talk that I bring banana skins, and he's just had his brand-new beach kablooied by a blue whale, something no one in the country can recall happening, scientists want to fly out and get in on the act and one of his most important customers has been killed by a tiny, usually harmless insect. The thought of dynamite on the premises makes him wobbly. To be frank, I don't want to go anywhere near the stuff either. So Suwat and I kick back in the restaurant, a quarter of a mile from the whale and Suwat reassures himself that he has the finest collection of French wines east of Dijon, when the whale blows.

'Perhaps I should know more about explosives, or maybe the blaster should have known more, but to me it looked like a nuclear explosion. The whole beach shoots up into the sky. You understand this is very, very bad. Then you hear these thumping sounds getting closer. It's chunks of burning blubber landing. Suwat copped one. Torn between a pinot noir and a cabernet, he was mullahed by a mysticete. Every room in the hotel was varnished with sand and oil, but the whale was mostly intact, it had just shifted ten feet. I looked for employment elsewhere.'

I was a little disappointed to see Heidi and Walter hanging around together. It wasn't a jealousy beef. Maybe it was. I had tried to be friendly to both of them, but hadn't made any inroads into their company, and no matter how you shrug it off, having your friendship left unwrapped on the counter is a little wounding. Most of us, Vlan for example, would be as happy jabbering away in a room of complete strangers who didn't speak the same language. But it matters to me whom I'm speaking to.

You were never short of company at Babylon, but I didn't have a shadow. I didn't have the acting best friend. Studying the group on the roof I tried to guess who I would stay in touch with when I went back to London. I had thought about looking for proper dance work in Barcelona, but I didn't know anyone. I knew enough to know that, without introductions, it wouldn't be worth it.

Heidi didn't really mix with anyone. The gossip was she had been dumped on her grandparents as a kid and endured years as an expensive nuisance, poor, unwanted, until biology came to the rescue. Psychologists are all imbeciles, there's no argument about that. The notion that you can fish out some detritus from someone's past and divine everything is the highest hokum, but in Heidi's case you could tell a seriously peeved six-year-old was at the wheel and that the world didn't have enough payback. Walter was more approachable although he'd never start a conversation. And you only got back a fraction of what you put into Walter.

Richard livened things up by calling Vlan a French ponce. Then reconsidered and called him an arrogant French ponce.

'Is it arrogance to want to understand?' Vlan countered. 'What's the point of having intelligence if you're not meant to understand? And is it so arrogant to understand? I can understand how a plane works without being able to build one. I can understand an earthquake without being able to do anything more about it than a ping-pong ball.'

'Ponce,' reiterated Richard. 'You're all badly dressed and you carry handbags. And why do you have a foreign legion? Because no one in France is hard enough.'

I overheard Walter chatting with Heidi about how he had been searching for years for an obscure reggae CD that he had heard once in the back of a taxi. He had offered to buy it on the spot to no avail. He had trawled record shop after record shop, but couldn't find a copy. He couldn't find anyone with a copy who could make a copy for him. He was saying he couldn't figure out why he was so obsessed with it, whether it was because it was as good as he remembered it, or because he couldn't find it.

I considered when to make my move. I had brought this CD with me. I didn't consider it at all obscure or rare because it had been in my sister's collection for years before I had helped myself to it. I did consider it good. This was clearly a sign that our friendship was meant to be. I wouldn't be given an advantage like this by accident. Sex obviously was nothing at the Babylon, but friendship was something. I was tempted to get the CD straight away and hand it over. Then it occurred to me it would be better to get Walter on his own so his gratitude could have time to expand. Then I reconsidered giving it to him at all. Walter had always been perfectly correct with me, but he hadn't made any effort to get to know me. If he didn't have any real interest in me, was it worth attempting to, as it were, buy his friendship?

Heavy whomping preceded the arrival of the police helicopter. The helicopter would regularly scout us out, though why they were so curious about us was a mystery. If peeping was your thing, the beaches were filled with the fullness of flesh of all sorts. And if you were gathering material for solitary activities the shops were full of high-quality goods in various formats at reasonable prices you could enjoy in the privacy of your abode hour after hour. Indeed, admission to the club wasn't that much if you wanted to see us in action.

But there was something about our roof that drew the helicopter. Slowly and deafeningly, it would buzz around almost every day. Perhaps it was that you could only see the roof from the air, that we weren't meant to be on display, the keyhole factor that was the high. My eyesight's not so great but even I could make out in the cockpit that sight so familiar to women the world over, the distant or not-so-distant male figure playing with himself.

'Give him the look, Heidi,' said Richard. In the show Heidi's numbers always ran to time. Other couples might stall for desperate minutes now and then, and as a woman, performer or not, it's tiresome to have a dick that doesn't work but Heidi's boast was that she could, on demand, make any man shoot in under thirty seconds. The evidence backed her up; you could set your watch by her number, which ended seamlessly with the music, ten minutes and forty seconds every evening. It didn't matter which jaded trunklet she was working with (and generally the guys were as interested in us as they were in last week's newspaper), the countdown was always faultless.

'I just have to look at them,' she said. There was much speculation as to how exactly she could do this, but having quizzed Rutger and Rhino about it, I wasn't greatly enlightened.

'You want to know the secret?' Rutger asked. 'Okay, as a special favour to you, Oceane, I'll tell you. It's the look.'

'Rutger, I know it's the look. How does the look work?'

'This sounds weird, but it's as if six women are making sex with you at the same time.'

'How would you know, Rutger?'

'You asked, Oceane.'

When I asked Rhino he stared vacantly for so long I thought he had forgotten the question or didn't want to answer. 'She makes you the most important person who has ever lived,' was his judgement.

Heidi stares up at the helicopter pilot, and if I hadn't been there to see it I certainly wouldn't have believed it. The helicopter veers off suddenly and sharply out of our view. Some harsh snapping sounds follow, before a thunderous bang and, last of all, a plume of greasy black smoke squirming on the horizon.

No one says anything. It's as if no one saying Heidi made

the helicopter crash will ensure that the helicopter hasn't crashed. No one moves. It's not something you're prepared for. You get advice about what to do for heart attacks, snake bites, bear attacks, earthquakes, all sorts of crises, but helicopter downed by blonde isn't on any leaflet I've ever seen.

Heidi reaches for her tube of factor thirty and slaps some more on her arms. I wonder whether she's hard of hearing. I want to say something, but I don't, because if I say, I think the helicopter has crashed, it will mean the helicopter has crashed, and it won't be some blunder at a nearby building site or a car overheating.

We were expecting there to be some questioning, but there wasn't. We sat on the roof day after day with no visit from the police, to our relief. What could we say: 'My friend Heidi's so dirty she can take out a helicopter with one glance'? What would the pilot have said in the final seconds: 'Mayday, I'm being muffed to death'? And what would the investigators have been able to conclude? 'Officer Diaz died the way he wanted, with his manhood in his hand?' That the questions never materialised made sense.

I was waiting to get a right moment to present Walter with the obscure reggae CD, but circumstances were conspiring against me. I spent hours sitting by the pool waiting for a one-on-one with Walter, while Lou and Sue would rabbit on endlessly about how only women could really pleasure women and that I was missing out. It was a drip-drip campaign and you can see why men end up henpecked, because women when they want to can really go on. It was getting to the point where I felt like saying, I'll give you half an hour, but shut up will you? My main objection to lesbians is that they're unable to talk about anything else. I was standing in occasionally as nipple-licker in one of Christiana's numbers, and having to work her breasts for a few minutes was as erotic for me as licking an armchair and let me add I really don't find licking an armchair erotic at all.

'You can't be a lesbian,' interposed Vlan.

'Excuse me?' responded Lou.

'You can't be a lesbian if you're a lesbian,' continued Vlan, 'only a straight can be gay.'

Vlan was saved from sapphic fury by Christiana sobbing in the pool. She had noticed Hamish at the bottom of the swimming pool, and that he had been down there so long he was doing more than inspecting the pool floor, he had left earth. Christiana found her voice wasn't on duty. She hopped around and pointed, not quite in the way you hope you'd behave in an emergency.

The consensus was that Hamish had overdone it with some stimulant. However, they found no drugs or alcohol in Hamish's body, well, naturally they did, but not in any contributory way. No signs of foul play were discovered, it was as if he had chosen to fall asleep on the bottom of the pool. No one had noticed anything, no one could even remember Hamish getting into the pool. I had been too preoccupied by the recruiters to have anything worth saying to the investigators.

Jorge asked me to sort out Hamish's effects. At first, you are honoured to be entrusted with such a delicate task, to be considered adult and unflaky enough for such a mission but then you quickly become irate about being lumbered with it.

The box of tissues, the rank footwear, the half-drunk coffee, the wooden word 'STUD' were no longer a box of tissues, a half-drunk coffee and a wooden word, they were the box of tissues, the rank footwear, the half-drunk coffee and the wooden word of a dead man and as such had acquired an unremovable veneer of bleakness.

The lumpy coffee was easiest to get rid of. It went down the sink. Getting rid of the other items was more troublesome and unsettling as I was abetting Hamish's removal. Most of the clothing was so worn it could only go to a dustbin. I can never fathom with men whether they keep a T-shirt for twenty years out of some sense of loyalty or whether it's a fear of shopping.

Hamish only had one suitcase, which strongly influenced my decision to send on a suitcase-worth of his belongings to his family. There were no murky pictures of Hamish rogering ladyboys, or tapes of Nazi marching songs, no organs of former lovers drifting in pickle. There were innumerable offers of credit cards and photographs of Hamish in rooms, bars and beaches jammed with acquaintances, cheesing it into the camera, waving cigarettes and glasses. Photos whose value had been excised. One of the reasons why I said yes was that I was curious about catching Hamish with his spiritual trousers down. What would it be like if we could all see into each other: would it be shocking and depressing, or merely dull? Are hidden depths a yarn? Is it that we do get to know each other very quickly and that's the snag?

The room was waiting for Hamish, as if he had popped out for a minute. A number of typed creamy pages in some foreign language were contained by a huge paper-clip. There was a covering letter in English from some old woman (you could tell that from the neatness and formality) to Hamish saying that perhaps he could find someone in Britain who might be interested in these letters by her great-aunt. The letter was dated four years ago. 'Easy to say, hard to live,' I murmured. I held the pages above the bin. I had no idea what to do with them. No idea how to even start to deal with them. No idea whether they were worth dealing with. No one wants to disappoint a little old lady who writes a nice letter. Were these the equivalent of an undecipherable shopping list, or the best words ever assembled?

Rutger walked in with a log. I was tempted to ask, but Rutger had an ask-me mien.

'Anything good going?' he enquired, leaning the log in a why-don't-you-ask-me-about-the-log way.

'You can't just help yourself.'

'No one's going to need this,' he said, picking up Hamish's tube of shaving foam. He fiddled around with the nail scissors, and then took a packet of travel-sickness pills. 'I'll take these,' he said.

'Are you going somewhere?' I asked.

'No, but I might be.'

He picked up his log with exaggerated exertion. He looked at me in puzzlement as to why I didn't ask him about the log. 'I've got this log,' he said.

I smiled.

'This is history,' he said.

I rummaged one of Hamish's drawers.

'This is where music started,' Rutger continued. 'This is the source of all percussion. This will be my first album.'

'I thought you wanted to be in films.'

'Yes, but I want a creation empire. The many moods of the log will be a crucial step.'

'So can you play it?'

'No.'

I examined the word STUD; it had cracked in two: ST and UD. It was acting as an elastic-band holder to keep itself together. Rutger was still there. He was fingering some shirts. I thought how annoyed Hamish would be at his clobber going to Rutger.

'The red one's good.'

'You can't have his shirts.' I wouldn't want someone's clothes if they were dead, especially in this misfortuned way. It occurred to me that of course since I had bought stuff from charity shops I might well have some dead woman's clothes. But I didn't know.

Rutger stripped off. 'Anytime you want loving you just shout.' He put on Hamish's shirt: far too large for him.

'It's too big for you,' I said.

'But it's red and it's free.'

'It should go to a charity.'

'There is no better cause than me.'

I went for terror tactics. 'Aren't you afraid of bad luck?'

'No. Oceane, why doesn't anyone like me?'

'Everyone likes you, Rutger. Now, would you fuck off?'

'Will you be my friend, Oceane?'

'This is your friend saying goodbye, Rutger.'

'I have something to confess, Oceane.'

'Don't confess anything.'

'I must. Do you know why I like you?'

'No.'

'Because you see deep down I'm an arsehole.'

'Hmm.'

'Why isn't my profile high enough?'

I sat there and reflected. When someone asks 'why doesn't anyone like me' what are they asking? Are they hoping for an assurance that they are liked, however bogus, or are they genuinely inquisitive about the reasons for their unpopularity. Had I let Rutger down? Could I have mapped out for him the disagreeable in his soul?

I stared at Hamish's effects. I noticed two hours had gone by and all I had really done was pour the coffee down the drain. There was a large, half-used tube of toothpaste. I couldn't bring myself to use it. You couldn't take it to a charity shop. Certainly the toothpaste could find a new home out there if I didn't reveal its history, but I didn't know how to find one. I put the toothpaste in the bin.

I was up on the roof with Constance. Constance was a professional benefits cheat who had two homes in London that she let out to French painters while she lived in Barcelona. Janos had picked her up at the beach. She didn't need to work, but she had got a taste for working at the club.

Janos and Sergio were loafing around as well. They had become a unit. Sergio didn't speak anything apart from Italian, and Janos who had a smattering had become his outlet to the world. Janos was always in a good mood; he was doing what he wanted. Paid lots of money to slip a length to beautiful women all day. Rhino would be professional, but would be grumbling about this and that. All Janos wanted was a beautiful blonde wife, a big house and a big car, and he'd be happy. He wouldn't want a bigger blonde, or a bigger house or a bigger car. He might fool around, but he'd be the type to turn up on time for supper without lipstick on his collar. He was pure upness.

Sergio was disturbing. No, he was very disturbing. Skinny, smaller even than Rutger, his selling point was that he'd do anything to anyone, anytime. Let me repeat this. Anything to anyone, anytime. We'd seen the pictures. He was successful in the business because the phrase 'I'm not doing that' would never pass his lips. He was admirably omnivorous in a way, but you couldn't help agreeing with Vlan when he said that the man who fucks everyone fucks no one. Health concerns were always paramount at Babylon, but I'd firmly made up my mind, whatever the blood tests said, I wasn't working with Sergio ever. He'd been raised in care and had been seduced by his swimming instructor when he was twelve.

'That's terrible,' I had sympathised.

'No,' Sergio elaborated. 'It was fantastic. He loved me and gave me lots of presents.'

What was disturbing about Sergio was that he couldn't see

any difference between a question like 'Shall we have a beer?' and 'Shall we kidnap someone and hogtie them so they slowly asphyxiate, while we drink a beer?' When we had discussed getting rid of Rutger, Janos's Italian idiom had failed him, and Sergio, misunderstanding our intentions, calmly suggested in mime holding him under the water in the pool. Janos laughed, but we all grasped in horror that Sergio hadn't been joking. None of us could look at him. This had been shortly before Hamish's drowning.

'They're so greedy and disgusting,' Constance was saying. I can't remember which set of politicians she was talking about. Politics didn't figure much on the roof, but whenever they did and Constance was present, the bile would pour out. There wasn't a political figure of any party, ruling or in opposition, in any country who didn't qualify as evil, greedy, disgusting or – her favourite epithet for the rulers – loathsome. Much ire would be expended on 'the system' and 'the establishment'. For someone with a string of properties, whose only worry was which thong to put on in the morning, she was highly furious. Wetwork was the only other subject dear to her heart. Somehow, I'm suspicious of someone who within a few minutes of being introduced announces she has slept with a hundred and seventy-eight men. Why the count? Why are you telling me? Perhaps my thighs have been more open than they should have been, but, for an amateur record, in your early twenties, that's some going. But, you know, finally if you want to get numerical, a coachload of rugby players is never more than a phone call away.

Sergio and Janos were chuckling again over an advertisement about Rutger. Sergio and Janos did a lot of film work, and Rutger had attempted to break in, but had been found wanting in the timber department. Rutger had accompanied Janos on one shoot, insisting that the director provide him with two or three women, because 'one wouldn't be enough'. As Janos remarked: 'He was right. One woman wasn't enough. She was too much.' His failure to raise cane on camera left him undaunted. He flew all over Europe and America to get on sets, reappearing under aliases and wigs, but invariably failing to raise cane when it counted. Paradoxically, although he had never thrust on screen, he was well known in the business. Well known and well disliked. To the extent that a director had taken out a quarter-page advertisement in the trade journal, complete with mug-shot of Rutger, a list of his aliases, and the headline: 'Why you should never work with this man.'

When I first arrived Rutger had conned me into viewing his showreel. The showreel was not long.

The first section, some three minutes long, had only two shots of him. He played the outraged boyfriend of a beautician who is ravished by the pizza-delivery man, while he looks on. This first clip amply illustrated why Rutger was angling for a career in this branch of the cinema. He had an anti-talent for acting. He drained away the talent from the other performers. His entire task was to look on, but he looked like exactly what he was, someone trying to look like an outraged boyfriend, disappointed with life.

Janos later explained that even this part had only been obtained by Rutger paying the director and buying the pizza.

The next clip was also mercifully short. A septuagenarian woman wearing only the top half of a nun's habit was struggling to insert a towel rack into Rutger, while Rutger struggled to look as if he enjoyed it. His acting was improved by his wearing a gas mask. The half-nun had a disappointed-with-life expression.

Then Rutger appeared as a pig-handler, while an elderly woman who had evidently never considered the benefits of exercise, a good diet or cosmetic surgery cavorted with the pig. The pig had a disappointed-with-life expression.

The final sequence consisted of Rutger roped on to a Formula One car while a bored blonde with a poorly tattooed scorpion on her buttock had a dump on him.

Apparently Rutger had only got that role because he had supplied the car. Janos explained that Rutger's father was the deputy minister of something in Germany and regularly forwarded money to Rutger in the belief that his son was a smackhead.

'I'm going for a swim,' I said as I went into the pool, in case being forgotten about caused me to sink to the bottom. The pool was so small and shallow it seemed impossible to have a misfortune in it, but then drownings happen in bathtubs. I hoped to enjoy my swim, but I couldn't. All I could think of was that I was splashing merrily in the sunshine and that Hamish wasn't. Being gloomy is futile, but it can be hard to shake off.

I watched Constance laugh it up with Janos and Sergio. I was a little envious of the ease she had with other people. I was too young to realise that many people like people whom they don't know very well, because generally those people don't know them very well either. It's the charm of the stranger. The stranger has to make do with the information you provide and is unlikely to refute you with yourself. It's not always major deception. It's not pretending to be a fighter pilot or the fifth richest woman in Spain. It's more omission, and realigning your past in a favourable light. It's saying 'I love New York' and no one saying 'But you hated it and moaned constantly about it during the five years you lived there'. New life through new ears.

I thought about Constance's a hundred and seventy-eight and then, by way of opposition, Tina came to mind. Tina and I had become friendly at school, because, simply, we all sat in the back row in maths. Her, me and Azra. Azra and I wouldn't have bothered talking to her otherwise. Tina got married at nineteen to the first man she went to bed with, Phil, an inoffensive helicopter pilot. It was embarrassing. I wanted to say 'don't' but it would have been horrid because she was so intransigently happy. Azra had had more adventure in one Friday night ('His brother was staying with him. He asked nicely'). I also suspected that Phil might well have been the first man Tina ever kissed. She wasn't unattractive, but she had extremely strict parents and was wallflowery. We enjoyed the wedding, because you always do, but we did feel sorry for her. It was like seeing someone go down with cancer. Finished at nineteen. They went to live in Malta.

I had lost touch with Azra. There's very little sadder than a friendship terminating. And although I was too young to realise it, it was sad precisely because there is nothing you can do about it. It's not that you didn't phone up enough or that your Christmas card was too cheap. I discovered that, after all, perhaps we had been friends because we sat together in maths. Not that Azra really needed anyone. She had breasts. Voted as having the best breasts in the school. Naturally, like anyone with mammary supremacy, she couldn't stop getting them out; I suspect that when she was staring vacantly during maths she was trying to concoct a plausible pretext for breaking them out during set theory.

But then again everyone had lost touch with Azra. She had been, on a smaller scale, like Heidi, an absolute ruler. Perfectly respectable men would start fiddling with themselves as she walked by. And what does the woman who has everything want? Other women's possessions. We're all warned against married men, but it does no good. We're all warned against office affairs, but that does no good either.

Then, naturally, Azra got angry with her married man for being married. She employed none of the standard measures. She didn't phone up the wife. She didn't pour acid on to his car. She didn't arrange for large, hard-to-dispose-of dead animals to be dumped in his garden. She didn't consult contract killers. She went on holiday.

She had ascertained the details of the family holiday and as Mr Married and wife and kids walked up to check in at the airport, Azra was right behind them with an elegant suitcase. If you start screaming at the top of your lungs and hurling objects around at a check-in it might be very satisfying (and unpleasant for the target of your abuse) but that behaviour upsets airlines. If you stand meekly behind an adulterer, like anyone else in the queue, it's not possible for an appeal to be made to the forces of public order.

Mr Married sees Azra and is plunged into a hermetically sealed terror-suit. Is Azra about to go off on one? Is it merely an outrageous coincidence? He doesn't know what to do. His tiny assets are about to be pulverised. He knows the unlimited penalties wives can impose. He understands the ant fearing the sole. Standing in the queue has suddenly become the most gruelling ordeal in the world. Sweat ivies down his face and he is concentrating so hard on not collapsing that when his wife asks him what the matter is, he can't even croak 'nothing'. The assistant at the counter considers not allowing him to board the plane, he is so filleted. Is Azra's presence merely a warning? Glancing back, he sees her check in and accepts it's going to be a very bad day.

Yet he is heartened by Azra's silence. If she were going to denounce him why wait? He is very ill nevertheless and considers baling out of the holiday. His wife is watching him with the suspicion and utter lack of sympathy only a wife can muster. If he tries to duck out now he will be accused of dropping the family to spend more time with the mistress, because inevitably, she knows; she doesn't know it's Azra, but she knows. And cancelling the holiday would be money down the drain.

This is the worst aspect of married men: no money. They drone on about mortgage payments and ballet lessons for the kids until you offer to pay for the meal you're eating.

They all fly to Ibiza, Mr Married tortured over his future. He's not earning anything like the money he'd like, but his wife's family owns some small trees in Perthshire which in twenty years will be big trees and a tidy sum. There is no other comfort in the coming decades. At the airport in Ibiza, Azra vanishes and Mr Married slumps at his hotel. The next morning, as his family deploy themselves on the beach, Azra unfurls her towel next to them, introducing herself to the wife: 'I'm Azra, I'm sure he's told you all about me.'

The family move to another hotel on the other side of the island. It takes Azra fifteen minutes to locate and join them. Mr Married tackles the crisis by lying in a darkened room, chain-smoking and sobbing, while the two women bandy nonchalance by the swimming pool. On the fourth day Azra is no longer in sight. The assumption is she has got tired of the battle.

Back home, Mr Married is consoling himself with the knowledge that, at worst, he'll be dead in fifty years and that things couldn't be any grimmer when the police visit to question him about Azra's disappearance. None of her gear ever left her hotel room in Ibiza. She was last known of at the hotel.

I towelled myself down and rejoined Constance. My shoulders had tightened pleasantly from the swim. Janos and Sergio had wandered off to bait Rutger. The mellowness of the afternoon started to permeate me. I heard Constance clear her throat. Once might have been a throat-clearing, but twice was throat-clearing as intro.

'Oceane, everyone says they can talk to you.'

'Yes . . . ?' I didn't know this. It was, I suppose, a compliment: 'everyone says they can't talk to you' wouldn't be a very desirable accomplishment.

'There's something on my mind.'

'You're not going to confess something are you?'

'No. But I need you to tell me I'm stupid.'

'If you insist.'

'No, listen to me first. My mother had me very late, and whenever it came up I always pretended that she was ten years younger. After a while I got this idea if I ever told anyone her true age something terrible would happen to her. Then she had her sixty-fifth birthday.'

'Why are you telling me this, if you're worried something will happen to her?'

'Because I told someone else.'

'Did anything happen?'

'She died. I want you to tell me I'm being ridiculous thinking it's my fault.'

'You're being ridiculous.'

The sound system in the club was extremely powerful and so it was that evening, as we were comparing nail varnish backstage, we couldn't hear Mervyn being shot. We gradually became aware of the audience being ushered out and unusual goings-on out front. We learned that a group of Lebanese had turned up for the first show and had got chatting to the chatty Mervyn. They exchanged pleasantries about Lebanon. One of them asked Mervyn what time he finished work as he wanted to continue this so-delightful conversation but had some business to attend to first. Mervyn confirmed he worked late. The Lebanese guy then spent four hours trawling Barcelona's grubbier districts until he found someone who sold him a gun. He paid for readmission and shot Mervyn five times point-blank and as he sedately walked out shot the Doormat in the arse with the injunction 'idiot' before merging with the night.

'You heard?'

A week later, Christiana found Moany Patricia at the bottom of the pool. The mood was not good. It was now September. Originally I'd planned to go back to London after three months. Quickly I'd reconsidered Christmas a more suitable date. Now I thought about talking to a travel agent immediately. Jorge was gutted.

'Ten years in business. Not one fight. Not one customer fainting. Hardly a spilt drink. Now this.'

Closing the club for a week or so was discussed. It was a sensible solution. No one wanted to work, but sitting around doing nothing wasn't any better. And you didn't get paid for that. I wouldn't have minded a week off, but bills had to be paid, and almost everyone urged Jorge to carry on.

We still went up to the roof to sun, but the only person who would go swimming was Rutger. He'd splash about ostentatiously, while the rest of us kicked the gloom around. While none of us had been close to Patricia, it was unnerving to see someone so young, so irritating and with such attention-detaining breasts just go. The circumstanceless circumstances of her drowning caused us to provide some. Without any medical training whatsoever we were willing to list dropping-dead scenarios gleaned from television and half-remembered conversations. 'It happens just like that. Some-one young, healthy, carefree. And your last thought will be, do I need to wash my hair tonight?'

I had an impulse to do something for everyone. Vlan was always managing the paraphernalia, Janos and Sergio were always going down to the beach for shareable young ladies, Rhino's mother was sending hampers of ham and strange nougaty stuff that got passed round and Extremely Moany's sister was in the wine business so crates of surprisingly good red were much in evidence.

I offered to cook Sunday lunch for everyone. There was one small kitchen on our floor which was as basic as you could get. I chose to make a chicken curry because of the limited facilities, because in a wretched foreigner-abroad way I had brought a small sachet of spices with me in case I needed to do the cooking, and because while a great chicken curry is hard to make, chicken curry is hard to ruin. I didn't plan a dessert, because at home I'd always done the main course while Julia had been responsible for the desserts. Fortunately the paucity of kitchenalia gave me an excuse for not attempting a chocolate soufflé.

Fifteen of the team were invited, even Rutger. I really didn't want to invite him, but somehow I couldn't bring myself not to, though at least eight of the fifteen raised the non-inviting of Rutger as a very desirable measure. I hoped, somehow, I would simply not see him for the next five days. It's one of these strange phenomena that you can live very close to someone and not see them for a long time. But Rutger crossed my path every five minutes. I felt this was a test. Praying he would have some prior engagement or a deep-seated aversion to chicken curry, I issued the invitation as unappealingly as possible.

'Great,' he said. 'You'd better be good though. I'm a fussy eater. But my orectic potency is more than satisfactory.'

'What?'

'Orectic potency. Hey, it's your language.'

It was on Sunday morning as I fiddled with the turmeric that I could no longer conceal from myself that I was nervous. The drawback to cooking is that you only need one miscalculation or to lose your concentration for a few seconds and you have 'klutz' stamped on your forehead. Like anything else if you don't practise you lose your edge and I'd never cooked for so many at one go and I was learning some lessons of scale.

Soon I could no longer conceal from myself that I was terrified. I told myself that even if the chicken was blackened and the curry only fit for spitting out, it didn't matter. We could all laugh about it. I told myself this a lot, but I didn't believe myself. I was visiting the toilet repeatedly and I was almost doubled up with fear at the prospect of my guests not turning up and social extinction, and the fear of my guests turning up and not being able to force-feed themselves.

Why had I done this? There'd been no obligation to do this. And it wasn't a nothing. It was a cashing-up, I was on the line. Whatever I said about it, whatever anyone else said, it was about me. I was putting myself in the balance. It was what I was worth, no matter how you draped it in insignificance.

I knew I could count on Janos and a few others. Janos would eat a tyre if you gave him a sharp enough knife. I attempted to allay my terror by thinking of Janos troughing his way through my cooking. Lunchtime arrived. What would be the etiquette with such an international crew? How many minutes late was it considered polite to arrive? I had set up the serving space in my room and I waited. I could hear movement in the neighbouring rooms and I assumed appetites were being finalised. I sat with my pans of curry and rice and waited. I served myself a small portion. It wasn't great, but it was okay. It was definitely okay; I had dodged the buzzsaw on that one.

Where was everyone? Should I knock on some doors? It was too late for a lie-in and I could detect the sounds of uprightness. I didn't go knocking because I didn't want to look as desperate as I was.

Finally an invitee. Rutger carrying a box with dials on it. I wasn't going to ask. I served him a portion and he tucked in appreciatively. Our conversation petered out quickly so against my better instincts I asked him about the box.

'It's a Geiger counter.'

Right, I wasn't going to pursue that any further. We silenced for a while then Rutger said:

'We could make sex while we wait.'

'We could.'

I gave Rutger a second helping which he again wolfed down with abundant noises of pleasure. I had intended to get rid of Rutger as quickly as possible but now I needed him to stay. Failure was caking on me like a mudpack. One guest is an immeasurable improvement on no guests. I could hear the others out of sight, but no one came. Over the previous days I had repeatedly reminded everyone about this.

'This chicken curry is the best I've ever eaten,' Rutger said. This is what is terrible. A compliment, probably insincere, from someone you despise, and you melt.

Rutger stayed for another half an hour out of what looked suspiciously like sympathy. He even had a token third helping. No one else turned up. I waited another two hours before binning the chicken, because I knew I wouldn't be eating it later.

Of course, it's a small thing. Especially after the events of the previous weeks. But even now the shame burns. Because I had learned something. This was the first time I learned that the truth isn't welcome. Truth gets a good press, but like most celebrities it's capable of behaving badly. I didn't really want to know that my friendship meant so little they couldn't walk several feet and have a free meal.

I thought about the group spirit. It occurred to me that Janos and Sergio shared their pick-ups because they were cast-offs. Rhino passed around the nougat because he didn't want to get fat. The wine cost Extremely Moany nothing.

This was an avenue of thought I didn't want to go down because I couldn't see it leading anywhere good. I could hear the others, going up and down the stairs, having far-off conversations. They were around but they didn't turn up. I was hoping that one by one, there would be apologies or mitigations later on to balm things over, but there weren't.

I'm sure it wasn't a worked-out policy. There was no consultation, no boycott. Just a series of individual decisions. I examined my behaviour. Had I failed to return someone's hairdryer? Or vilified anyone's character? In some ways that was more hurtful. If they had snubbed me, I could at least have had the satisfaction of justified rage. If someone treads on your toe on purpose, you can treat yourself to revenge, but if someone merely takes a step backwards carelessly and crushes your foot, even though it might be excruciating it's hard, for me at least, to harbour revenge. One of the reasons I didn't grill the others over their absence was because none of them knew that Rutger had been my only guest. The phantom lunch could live on, if questions weren't asked.

'Don't worry,' Rutger had said as he left, 'there will be one or two friends in your life who won't betray you. They'll be the ones you'll betray.'

There are only two things you can do when your friends disappoint you. Remember or forget. It's indisputable which is healthier. Or is it? You have learned an unpleasant truth. If you have a faulty item of clothing or a defective electrical good you can return it or exchange it, but few of us are in a position to change friends even if we are determined to do so. We are stuck in our vats. Some of my friends from home had speculated about coming to visit me, but even with a free floor on offer they hadn't. You begin to wonder if you're doing something wrong. I was beginning to discover I wasn't like most people: I had feelings.

I thought of what Piotr had told me about what one aged counterfeiter had told him after serving ten years in jail: 'The universe is billions of years old, but it can all change in a second. You get ten years of shit, and then suddenly, you don't.'

A few days after that, I went up to the terrace and saw another ambulance crew, Richard and Vlan standing aghast. Extreme misery has an unmistakable aura. You can actually stand miserably.

Rutger looked as bouncy as ever. Vlan indicated the pool and croaked, 'Marina.' I thought the ambulance crew was there on some sort of exercise. I still didn't quite get it until Rutger spelled it out for me. When does panic become terror? Or is it terror that blossoms into panic?

We were freaked into outer space. We had soldiered on to some extent, congratulating ourselves on our fortitude, partly because none of us had been that close to Hamish or Patricia. We were all friendly, but none of the performers had been there that long, and you have some spiritual stamina locked away for the odd vicissitude; if nothing else, at the deepest level, you can rely on wondrous reserves of selfishness and disregard for others. This was too much.

The verdict was the same. No sign of bad temper, no sabotage from booze or drugs. Patricia and Marina had failed to stay awake in the pool.

Jorge closed the pool permanently, as if anyone, apart from Rutger, would have thought of using it again. We didn't know what to do. You keep on telling yourself the show must go on, and we did that the first time. Our emotions weren't all to do with sympathy for Marina. Very little of it was.

'You are firing Richard?' Ewa asked Jorge.

'Now it's Richard? Last week you all signed a petition to fire Rutger.'

'He works for death.'

'What?' asked Jorge.

'He came here because everyone he teaches drowned.'

'No. Don't forget the shark attacks. And two died from bends,' Vlan added.

'First the helicopter crash. Then Hamish. Merv. Patricia. Then Marina.' Ewa was waving her hands around.

'How did Richard do that? Did he pull the helicopter down with a piece of string? He wasn't even here when Hamish drowned.'

'He's bringing death here. Either he goes or I go,' said Ewa.

'You're being foolish,' said Jorge. Ewa, oddly, didn't sound foolish at all. We were all being asked to shoulder too much reality in one lump. 'What should I do? Behave like an old woman?' said Jorge waving his arms back. I've never understood that expression: in my experience, old women are history-fed toughs who aren't afraid of anything. The analogy should be a young woman or an old man.

Time had slowed to syrup. I didn't offer to help sort out Marina's effects. There are truths you know, but you don't feel. We all had been informed of mortality, but there's a difference between knowing it, and having the reaper come and sit on your face.

'My wife thanks you for the overtime,' said the detective as he left.

'We make a great team,' replied Jorge.

The sound system may well be the pinnacle of human achievement. Having the club to ourselves, loud music and intoxicants had achieved remarkable mood gains before. But even that wasn't enough to cheer us up. This time the show didn't go on. 'I like to think of them in heaven, performing for God,' Nadia remarked.

Ewa and Piotr quit. They had been talking (interminably) of staying for another six months and saving enough money to buy a disused convent in the Tatra mountains and converting it into a swingers' club. 'I'm not dying alive,' said Ewa and we thought we understood what she meant. We all congratulated ourselves on our bravery for staying. There's nothing like seeing someone bolt to make you feel brave. Lou and Sue, who had been talking (interminably) about leaving, stopped, and now got to do another ten minutes in the show using a food blender. But we were still lollipops for fear.

For several days everything was quiet. We had some immemorable performances and we managed to unwind a little. Nadia and I walked up to the roof to catch some sun. Jorge had had the pool filled with soil and had planted some saplings.

Nadia and I stopped in our tracks when we got to the roof because there, next to the one-time pool, was a large Friesian cow, on its side. When I say large, of course, I'm no authority on Friesian cows, particularly out of the pasture context, but it looked very large. The lifeless legs that protruded from underneath the cow looked rather small. We recognised the frayed orange sandals on the feet. They were Vlan's.

'It's a cow.' I said.

'I could have told you that,' said Nadia.

I won't go into the details but there was no doubt at all about the deadness of the cow and Vlan. We were so shocked we could barely raise the alarm.

We fizzled with fear. I ran my bath one inch deep to make sure I couldn't drown. I handled my nail scissors with enormous care in case I tripped and impaled myself. I announced I had to go back to England to work on my dance career, which was true, but I was glad I had a dance career to think of. It had been fun, but all I had to show for my time at Babylon was better definition in my arms from hours spent in the doggy position on stage.

We never found out more about the cow. Vlan had met with some uniquely bad luck. Cows falling out of the sky are rare. No one owned up to losing a cow; but then if you'd dropped a cow over Barcelona which flattened someone would you want to put your hand up? Janos came up with a theory that the police were retaliating for us downing one of their helicopters by bombing us with beef. No one came up with anything better.

It was the middle of my night when Rutger hammered on my door.

'Quick! Richard's tried to commit suicide.' I got to my

feet, not very successfully. An anvil of awfulness was in my stomach. I was being asked to do something I couldn't do: deal with more misfortune. I was attempting to rustle up a thought, when Rutger said:

'No, I'm only joking.'

It took me several seconds to slam the door in Rutger's face and issue a grunt before falling back into my bed and leaving punishment for a future instalment of consciousness.

Rutger knocked again. 'No. Okay. I was joking. Constance's tried to commit suicide.'

She had swallowed a load of pills, thrown up, wandered about, been discovered and taken to hospital where she had been depilled, pilled and shown the door. There's this strange idea that if you both come from the same island you must have some sense of responsibility for each other. Again it was flattering to be seen as a reliable person who can support others in distress, but that effect soon wore off.

They put a camp bed and Constance in my room so I could nurse her.

'Depression was it?'

'No.'

'Then why take the pills?'

'I was very happy. I thought, why commit suicide when you're miserable?'

Constance was afraid of the dark, so we slept with the lights on, or rather she slept while I did my best to fall asleep. We all have our little foibles. Well, I don't. Lots of people do though. Azra used to have a fear of melting butter. She'd always put the butter back in the fridge after carving off a strip. The prospect of butter achieving room temperature distressed her.

I can understand being afraid of the dark. I can't understand telling anyone about it.

But I humoured her. Constance also smelled badly. I hinted a few times, then saw a direct approach was needed.

'You need a shower.'

'That's right. Tell me what to do. Why is it that women are always being told what to do? Do this. Do that. Or if we're not told what to do, we're told what not to do. Don't do this. Don't do that. Why don't we have any freedom? Men are allowed not to have showers.'

The only way I could get her out of my room was to lend her money for shopping, her pharmaceutical debacle having severely disrupted her going-to-the-bank skills. I put up with it for a while because an event like that just isn't funny: life is sacred – that had been clearly explained to us.

After three days, however, the compassion was gone and I sincerely wished that she had succeeded. I suspected that I had been nominated to nurse her not because my compassion shone out, but because I was a mug. You don't get thanks, and even if you do, thank you is just quick sounds. On the fourth day, after she had stubbed out her cigarette on my bar of soap, I went to Jorge to explain she had to go to another room or I'd injure her.

I raged in, scolded Jorge and only then noticed the new boy standing in the corner.

'This is Juan,' Jorge said. 'Perhaps you'd like to show him round.' Jorge knew full well I would. I don't like pretty boys, but Juan had made himself an exception. He was too good-looking to be working in the Babylon, indeed he was too good-looking to be working anywhere. He should have been given a grant for being Juan. I found myself shifting from foot to foot, and playing with my hair and cursing myself for not having applied the best make-up. He was younger than me. I was twenty-one, but he was nineteen – enough for a distinct thrill of toyboy action there.

I conducted Juan around, swallowing the drool. I assumed Jorge hadn't burdened him with information about the deceased, so I accentuated Babylon's other features.

'What's at the top?' he asked.

I had been planning to omit the roof, but I couldn't risk

pretending it wasn't there in case Juan had a deep-seated aversion to falsehood.

'The roof terrace.'

'Let's look.'

Going up to the roof was not something I ever wanted to do again, but I had to humour Juan and spend more time with him than anyone else in Babylon until I had conclusively demonstrated to him that no one else would provide him with such a wonderland for his willy.

When I saw Richard on the roof, my trepidation was upgraded to stifled hysteria. Among us survivors he was now referred to as The End. I found myself hunching slightly as if to parry the effect of a falling cow and I gravitated to the centre of the roof in case there were any sudden powerful gusts of wind that might sweep me off.

'I need to talk to you, Oceane,' Richard said.

'Later.'

'No,' said Juan sauntering off. 'Don't worry about me.' Courteous to boot: I vowed to make him groan.

'So?' I asked, wanting to say can't you see I'm occupied, but not.

'You have comfortable ears,' Richard said. 'I can't go on like this.'

'Like what?' I almost managed to say this as if I didn't know what he was talking about.

'This is all my fault.'

'This is all my fault? How could it be your fault?' I said this because it was what you were supposed to say, although I couldn't make myself sound convincing, and what I wanted to say was, you have a point.

'I don't want to be me,' he said. 'I'd give anything not to be me. Wherever I go . . . I want to check out.' I wanted to say something healing but I couldn't manage anything better than:

'Come on.'

'I'm too much of a coward.'

'Don't talk rubbish,' I said, because it was what you were supposed to say.

'I need to find a good way of doing it. Something memorable like tying myself to an insurance salesman and then jumping into deep water. Something that would make amends.'

I didn't stay on the roof too long with Richard. He sneaked off that day, saying goodbye to no one, his exit unobserved. Most of his stuff was left behind, but some packing had taken place. Lou and Sue were now given almost half an hour on stage to pad out the show. They hit upon the concept of guest stars and would go down to the beach to offer young sunbathers a climactic education. Either there were a lot of takers, or they did a lot of asking. Performance must be the only endeavour where you could pay less the more that's done.

Before I left I swapped addresses with everyone except Walter (whom I kept on missing) and Rutger. I was lucky, I didn't bump into Rutger in the days before my departure so I didn't have to deal with the dilemma of whether to provide or not to provide. Oddly, as I handed out my carefully written address to the survivors I had the premonition that I would never see them again, but I was confident that I would see Rutger again. Rutger would turn up whatever I did. He was a turner-upper.

I never did hear from anyone to whom I gave my address. It's disappointing when you don't hear from your acquaintances. You tell yourself it's simply pressure of the daily drizzle of frustrations, the washing-up, buying groceries, grouting bathroom tiles that prevents a response to your card, letter or phone call. A change of address, the loss of a handbag and Filofax are the setbacks you imagine silencing your correspondents, but you dread that it's because you don't merit any effort or even worse that you merit the effort of not responding.

Although I didn't realise it, I was living at the close of a huge era. It was the last days of losing touch. Those most human of emotions: loss and curiosity. Whatever happened to? From the caves to the clubs, your intimates would vanish leaving you with unfinishedness. It's still possible. Mobile numbers and e-mail addresses change, but unless you are really hiding, you can be easily tracked. Most gerbils have their own web site now. Then you could still choose to lose or to stay in touch in a way you can't now. At least you know where the finished versions are now, which often makes them less alluring, and can choose whether to look or not. Being forgotten is much harder to do, and therefore much harder to take.

I bought the expensive pair of shoes. I was certain that they would laugh at me in the shop (two doors down from the Babylon) for spending so much on a pair of shoes, but they kept a straight face. As the shoes were packaged it occurred to me I could still run out. As the money hit the till, I had a spasm of nausea. The following day, I zigzagged between exhilaration at owning the shoes and shame at the price. I also realised that I liked the shoes so much that, in order to protect them from wear, I would probably never wear them.

I had seen them in the shop window months earlier. It's very rare for me to see an item of clothing that I can flip over. But these shoes would make me a better person and spread my importance all over the universe. In these shoes, I'd always be pleased to see myself. It was purchase at first sight. Except it wasn't. I stalled on the purchase to enjoy it all the more. I enjoyed pretending to myself that I wouldn't spend that much on a pair of shoes, that I was too sensible. But extravagance . . . extravagance, it's always going to be a crowd-pleaser. A two-hundred-pound bottle of wine isn't ten times better than a twenty-pound bottle of wine: you're not paying for the wine, you're paying for the paying.

There are those who say clothes are frippery, jumped-up nothingness. They're wrong. They say that style only makes you feel invincible and successful, but if it makes you feel invincible and successful, isn't that enough? Which is easier, buying clothes or becoming invincible and successful? And the bonus of feeling invincible and successful is that others think you are too.

I had my bags packed. The taxi was booked. My make-up had been retouched. I was ready to leave and I was regretting going home. I missed it but I still wanted to stay.

Juan came to mind. I had slipped him my address and urged him with the big smile to visit, but I was concerned I hadn't been graphic enough. Why bank on some future visit to London? The man was upstairs. Let the fox see the rabbit. I didn't know which room number, though. I'd ask Janos.

On the landing, Constance. I had been hoping for those quick sounds at least. One thank you for listening to her ceaseless dissonance and the toil of trying to will her into a better mood. It's easier to roll an elephant uphill than to pull someone out of the gloom. At the end of the inventory, she had nothing to complain about. Obviously you don't stuff a bottle of pills into yourself if you're completely all right, but, frankly, she had no grounds for complaint. She was young, healthy, more attractive than some and she hadn't had any major trauma. She didn't have a painful illness. She wasn't facing starvation. In light of what had ensued at Babylon her actions were obscene.

'Haven't you left?' asked Constance, wearing one of my tops.

'The countdown's begun. Which room is Juan in?'

'I don't know. Anyway, he's gone off for a few days.'

If you're clever you say thank you. It takes a second, costs nothing and then it's harder to be hated. No one can say 'and you didn't even say thank you'. Annoyed with myself for not putting myself on a tray for Juan, I picked up my luggage. Then it occurred to me, I could do Juan another note to leave him in no doubt about his reception in England and where to get cut-price flights. I wrote the note with lots of underlinings and exclamation marks, which I find silly, but this was no time for restraint.

Janos told me which was Juan's room and, as I slid the note under the door, I heard a stirring and the door was opened by Juan, his door-opening prowess unhampered by any clothing.

Half an hour later, unable to walk straight, I said goodbye to Juan and collected my bags and stuck them in the taxi waiting out front. My eyes were streaming. It was quite blush-making, because I wasn't emotional, something was irritating them. I looked in my mirror and I could see my eyelids swelling up chameleonly.

'Airport?' asked the driver.

I didn't answer. I was thinking about Juan's cock, lying on his belly like some superb sunbather on a fleshy beach. In general, men's tackle is a reliable source of hilarity or disenchantment: you tire of the slugs and distressed sea-urchins. Juan's sweat was sensational too. Even now I wish I could go down to the supermarket and buy a pint. With difficulty, I studied my watch. About an hour to get to the airport.

'Five minutes,' I said, going back up to Juan's. I knew it was going to be more than five minutes, but when a taxi driver says he'll be arriving in five minutes he doesn't mean it either.

Juan was far too good-looking for any hope of a long-term relationship. When you're that formidable at helping women with their sexual enquiries, you're never going to settle down. No woman can never have outright ownership, only timeshare. Moreover, he really liked women. Rhino, for instance, didn't. Rhino only liked Rhino. Janos only liked very attractive blondes with lots of hair who would quickly agree to get climactic with him. Juan was perhaps too easy-going for me. It's like training dogs. You want the dog to obey you, but you can't have any real respect for a dog that always obeys you. You want a dog that occasionally goes over the wall or bites the postman without your permission; you want to be reminded that you command a subdued yet wild animal, not a crawler. A man should be strong enough to kill you with his bare hands.

Nevertheless I considered marriage and raising a family with Juan for the duration. By the time I got back to the taxi, I needed luck to catch my flight. I didn't know what I would do if I didn't. My savings had largely been blown on the shoes, and the taxi meter was already frightening.

Saving money has never been me, but saving up expectation has always been one of my traits: that's why I waited till the last day before buying the shoes. It could be that's why I waited ten minutes before telling the taxi driver to turn around and return to Babylon. There was pleasure in delay and pleasure in imagining having another go with Juan. Imagining is what it's all about; and there's nothing like actually making love with someone to help you imagining making love to them.

As I progressed by touch up to Juan's room (my eyes watering so much I could barely see) I calculated that by then, back in England, my parents and sister would have already left home to give me the big family welcome at the airport. Inching their way through traffic somewhere. This racked me a bit. I didn't mind messing Julia around, because somehow that's part of the deal with a sibling. If Julia had been going to the airport by herself it would even have been funny. But nettling my parents was different.

I got on with them very well. It took me a long time to notice that this was quite unusual. First of all having parents, as opposed to one parent and someone else passing through. Secondly, they never made me do anything I hated. I was never made to reattempt their own failures. They never embarrassed me. My mother didn't traipse around sucking on a gin bottle. My father didn't greet my friends with his dick hanging out. They looked after me with only a few skirmishes over discipline. We were freaks.

One Christmas when a boyfriend and I had come to stay, our car, full of our presents, was stolen from the family driveway. The car and the presents weren't worth much, but it was upsetting. My father spent the next day driving around trying to spot the car, which of course he didn't. His quest wasn't propelled by an outraged masculinity or a fanatical adherence to law and order, but simply because he wanted to get his daughter's presents back.

The terrible consequence of being raised in a civilised and loving household is that you are poorly prepared for everything outside. While selfishness never lets you down.

'Back so soon?' commented Juan. In a blurry fashion I could see he wasn't alone. His groin was curtained by Constance's hair; she was nodding away, using those little extras to remind the recipient that what is happening is happening, with a smugness that suggested she thought she was the sole proprietor of those little extras. Juan really was going to have to buy a big stick to beat off the women.

'You have been crying,' he said. There was no need for the truth. I looked as if two peaches had been fixed over my eyes, and normally I would have wanted to hide in a dark room with a bag over my head, but I was stuck on rut.

'Isn't this the best thing in the world?' slobbered Constance, interrupting her work. This, of course, wasn't the question she was asking. And this was the answer she wasn't wanting:

'No,' replied Juan, without hesitation. 'The best thing is going for a walk with a friend.'

I assumed the position while Constance showed herself out. No woman likes to gear up for the five-star fellatio with deluxe filth to have it lightly dismissed. Climactics is the one enterprise we all want to be good at. No one minds being bad at something, and most of us can joke about our fiascos in the kitchen, on the dancefloor, in the office, in exams. But no one is going to say, 'Don't bother taking me home. It's not worth it.'

Irresponsibility had reorganised me. Why was I doing this? All the trouble had unhinged me somewhat, and because, like most things, I was doing it because I wanted to, I suppose. Nevertheless even immense pleasure has some consideration; it can leave a little room in your mind for other thoughts. Which set of traffic lights would my father be fuming at now? I had flung my blouse aside; I could see it would get creased. (Again, now, it wouldn't be a problem. Three in a car, there would be at least one mobile).

During that final final goodbye, Extremely Moany knocked at the door to try the 'I've run out of toothpaste' ploy, but heard it wasn't a good time to ask Juan.

As I made my way down to the taxi for the last time, Rutger was leaning against it.

'Goodbye, Oceane,' he said. 'I only wanted to let you know I told everyone the curry was cancelled.'

Going out to the airport, I didn't see much. My eyes were still puffed up, my mind nebulated. Now that I had missed the flight, I no longer had the compulsion to go back for more of Juan. I tried to prepare my speech. I'm always inclined to tell the truth, whether this is because I don't like lying or whether I'm no good at lying, I can't say. Certainly, I don't like lying, but that's because I'm no good at it.

And surely the fanfare of the truth, the incense of candour should earn you something? I'd never committed an irresponsibility like this before. Regrettably, the good conduct of the last twenty-one years didn't count for anything in the present situation. I couldn't stroll up and say, 'I have never let anyone down in my life so now I'm claiming my free flight. Here is my certificate to show I'm not a habitual bunglehead. Thank you for your under-standing.' I ought to be able to say, 'Look, I was obliged to rut my brains out this morning,' and get some sympathy, because I think we've all had lust beasting in us, and again as long as you don't make a habit of it, there should be some tendency to pardon.

The female stand-by of bursting into tears was what I settled on. Men always have the recourse of threats and violence in a sticky situation. They start swinging, we start crying. With my face the way it was, I fibbed up a scenario of mugging and assault *en route* to the airport with loss of all my money and ticket. I considered throwing in a string about hospital (visiting a friend in a coma) or a funeral (my sister), but judged it over the top.

I miseried up to the counter and when I explained I had missed the flight because I had been mugged, the woman said to me:

'You're very lucky.'

I thought she had meant unlucky, but she did mean lucky. I hadn't missed a flight. I had missed a crash.

YUGO

It wasn't that much of a test, compared to where Audley had to go, but we had to have a test.

We went for a stroll around Sunk Island. It's flat, with nothing going on, almost a vast badly kept lawn. The Humber Mouth is uninviting this morning. Maybe it always is. Dampness and wetness abound, either because of the river or the sagging clouds. The greyness doesn't do the region any favours. But then, as Audley confessed, it's nearly always grey.

'I didn't see the sun until I was six.'

Why does anyone live here? It's peaceful, certainly, and if you want to be a farmer, land's land. But it's miles to the nearest shop, which will have twenty packets of cigarettes, ten tins of baked beans, five bars of chocolate and a tabloid newspaper.

Audley identifies the lifeboat station across the water. 'My father was on the lifeboat.'

'You must be very proud of him. Saving lives.'

'I am. They risk their necks time after time to save, in the normal course of events, chuckleheads. My father saved some nautical dunces, but what I'm proudest of, is the one he threw back.'

'Threw back?'

'They were called out in a force ten. Some banker who

157

ignored all the warnings had capsized his yacht. They almost went over several times. My father said it was the worst ride he'd ever had. When they pulled this chucklehead out of the water, all he said was, "Why did you take so long? I can't wait to lodge a complaint about this." My father said, "You get one chance to say thank you. You're not obliged to be sincere." "Thank you? What for?" "You're right," says my father chucking him back in.'

'Didn't he pull him out again?'

'No.'

'Didn't he feel bad afterwards?'

'No. As he put it, why should he feel bad about throwing someone into some water? The North Sea's business is its own.'

We move down to the bird sanctuary. There is something soothing about watching birds. For a few minutes. The air would be very bracing probably, if I could breathe it.

'It's very tranquil.'

'Not always,' replies Audley. 'It can get wild. I was mugged by a pensioner once.'

I laugh.

'I'm serious. I was walking home late one night, and this small old fellow dodders up, and I'm thinking he shouldn't be out by himself. He must have been eighty, and not in good condition for eighty either. He stops in front of me and says, "Give me your money, if you know what's good for you." Poor old sod must be mad or on something. I sidestep him and carry on, but he's sticking his hands into my pockets, so I give him a shove to get rid of him. "If you don't give me your money," he says, "I'll call the police and tell them you mugged me." It's an uncomfortable situation; three in the morning, me, young thug in rude health well known to the local constabulary, collapsing geriatric; who would you believe? Even if I get cleared, I'm spending the night with the police. I start running, but I'd been out on the dancefloor showing off, so I have a sprained ankle and I can't move fast, the old git chases after me, shouting, "I've got a razor and I'm prepared to use it. Stop or I'll cut myself." So I figure it'll be easier to give him something. So I hand over my fiver, and he says, "Is that it, you pauper?" He made me give him my shoes as well.'

'That must have been embarrassing.'

'I've had worse.'

I hear a thump and Audley curses.

'What's up?'

'My nervous tic.'

'How long have you had that?'

Audley snorts. 'A long time.'

'Did it just start by itself?'

'No. I was at home thinking about having a second lunch.'

'How does thinking about food give you a tic?'

'Can I finish? I was eighteen at the time, and I was desperate to get bulky. I'd always been skinny, but I kept on praying when I'd stop growing that I'd get bulkier. But I didn't. I pumped iron, I did karate, I did everything and hell, was I hard. My muscles were like metal. But I was still skinny. I wanted not just to be hard, but to look hard. I ate. I ate. I ate. Everyone I knew spent their money on girls, booze or clothes. I spent every penny on food. I got up early to have a big breakfast. Then I'd snack. Then a big lunch. Then more snacks. Then a big supper. Then more snacks. Day after day. I hated meals. I hated the sight of chocolate. I never wanted to see another sausage. I shat epics. After a year of this regime I'd put on three pounds.'

'That gave you a tic?'

'No. I was at home thinking about having a second lunch, but I was also worried about missing the war. It was the first good war, you know, with the good guys on one side and the bad guys on the other, with proper fighting, all the toys. A war you could understand. A war on our doorstep. When I saw the first pictures on the news I couldn't believe it. In Europe. A war in Europe. I thought wars only happened in shitty third-world shitholes. Not in Europe. Although in a way I was right.

'Everyone was talking about the end of history and I thought this'll be the last one. It had been simmering for weeks and diplomats were emptying hotel minibars all over the place. I wanted to get there double-quick, but I had problems. Like where the fuck is Yugoslavia? What is a Croatia? On top of which I had no money. The day the fighting started, I'd bought this rowing machine. I'd figured out I needed more work on the upper body. I get home with this sickeningly expensive rowing machine, and Scargill's watching the news.'

'Your brother in the Paras?'

'Yeah. "It's going to be a nasty one," he says. "Oh, yes, why's that?" I ask. "Because they're exactly the same," he says. "It's like Northern Ireland. You try explaining Northern Ireland to a barman in Belize who knows nothing about it. The inhabitants speak the same language, have the same God, are as thick as each other, and they can't get enough of watching each other die because some of them want their taxes, which they don't pay, to go to parasitic, useless fuckers who don't give a toss about them in Dublin, while others want their taxes, which they don't pay, to go to useless, parasitic fuckers in London who don't give a toss about them." He got up, farted, and left the room. That memory's well vivid. He was right as usual. Spot-on. I always wanted to be like Scargill. Not even like Scargill, I wanted to be Scargill.'

'He was in the Falklands you said?'

'But he never talked about it. I once went to the pub with him and a load of his mates and when Scargill went off for a slash, they all leaned over to me in the way you do when you have something very important to say and they said very hush-like I bet your brother never told you he won the battle of Goose Green. It was all going very wrong, they were taking withering fire, and no one much fancied it.

Scargill gets up and shouts, "Who's with me?" It didn't surprise me. There really are people you'll follow anywhere. "Why didn't they give him a medal?" I asked. His mates just laughed.'

'It's not surprising that you wanted to be like him.'

'But that's the trouble. You want to be like someone because you're not. Scargill couldn't do anything wrong. He'd always know what to say to a girl, he'd never buy a crap rowing machine that didn't work properly. He had this closet at home; it was beautiful to look in there. Everything was immaculately folded. Scargill could iron a shirt in under two minutes so it would look as if it had just left the factory. Colour-sergeants would choke up at the sight of his creases. He'd be away from home for months, but there wouldn't be a speck of dust in the closet. I'd go in with a magnifying glass and a torch, but I couldn't find a single speck. Dust respected Scargill.'

'Why didn't you join the army?'

'Why didn't I join the army? That was all I wanted to do growing up. I was a cadet. We used to parade outside York Minster. I loved everything about the army. Not just the guns, but belonging. The order. But I gave up on the Paras.'

'Why?'

'Because they gave up on me. I was the best-prepared applicant they must have had. I knew the regimental songs by heart. I'd counted on joining Scargill. Then they discovered I only had one kidney.'

'What happened to the other one?'

'Nothing. Just AWOL. I failed the medical. I could have been in the reserves, but I didn't want second-best. I was pissed off. I was concentrating on getting my qualifications as a fitness instructor and doing a bit of work as an ejectioneer when the war started. I'd forgotten about the military. Then suddenly I thought, here's this good old-fashioned war where the good guys need help. I had no idea how to get there, I had no money. I was worried about what to wear.

What do you wear to a war? If you turn up in a uniform, which uniform do you choose? Then I said to myself: it should be like this. It shouldn't be easy. Just go. Just go.'

'How did you get there?'

'Hitched. Hitched and walked a lot. The hitching didn't go well. I told the family I was off to work in a campsite in France. I was stuck at Birmingham for eighteen hours trying to get a lift, watching attractive and unattractive girls getting lifts, in the rain, but then I got one that took me as far as Austria. The driver tried to recruit me to the Peruvian Communist Party.'

'Peruvian was he?'

'No. Some housing officer from North London. Seems that most of the Peruvian Communist Party is there. In Austria I end up walking about a hundred miles, mostly in the rain, without getting a lift. Obviously I'm doing something wrong, but I can't figure out what it is. But I'm not a quitter.'

We go into a pub. Audley orders himself a pint. I put the kettle on and make myself a cup of tea. When I get back, a ginger-haired man is insisting on buying Audley another pint, although he has barely tasted his first.

'Friend of yours?'

'No. Someone I beat up once.'

'I don't understand.'

'That's how it is. Back to the war. I'm sitting in this run-down café in some sleepy town in Hungary, watching the town's three hard kids gathered around the town's only motorcycle, not a very big one. My feet are killing me, I'm about to spend the last of my money on a meal, but I'm not far from the border. No one speaks English, and I don't understand a word of the language, but I can see from the pictures on television that military stuff is still going on. I'm studying my guidebook when a voice asks: "Going south?"'

'There's this Scouser, late forties, wearing combat trousers and a bomber jacket, cropped hair, with the look of ex-military. "Yes," I say. "Journalist?" he asks. "No." "Good. I hate journalists," he said sitting down. "I'm Real John. There are lots of Johns, but I'm the real one. You're on holiday are you?"

'"No," I said, not knowing what to say because "I'm off to the war" sounds stupid. Then I twigged he was joking. With a laugh he sat down next to me saying, "I'm not either. The Brits are here, have no fear." It was clear he had the same plans as me.

'I was overjoyed to have some company. I didn't mind Real John molesting the waitress because I'd been on my own for the last few days. Real John kept on drawing the waitress's hand over his scars, including the ones under his clothing, saying "Kolwezi", "Belfast" etc. The waitress was well disgusted.

'"You're in good hands, son," he said. "You're lucky you met me." And it felt like it. Real John had a car he'd rented in Vienna; after my hitching, it was paradise. Everything, with a bag of chips. It was sunny, we had the music on, we were driving to a war. We stopped at a small bar to get a drink and this American comes up to us and asks us if we're going across the border.

'He had this Biblical name . . . Jeremiah. I only knew him for about fifteen minutes but I found out a lot about him. He came from Florida, St Petersburg, and he sold needles to hospitals. He was very proud about that; he had shifted more needles than anyone else in Florida. "But I'm kinda multitalented, so I'm exploring photography now." It's easy after all to become a photographer, you get a camera and go to war.

'I felt much less original now about my idea of going to Yugoslavia. I was expecting to find coach parties loitering at the border. I wasn't happy when Real John offered Jeremiah a lift because it was damaging our cool, but it was his car and maybe Jeremiah could get my picture in the papers.

'We're speeding along when Jeremiah says he needs a piss.

So he gets out, strolls over to a bush, and Real John drives off, slowly. Jeremiah chases after us, he's a pudgy soft fucker, forcing himself to laugh as if he finds our prank hilarious. Real John stops every few hundred yards, but just as Jeremiah puffs up, he pulls away again. After we've done this several times, Real John puts his foot on the floor and we're gone. All of Jeremiah's stuff is in the car. I don't know much about photography, but I know a shedload of money when I see it. Real John is laughing like a bastard, and so am I. We reach the border, stop for another drink, and each of us does an imitation of a desperate Jeremiah.'

'It's terrible to find that funny,' I chide.

'Funny? We laughed for an hour. We laughed so much we got back in the car and drove back to have another look at Jeremiah. He was more or less where we left him, no money, no passport, crying by the side of the road. We offer to give him back his passport if he gives us the trousers he's wearing. "You want to rip me off again," he goes. "No, give us your trousers and we'll give you back your passport." So he gives us his trousers and we drive off. "We're doing him a favour. He should fucking thank us," said Real John. "He wouldn't last five minutes in Yugo." Was he saying that for my benefit or is it that real bastards never like to think of themselves as real bastards?

'We reach the border. The traffic is mostly in the direction of out. Hardly anyone going in. I'd been mulling over my application: "Heard you've got a war going on. Room for one more?" Real John said leave it to him. He waved my guidebook: "We're food critics. Come to review restaurants." They gave us a funny look, but we were waved through.

'In Zagreb, Real John immediately sells the car – he says it's on his mother-in-law's credit card – and the cameras and gives me a small cut of the proceeds. I was in love with Real John. We went to visit big buildings that looked important for a couple of days, trying to find someone in charge, but no one was at all interested in us. We could get papers in English, so we knew things were getting nastier, otherwise it was just a hot summer.

'We were sitting at a café, I was eating a raspberry ice-cream. There was some noisy Euroarse at the next table complaining about his favourite flavour of ice-cream having run out and across the road three guys were having a row about how to put a windsurfing board on to the roof of a car. That was the first lesson: usually, when a country's at war, it boils down to a few people being delegated to eat shit on its behalf.

'"All right," said Real John. "Enough arsing about. This isn't what we're here for." He hailed a taxi. "Take us to the war, pal." It took a couple of hours to get to the outskirts of Osijek, which was under siege. One officer who spoke some English told us there was a sort of foreign legion forming in a small village. Taxi drivers are usually shits, but I have to say this one took us right to the action.

'The group was based in the village school. There was a guy outside stripped to the waist, with bits of stripped Kalashnikov around him, like a very unorganised guard. He had "Fuck U" tattooed on his forehead so it was reasonable to assume he spoke some English.

'"We're here to volunteer," said Real John.

'"Too late," said U. "Full. Go away."

'"Don't make me laugh," said Real John walking past. "Where's the gaffer?" If Real John hadn't been there I think I would have jacked it in.

'It was disappointing to see that my plan wasn't at all original. Dozens of volunteers were sprawled around, and it was also dispiriting to see they were nearly all fuckwits of one species or another. Apart from U, who either had a lot of emotional baggage or had been the victim of a vicious stag-party prank, the calibre of the group was summed up by Rico, a Yank. He had flown into Belgrade first, sporting desert fatigues, demanded to see a general in the Ministry of

Defence and had assured him, at length, that he "really fucking hated the Serbs" and wanted to kill "as many fucking Serbs as possible" – because he "really fucking hated them". It says everything about Rico that he was politely redirected to Croatia and given every assistance, and then told everyone about his adventure. I mean I couldn't have told you Belgrade was the capital of Serbia before I went out, but you look at the map before you buy the ticket.

'The gaffer's command post was in one of the school offices. We go in and find two lean, mean, seriously professional guys in black next to some maps and one tubby short-arse, who's the fat kid from school who was always bullied and who ends up as doorman at a massage parlour. Real John salutes the men in black and announces we're reporting for duty. The men in black direct him to tubby.

"'I'm Roberto Diaz," short-arse says.

"'Spanish?" asks Real John, trying to recover.

"'He's Hungarian," says one of the men in black.

"'It's nothing to be ashamed of," says the other guy in black.

"'Spanish," replies Roberto, giving them a dirty look. "I have a Spanish passport."

"'Only one?" asks Black One. "I've got at least half a dozen." Then he starts gibbering away with Black Two in what I assume was Croat. The two of them are hunched over in concentration, fiddling with a wristwatch.

"'Tell me," asks Roberto, "do you know anyone rich or successful who was decent? That you really liked?"

'Real John and I are going ummm, thinking this over. What's the answer, and why are we being asked this question?

"'Don't worry," Roberto says. "It's not a test. I like to ask that question."

'So we were recruited. A supply lorry came the next day and Real John and I were issued with kit. Judging from the military wisdom that was constantly being aired around camp, the Serbs had no chance. Because of my expertise I was put in charge of fitness, and I had everyone running uphill carrying jerrycans full of water and I broke the hard men in squat hell.

'I felt at home. I was a hero, getting a tan, and quite safe. There was nothing going on near us. It was like being in a resort, apart from the fact there were no women, no clubs, no bars, no swimming pool, no proper food and the conversation revolved around how many angles there are in knife fighting. I got to know the others: three security guards from Gosworth, Bazza, Gazza and Lazza, a ticket inspector from Inverness, lots of Scandos and one German who had brought his dog with him and who was living on his own in a tent with every imaginable gadget, including that thing for cutting tomatoes into funny shapes.

'The motives were mixed. Bazza, Gazza and Lazza needed a break from their wives. One or two were, even for those of us with no formal training in pyschiatry, obviously mad. U, for example, or Dr Death, who had been a photocopier demonstrator in Lille, who couldn't even do ten push-ups, and whom everyone beat up in the unarmed-combat sessions.

'It wasn't obvious straight away, but I soon realised that we were where we were because we couldn't do any harm. The real fighting was at Vukovar and Osijek, the big towns. No one was concerned about our out-of-the-way village and if the Serbs did come we would slow them down for about five minutes. The Croatians, Black One and Black Two, weren't really there for liaison, they were babysitters to make sure we didn't do any damage.

'Real John asked about money. "There isn't any," Roberto said. "But what's good about this place is that you can do what you want." That turned out to be the case. One morning six Serbian prisoners were delivered. The rumour was that Roberto had bought them for the complete back catalogue of Stax singles. The prisoners were then loaded into a helicopter, which Roberto had hired in exchange for a number of washing machines. Real John, me and some others were ordered to go along. The prisoners weren't very cheery, but they had no idea how bumpy their day was going to be.

'"This is scientific," said Roberto to me. "Every country has the expression the rich get richer. Many think this is because wealth brings advantages. I argue wealth is only a side issue. Something else is going on."

'Roberto explained that five of the prisoners were losers, but the sixth was the Patisserie King of Novi Sad. According to Roberto's theory, the universe would always back up the rich. As he said this, he shoved one of the prisoners out of the helicopter. We were about sixty feet up, so there was a remote chance of surviving, though I wouldn't have fancied having a go.

'"What do you want?" screeched one of the Serbs, mistaking this for some extreme interrogation technique.

'"I want to see how lucky you are," said Roberto as Real John helped him bundle the prisoner out of the helicopter. I was having doubts about Roberto and Real John. It was war, and the Serbs had done disgusting things. But . . . I couldn't have done anything, but I could have said something, but I didn't.

'Roberto was pleased with the results. The five losers were squashed, but the rich bastard landed in a swimming pool. He broke both legs but he was rescued by two topless teenage girls. "There has to be a Nobel Prize in this," Roberto kept saying.

'Black One and Two were furious, however. One of the losers had trashed the car of the man who supplied us with fresh rolls. Roberto had an ugly exchange with them in four languages.'

'So food wasn't that bad?' I asked.

'Yes, it was. It was spaghetti and caviar most of the time. This Serbian lorry full of caviar had been seized for the war effort. At first, latecomers like me and Real John weren't allowed any, but then everyone got so sick of it they insisted on sharing it. Even now the word caviar makes me queasy.

'Then we had our first casualties. There was a Portuguese guy who claimed to a body-piercer. As a sort of regimental marking, several of us had a nipple pierced. Two days later four of them went down with blood-poisoning. It looked as if someone had sown a purple hi-fi under their skin. We said goodbye as they were taken away to Zagreb, but we could have been Japanese princesses for all they knew.

'We were now "holding our position", the military term for doing nothing. We'd set up roadblocks; we'd constructed these makeshift barriers of concrete and iron piping, which the locals would make us take down. The villagers looked on us as a nuisance who damaged their tomatoes and it was no use stressing that we were there to protect them. The problem was that it was so peaceful.

'We also spent a lot of time trying to fix Guillermo's watch. Guillermo had come from Madrid, but the strap on his watch had snapped at Zagreb airport. Time-keeping's always important in a war, so Guillermo immediately bought a new watch-strap at the airport.

'Furious controversy raged in the village about this watch-strap. Some said Guillermo had been done by the sales-woman and sold the wrong strap. The other camp maintained that the strap was okay, but you needed a special tool to fix it on. The watch-strap had to be fixed on by a pin with retracting heads, and although the pin looked roughly the right size, no one could get it to catch on the watch. Guillermo, because we didn't have much else to do, would spend hours forlornly fiddling with the watch-strap. It was unbearable, because it looked so easy. Everyone would snap and take the watch from Guillermo, but would then be reduced to a black fury because they couldn't fit it in either. No one likes to be beaten by a watch-strap.

'The other great pastime was finding out about Roberto.

Everyone I asked had a different story. There was talk of service in the Israeli, Spanish, Hungarian and Uruguayan armies. He had worked for the Russians. He had worked for the Americans. Roberto was only in his mid-twenties, so only a fraction of it could be true. He certainly worked for Spanish newspapers. Using one alias, he regularly filed glowing stories about himself under another alias. There's really nothing like interviewing yourself. He also did restaurant reviews of Berlin restaurants by using an old guidebook and getting the restaurants to send him their menus. You'd walk into his office and he'd ask you, "What do you think about the *dicke Bohnen mit Rauchfleisch?*"

'Roberto looked like a tubby bed-wetter. But he had authority. Marcel, the German who lived in a tent, would show off the tricks he had taught his dog. Roberto was passing by during one of these demonstrations and says, "Why are you talking to that dog in German? All dogs speak Hungarian." And he growls a few things. The dog rolls over, begs, walks backwards. Marcel was livid since he had been going on about how the dog was a one-fuhrer dog and would only listen to him. I feared for that dog's welfare.

'Just as I was getting bored we got the news the Serbs were on the move. Eight of us were sent out on a long-range patrol. U was in charge. As we walked out, I realised I was windy. This was what I had come for and now I'd got it I didn't want it. It's one thing to get killed fighting in the luck of the draw, it's another to get killed because the unit's led by someone who can't tell his elbow from his arse. That's what I told myself, but I was scared. It wasn't finally about whether U was any good, it was about me.

'We walked for a couple of hours, and relaxed a bit. Staying alive is always reassuring. Then we passed through a village that had been cleansed. All the time I couldn't help thinking, was I in the safest position? You can discuss that one endlessly. If you're crossing a street where you think there's a sniper at work, do you want to be first? No. Sniper might be ready. Do you want to be second? No. If sniper wasn't ready, he'll have woken up. Do you want to be third? No. Sniper's definitely ready by now. Do you want to be fourth? No. Maybe sniper wants to split the unit. Do you want to be fifth? No. Sniper's really had time to fix the cross-hairs. Basically, you don't want to be there. The fear was so severe it hurt.

'I won't tell you about what we saw in the village. You don't want to know. We carry on into some woodland when, suddenly, it kicks off. Everyone's firing maniacally. I can't see anything apart from bits of branches flying around. I hit the ground so hard I get soil in my mouth. I pull my trigger. The gun jams. I clear the chamber. The gun jams again. I'm trying to clear the chamber again when I notice that everyone else is running like fuck.

'There's a style to running away from a battle. You want to run fast, so that you get away from it, so you don't get hit or taken prisoner; on the other hand you don't want to run so fast you overtake everyone else and leave them gagging on your dust.

'Our retreat took us to the top of a hill. Although I was the last to start running, I wasn't the last to stop. We regrouped because the others couldn't run any more.

'Frankie, a Yank, was missing. No one had seen him. No one had any idea why we had started shooting. No one admitted to shooting first. Had anyone seen the enemy? No.

'"What are we going to do about Frankie?" asked U in a very unleaderful way. He was waiting to see if anyone would suggest going back. No one did. We'd probably just had a nasty tangle with some undergrowth, but you never knew. We'd also burned up most of our ammunition, and if anyone was out there, they would know about us. Secondly, we'd bottled it, and running, once you start, is habit-forming. Courage is largely not running away.

'We agreed to go back and tell everyone Frankie had disappeared, because it looked so soft leaving him behind.

Just in case Frankie was alive, we'd hole up for a few hours before returning so we could pretend we had gone back to look. While we waited in the burned-out village I had the best drink of my life. It was plasticky water from my canteen, but I was alive and thirsty and I've never enjoyed a drink so much in my life.

'I was considering getting out. I'd ascertained I wasn't Scargill. Scargill would have sorted all that out in five minutes. Simple as that. I wondered how I could get out. The whole country was at war now, and getting out was probably as dangerous as staying put. I liked hiding in a burned-out house where I wasn't an open target, but I also ascertained beyond any doubt what I really wanted was to hide in a house in a country where there wasn't a war, and where there were several countries between me and a war, where I could go down the pub without anyone shooting at me. England for instance. I was in a world made of shit and I wanted out.

'When we got back without Frankie we were expecting Roberto to go ballistic. He was very calm.

'"What happened?" he asked U.

'"We were ambushed. We had to shoot our way out."

'"How many Serbs?"

'"I couldn't say."

'"Army? Chetniks?"

'"I couldn't say."

'"Where was Frankie hit?"

'"I couldn't say."

'"You don't seem to have seen much?"

'"I'm just being honest."

'"No, you're not. You're a failure at disguising your failure."

'The news we got was bad. The Croats were losing. Even Black One and Two who had spent most of their time guffawing and playing cards were crouched in a corner of the building with the thickest walls wearing helmets, clutching their weapons and hanging on to a box of oranges they showed no signs of sharing with anyone else. I got hold of a map and started memorising the route to the border. Our only consolation was that perhaps we were so insignificant no one could be bothered to come and kill us.

'That afternoon, a four-wheel drive pulls into the village square. This Italian gets out. I'm amazed he wasn't shot because there must have been thirty rifles trained on him by thirty brickers. "Hello. Buon giorno. Guten Tag,' he says with a big smile. He had this annoying habit of saying everything in three languages.

'He was a fucking salesman. He wanted to sell us body armour. We received him warmly because he said he'd come from Osijek which meant that the road was clear and we weren't completely cut off.

'Then it got worse. We were queuing up for our caviar, and I was about to reach for my bottle of ketchup. I asked Scargill once what was the most essential bit of advice for a soldier, the secret he'd like to pass on to a novice. "Ketchup," he said. I thought this was a mnemonic like Keep Every Thing Clean and Handy Upon your Person, but no he meant tomato ketchup. "Always carry some sachets of ketchup. With ketchup you can eat anything. Locusts, rats, overcooked veg. Anything." I'm reaching for my bottle of ketchup when the big Finn I'm next to slumps over. I think he's having a fit but then I see blood pouring out of a big hole in his back. We're in a war, and eventually I put two and two together. I want to shout sniper in a soldierly way, but it sounds like a six-year-old girl. Roberto takes charge, telling no one to shoot or move until they have located the sniper. He was a natural leader of a certain type, the homicidal thug.

'Eventually he leads everyone out in a sweep. I stayed with the Finn. Our medical supplies comprised some bandages and aspirin. The textbook says you talk to the wounded and reassure them, which was hard to do since the Finn was on the way out. Even if he'd been shot in the best hospital in the world he'd have been finished.'

'That must have been awful,' I sympathise.

'No. I didn't like him much. "Don't worry," I said. "You'll be all right."

'"I'm dying, idiot," says the Finn.

'"No, no, you'll be fine."

'"You are a bore," he says. "Go away."

'The others come back and Roberto looks in my direction and says, "You're a spy, aren't you?" I actually turned round to see who he was talking to, but there was no one behind me. Then I thought, this is warrior humour. But everyone was looking at me in an unamused way.'

'Why did he think you were a spy?' I ask. Audley gulps. He obviously doesn't enjoy talking about this.

'No reason at all. It was my turn to be the spy, that's all. I looked at this bunch who were right behind Roberto, and I understood why I hadn't formed any close friendships with the lads. Because they were a bunch of shits.

'"Why don't we have a look at that body armour?" says Roberto. I hoped for a moment that he'd dropped the accusation of spying. How wrong I was. They fitted one of the jackets on me and tied me to the school gate.

'"Who do you work for?" Roberto asked. My heart was pounding so much I could see it under the jacket. I'd have said anything or done anything to get out. I pleaded and grovelled.

'"Why do you think so badly of me? I wouldn't betray you."

'"I don't think badly of you," was Roberto's reply. "Loyalty's easy. Loyalty's for the lazy. Betrayal is an effort."

'I even thought about confessing, but I was too terrified to do it convincingly. Roberto took aim and shot me. At least he was a good shot; he hit the jacket rather than me. I haven't been kicked by a horse, but I guess it's like that. The salesman had a range of jackets, the cheap one, the mid-price one and the expensive one. He was concerned about the test drive, not on my account, but because of the wear on the jackets. By the time they fitted the expensive jacket on me, I was done, though I just managed to register what happened next.

'The Italian was negotiating with Roberto, language-hopping. He still seemed to think he could sell some jackets.

'"Why don't you speak Hungarian?" Roberto asked.

'"Very difficult. *Muy difficile*."

'"That dog speaks Hungarian," said Roberto, getting the dog to perform.

'"*Ongrois pas utile*. Not useful."'

'"Not true. Hungarian's very useful. I don't shoot people who speak Hungarian," says Roberto emptying a magazine into the Italian. Croatia wasn't the place for cold-calling.

'I thought that was it. But they dragged me off and locked me in a storage room in the school. I was in so much pain, I almost wanted to die. It occurred to me that if there were a spy in the camp he'd only have to make one report. "Leave them alone and they'll have killed each other in a month."

'Roberto came to see me the next day. "There are only two qualities that matter. Courage and humour. You don't have much courage, but perhaps you have humour." He was peering at me like I was a lab rat.

'This was all my fault. I had chosen to come here. What terrified me most at this stage was being put in a body bag. I was sure I would die, and I didn't mind what happened to my body, as long as it wasn't zipped up in plastic, like rubbish.

'"Most people aren't people," he said. "They believe they have character. They don't. You don't have to torture someone to break them. No sleep for forty-eight hours and you can bend them like elastic. Armies are all obsessed with fitness. Run so many miles with a rucksack. Anyone can be trained to do fifty sit-ups, a hundred sit-ups, two hundred sit-ups. Anyone. That doesn't matter. The interesting question is what do you have left, when you have nothing left."

"'Why are you doing this to me, Roberto?"

"'Because I like you.' Then he left.

'Locks are supposed to be easy to pick. There was a back door to the storeroom which opened out on to the yard. If I could pick the lock and sneak out at night, there was a good chance I wouldn't be caught. They hadn't searched me thoroughly, I had a secret belt with survival items in it. The survival items were, however, fuck-all use, in my survival. The fish-hooks, needles and matches were useless on the lock.

'I wondered if I could just kick the door down. It was a very old but sturdy door. If I hadn't been so weak and with broken ribs, I might have managed it. But even if I could have, the noise would have given me away.

'A lot of furniture was stacked in the room. One old desk had, I noticed, a very thin, hard-to-notice drawer in it. So I pulled out the drawer, and found a set of keys in it. No, I thought, that would be too ridiculous, locking me in a room with a set of keys. When night came, I slid the first key into the lock and it turned effortlessly in a well-oiled fashion. I peeked out cautiously into the night.

'The storeroom was at the back of the school. I could faintly hear some conversation from the front. Twenty yards away was a fence, and after that open fields. I could walk to the border in a couple of days if I was lucky. Our sentry positions were a long way off and the only night-sight was in Roberto's office, so as long as I moved quietly, it was extremely unlikely that I would be spotted.'

'So you escaped?'

'No. I stared out the open door. I continued staring for a long time. My future as a prisoner wasn't too bright. I was very lucky to be alive, and my situation was fairly hopeless. They would probably shoot me. But if I were caught going over the wall, however unlikely that might be, then I

176

definitely would look guilty and I definitely would get shot. I spent most of the night staring out the door. Courage is finite. I'd used up my bottle. I closed the door and locked it.

'Instead I concentrated on thinking about Scargill and his mates arriving to rescue me. No one knew where I was and even if they did, they wouldn't have been allowed to help me, but that it was impossible didn't matter. I felt if I wanted it badly enough, somehow it would happen, and thinking about it made me feel better.

'Roberto came in the next day. He took the keys out of the drawer and told me not to judge myself too harshly.

'"This war is a disappointment to everyone," he said. "You used to become a soldier for adventure, for travel, for loot. Now you'd be better off as an accountant. You travel the world first-class. You get all sorts of benefits. You can fiddle your own tax. You rarely get shot at. Better still, be an economist. Accountants have to get the sums right. While we are suffering, back in Zagreb, the . . . the . . . what's a good word in English for a complete freeloader, a disgusting, impotent, stinking, parasitic amphibian? All right, let's call them economists, back in Zagreb, economists who know nothing about this country, don't speak the language, who've probably read ten newspaper articles about Croatia, they're stealing everything."

'"You don't like economists, do you?"

'"No one likes economists, not even other economists. It's a very human failing, we all think we can live others' lives better. You imagine you could be a better Roberto and I think I could be a better Audley. It's Guillermo's watch; we all think we can put the pin in, until we try. We all have to help each other."

'"Can I go home, Roberto?"

'"That's a very profound question," he said and left.

'Then these two dummies walk in. "We are from Norway. We are journalists. We are told you will be shot tomorrow as a spy. How do you feel about that?"

'They asked some more genius questions while they ate salami sandwiches. I wasn't hungry, but I decided I should keep my strength up. Real John let the journalists out, and when I asked if I could have a sandwich, he said the salami sandwiches had been my last meal. I overheard the Norwegians asking exactly when I would be shot.'

'What happened?'

'I wasn't shot.'

'Did you escape?'

'I'd rather not tell you.'

'You can't stop there. About to face a firing squad of crazed mercenaries?'

'I've said enough.'

'Was it the Serbs overrunning the village?'

'No. Though that was another one of my favourite fantasies. The Serbs arriving and making Roberto and his gang eat their own genitals before shooting them. The drawback to this fantasy was when it came to the part where the Serbs found me. I'd say: "I'm spying for you." And they'd say: "No. You're not."'

'Roberto said it was a joke?'

'It's embarrassing.'

'I don't see how it could be any worse.'

'That's another thing. Never think to yourself things can't get any worse. I'll tell you how it ended. The next morning my mother walks in. Great, not only will I be shot but my mother's going to get killed as well.'

'What happened?'

'I was wrong as usual. Roberto and the others couldn't have been nicer to my mother. Marcel kept on making her cups of tea. Suddenly, the whole spying-shooting business vanished. And then we got into a taxi and drove back to Zagreb. They almost waved goodbye.'

'How did she find you?'

'As I was getting into the taxi in Zagreb with Real John, one of our neighbours who was in Zagreb on business saw me, and shouted at me, but I didn't hear. When he got back he told my mother how surprised he was to see me in Zagreb. There was stuff in the papers about the foreign volunteers, so she came out to look for me.'

'And she tracked you down in the middle of a war?'

'It wasn't as hard as it sounds. This is what it was like in Yugo. You'd go out in the morning and kill your neighbour because you didn't like him, because you felt it was your duty or because you were afraid he would do you first. Then in the afternoon, you'd put out the best tablecloth and offer the visitor from England your finest homemade jam because you'd want your country and your hospitality to be well thought of.'

'Why did Roberto let you go?'

'I don't know. Because he found it amusing. I've never forgiven myself for going out there. That's the tic. That's why I'm always kicking myself up the arse. The whole thing was utter madness, with a bag of chips. But however you judge Roberto's legion of chancers, undesirables and delusionists we were the only protection that village had.'

We've been on for five hours. Everything is working properly. The sound is an especial success. I can hear the ground crunching moistly under Audley's feet. Let's hope the system works as well in Chuuk.

CHUUK

AUDLEY TAKES the train down to London, and we have a final test. Once he's in Chuuk I doubt there will be much available in terms of technical back-up. Audley takes his seat, when a tall woman boards and fiddles with her luggage. She exclaims loudly and dashes about. Her handbag is missing. She has one of those roller luggage racks and the handbag had been secured on that. She has lost her ticket, her money, her sandwiches, all the key items. She wails to Audley and the nearby passengers. The conductor is summoned and she wails some more. Audley says 'oh dear' once. She has even lost her reading material and it's a long trip.

Audley reaches into the seat-pocket and pulls out a book on Micronesia. 'Here,' he says. The train pulls out. Ten minutes later she hands the book back to Audley. 'Do you have anything better?' Someone buys her a sandwich.

Audley has one advantage over me; he has a starting point. To travel you have to have somewhere to start from. Sunk Island might be dispiriting and bare, but it has one great strength: it has fixity. The farms and cottages have been there for generations and have the intention of remaining.

The name of the place where I grew up still exists; but the place itself is gone. Most of the streets persist, but the place has been razed. It was chipped away, day by day, disassembled, piece by piece. Men did this over twenty years. Most suburbs are like this, presumably, rebuilt out of recognition. Last time I went back, I had no idea where to find anything. Ironically, in many ways it was the same: the same services, but everything jumbled up and redesigned. Everything five or ten doors out of place. Someone threw my youth away. Even if the place had been carefully preserved I wouldn't have wanted to go back very often, but it's disheartening to witness how disposable your past is.

Elderly relatives lamenting change had always bored me, but at under half their age I find myself there. It's the small things that are often the most missed: the stairs you fell down, the alleyway where you had a kiss, the bench where you sat with your friends. You want something to hang on to, even if it's a dump.

Apart from the big attractions, London has become fluid: a big soup where the meat and veg might stay the same, but everything floats around. Companies move, employees move, everything moves, except the traffic. Responsibility of any sort seems antique. I have become the most stable thing I know. All you can do is watch.

Walter was usually late. That was bad enough, but he had a habit of saying as we arrived, casting a nod at me: 'Sorry, we're late. You can guess whose fault it was.' It got to the point where I'd go on my own to avoid the accusation of tardiness. One night at a dinner party I was cringing with embarrassment because Walter was over an hour late, when he showed up. He explained that the police had kept him away because a house was burning down across the street.

We all went out to have a look. The fire was too far away to endanger our host, no one was in the house and there was nothing we could do anyway, so we stood there drinking our champagne as the firefighters tackled the blaze. I had never seen anything on that scale – a burning house is a fearsome fire: the flames raced out of the windows almost making a cackling sound. Sometimes all you can do is watch, although I felt our host was enjoying the spectacle a little too much.

The second letter from Walter arrived three days later. Like the first it was postmarked London, sent the day before, so it couldn't simply be a question of the letter being delivered eight years too late, a not so infrequent occurrence.

Dear Oceane,
  Surprised, eh?
  By the time you read this I will indeed be . . . I don't even want to write the word, that's nonsense isn't it?
  You'll be annoyed with me, won't you? Allegedly, annoyance is good for the heart. It's important to be tested every now and then.
  I'm working in the dark so forgive me if I trip every now and then.
  There'll be more.
  Walter

I had been annoyed when I read the first letter. Was it a hoax? Joke? Mistake? I had been many things. Perplexed. Upset. Angry. Mostly moved.

Maybe it's my fault, perhaps it reflects more on me, but there haven't been many bodies of emotional weight in my life.

You're not immediately aware of it. At the time, you can't

spot the hollowness. Unhappily, as you get older, you can. When I think back on the men who pumped into me in my younger years, it seemed that we had broken the record for enjoyment, that global importance was taking place. In a way, it was: twin enjoyment in this universe is a result.

But almost any man with good skin, a rigorous tooth-brushing policy and a car could have gone to bed with me in my teenage years; the affection simply spills out of you on to the nearest object. You eventually perceive that most packets are empty. Fulfillers are few.

Nevertheless, more and more climactics reveals itself as the only worthwhile activity. Friends may desert you, money can be stolen, houses can crumble, but pleasure endures as long as you have memory. In and out is the only quality pastime. Time you can unreservedly designate as well spent. Things before, things after, you regret, but I can honestly say that the act, even if not up to the billing, is usually satisfying. It's a pity you can't spend the whole time doing it, no matter how athletic you are; that's when the disappointment and arguments start. The pleasure's never a problem, it's the emotions and the logistics. Yet even if you could lock yourself on a loop of pleasure, you shouldn't. You shouldn't be a slave to anything, even if the world is one large machine constructed to tribulate you.

That's the gamble of keeping in touch; it's disappointing when someone who used to relish slobbering on your thigh won't make the effort of walking across a room to say hello to you; but, alternatively, sometimes it's disappointing when they do.

Yet nothing is more pleasing than to see someone whom you are pleased to see and who is pleased to see you; nothing more touching than someone whom you want to keep in touch with keeping in touch with you.

But Walter did annoy me. But then he always did. You'd come home and find Walter lying on the ground, unconscious. You'd pick up the phone to call an ambulance, and then you would hear Walter's sniggering. Of course, the five-year-old embedded in men is a well-known phenomenon. And it isn't necessarily a bad thing. It's tricky. While you certainly don't want a man who behaves like a five-year-old all the time, especially in the whining and wanting-to-be looked after, the playfulness can be fun. And in a way, it's a compliment. Because the five-year-old, in worthwhile individuals anyway, is always locked away in the last room, and it's nice to know the guards have left.

Walter was also the most entertaining of my boyfriends. For several reasons. Firstly, he let me kick him. If he committed some infringement of proper washing-up technique, went to do the shopping and forgot items, bought the wrong items or substandard fruit in a predictably male way ('Did you look at this before you bought it?'), he'd bend over and say, 'Two kicks.' And if I didn't get a good swing in on his rear, he'd say, 'You can have one more.' It was fantastically satisfying.

He also understood the creation of language. When I rang his doorbell, he'd open the door fractionally, look me up and down, and say, 'No. Not interested.' And close the door. Four beats. Then reopen it and let me in. Every time. Week after week. It hadn't been that funny the first time, but it hadn't been meant to. It wasn't a running gag, it was our greeting.

And the real sustenance of any couple is how you are when you're alone together. Walter's amusement value was best illustrated by a game we used to play. For money, at first. On long trips or long waits Walter would bet me I couldn't keep a straight face looking at him for thirty seconds. To my shock I found I couldn't keep a straight face for more than one or two seconds. Walter didn't even have to get to pulling faces or doing anything stupid. He'd just have to look at me, and I'd burst out laughing. I lost a lot of money at first, because I couldn't believe if I blanked my

mind (and dwelt on illness, death, cold cabbage, or enumerated the flowers in my mother's garden, Aaron's rod, baby's
breath, hostas, etc.) that I couldn't last thirty seconds.
Walter's secret was that he never tried to make me laugh,
there was something in his facial muscles that was threatening
to be mischievous, or knowing, a confidence that he could
make me laugh, that made me laugh; and finally it was so
ridiculous that I couldn't keep a straight face that I had to
crack up.

I had been sitting in Soho with my friend Amber, playing
Address Book. The game consists of drinking at a café and
the winner is the one who has an acquaintance come up and
say hello. The loser or losers pay for the drinks. Strenuous
elaboration of and agreement on the rules beforehand is
advisable. We had been there all afternoon, when Walter
walked up, and said, 'Oceane, I've been looking for you.'
Amber refused to believe it wasn't a set-up, and her tongue
was hanging out when she saw Walter. I didn't recognise
him at first, because he had his clothes on, because it wasn't
Barcelona, because I had been drinking absinthe, and because
I wasn't expecting him. It was a few months after I'd got
back from Barcelona and I'd been regretting that I hadn't
been able to say goodbye to Walter.

He had arrived in London that morning. 'No one had
your address in Barcelona,' he said, 'but I wanted to come
anyway.' He had headed for the centre of London, and
spotted me at the café with Amber. What are the odds on
that one? That's a once-in-a-lifetime turn-up, but then
maybe it only needs to be once.

I felt at home with Walter. Perhaps that's the quality that
counts most, being relaxed. That you can be yourself, slob

down, fault freely, and that's fine. 'Why did you come for me?' I asked.

'Because I wanted to.'

'But why?'

'I was thinking about you.'

'You hardly knew me.'

'I knew enough.'

'Don't you miss Heidi?'

'Once you've had her five hundred times the thrill wears off. Wasn't I right to come looking for you?'

He was. I had been charmed by his reckless optimism, but he kept on impressing. Most affairs start high, then flutter down. With Walter, the more I saw, the more I liked.

Walter's letters always made a big impact on me. He had beautiful handwriting, something you hardly ever see in a man. He really drew rather than wrote.

His kiss-off letter to me had been very upsetting. Firstly, because it had been so unexpected. Usually you experience some juddering before the break-up. Everything had been fine until I opened his letter. The problem with individuals who make a big impact in your life is they usually make both good and bad impacts.

I had been furious that he had written: 'This is about me, not you.' Talk about cliché. I couldn't believe it might, in fact, be true. I judged his letter and departure as the worst sort of cowardice. In truth his actions, whatever they were, were not cowardice at all. I had noticed that he was losing weight, but he was a confirmed gym-goer, so I assumed he was going at it.

Five months after he corresponded his way out of my life, I got the notification of his death. There was another letter. There was one line that always stuck with me:

You will want to scream and weep: when you do, I wish I could be there.

His decision had an element of selfishness in it perhaps, but it's the bravest action I've ever come across. To choose to go from the light into the dark all alone, to go solo at the time when nearly everyone would want a hand to hold. Truthfully, there was a part of me that was relieved I hadn't had to go through the ordeal of sitting by the hospital bed. Real men are hard to find. Walter was the only man I could describe as a real man. It may be a stupid term, but I can't think of anything better. There are so many squirts and idiots who get attention and praise for nothing. But I've seen courage. Going into the dark, alone, unarmed, uncomplaining, fully aware you will lose is surely the highest warrior valour. It's rare but it does exist. When he left I didn't chase after him, but that was pride rather than strength. Sometimes I wish I had. You never know.

I mourned a lot. Mourning is pointless, but that's precisely its point.

Walter was the only one I thought about having children with. I still think about it, but even if the situation were right, I'd hesitate. Not just because of the terrible things that can happen out there, but because of the problem of education. What would you teach your kids? Be decent, honest, hard-working? All that's patently a waste of time. It would be dishonest and cruel to raise them in the expectation that behaviour like that would earn them affection or success. It would just make them into doormats.

And now more letters. I had no idea where the posthumous letters were coming from. Presumably someone had been entrusted with them. I doubted if it were one of Walter's friends: they were too flaky. Unless Walter had intended them to be sent years earlier, say five years earlier, then it might be one of his friends. No, it had to be a lawyer or a bank, some institution, primed to fire them off.

The third letter arrived.

Dear Oceane,

I have so much to tell you.

It starts with my brother. He went on a diving holiday and didn't come back. Sorting out the repatriation of your brother's body is about as miserable as it gets. I won't go on about it. It was while I was in Chuuk that I heard about the accidents that followed Richard around. A lot of my brother's stuff, money especially, had gone missing. Well, it's not the nature of money to hang around, but I was suspicious.

That's why I was in Barcelona. I had tracked Richard down. I wasn't convinced about the accidents. We all think we can play private detective, don't we? I wanted to catch Richard at it and then decide whether to give him a taste of his own medicine or shop him. That's what winds us up the most, isn't it, how powerless we are?

In case you were in any doubt, Richard certainly didn't have anything to do with the drownings. In the first case he was at the dentist's, and the second time he was buying a nasal irrigation kit at the market. I can guarantee this because I spent bloody hours trailing him. I didn't believe he was innocent the first time, but I had to concede that he couldn't commit two impossible murders. It looked as if he was just the world's greatest harvester of banana skins.

It was only then something else occurred to me. I used to stay up late to monitor movements, to do the old sleuthworks. This is why my conversational skills were not always what they should have been. One night something did happen. Your room was only a couple down from Richard's. I heard someone padding around softly. I saw a figure tiptoeing into your room. I was positive it was Richard up to no good, otherwise I might have waited to see what happened. I stepped out to challenge. But it wasn't Richard. It was someone else. And here's what's strange. He knew he'd been caught.

'Visiting Oceane?' I asked.

'No,' he said shutting the door. He was lying, and it was one of these situations where I knew he was lying and he knew I knew, and didn't mind at all but there was no way I could prove

it. His being in the hallway at that time of the morning was odd, but not much odder than me being there. Finally he could always say he was trying to get his leg over.

'I thought I heard the fire alarm,' he said. 'Did you hear it?'

'No. There was no fire alarm.'

'Perhaps someone tested it by accident.'

'No. There was no fire alarm.'

'Everything gets tested once in a while.'

'No fire alarm.'

'Maybe it was in my dreams.'

I realised I was dealing with pure evil. It was like going to the zoo and seeing the name displayed on a plaque, and then the creature pops up from some undergrowth at the back of the enclosure and you think, so that's what it looks like. I didn't know what to do. Being pure evil isn't, as far as I'm aware, a criminal offence anywhere, and somehow I doubted my word would count for much. Have you studied pure evil? Where are your qualifications? And you are by profession a mounter of blondes? You expect us to take your word for this? I had a word with Jorge but he didn't see it my way.

I know what I saw. I have the feeling I saved your life. I never told you this in case you thought I was loopy or was trying to make you grateful enough to do all the washing-up for a year. I could be wrong, but I know what I saw. I punched him in the stomach and told him to leave you alone. It's an achievement of sorts, I reckon, to have punched pure evil in the gut.

Maybe you know all this. Maybe now he's got the record for world's greatest serial killer. Perhaps you give interviews, 'I knew him in Barcelona.' I went to look for him in the time . . . But I didn't get anywhere. Should I have done more? I had nothing to go on.

I kept quiet about this, because it's a burden. A fright. I'm guessing after all this time, you'll be able to make a level-headed decision. There's one more letter that has all the information. Go to Chuuk, that's in Micronesia, by the way, not some backwater of Louisiana, and ask for Bruno. Bruno has the letter.

If you don't want to go, that's sensible. Whatever you decide,
I hope you are in several thick layers of happiness.
Love
Walter
PS Watch out for the comfortable coffins.

Who had he found? It must have been Rutger, in an earlier attempt or (who knows?) a later attempt to fit into me. Pure evil? Pure imbecility more like.

Walter was always very active. He was one of those people who leap out of bed wide-awake, who seemed to worry that they might be missing something if they're asleep at seven in the morning. He'd glare at me accusingly as I lolled in bed. 'You'd be quite happy to stay there all the time,' he said. I considered his remark and concluded that this wasn't entirely true, you can't have a dance career in a bed, but if you could it would have suited me fine.

One evening, after I got back from a performance, Walter had changed the sheets (he was cunning at thoughtful gestures like that) and greeted me with the in-house euphoriant. I was lying in bed, in fresh sheets, corely contented, and Walter said, 'You couldn't be more comfortable, could you?'

I realised I couldn't. I was laid out in a very comfortable bed, the mattress giving the optimum level of yielding, buoyed by the scent of fresh linen, the temperature was perfect, the light was perfect. There was simply no way I could have been more comfortable. Serenity and pleasure hand-in-hand. No team of comfort experts, no dispensing of money could have boosted the restfulness; no demented despot with years of bed experimentation could have topped this ease. 'You know what's tragic,' said Walter. 'Within two minutes you'll move.'

I might dispute whether it was two minutes or not, but I soon had to shift round. Comfort seems to be something that's always rolling away, like a ball on a slight incline. You have to move to catch up with it, to reposition with movementlets, though, of course, comfort can also, as in my case, prevent you from real movement.

So I had to go after the last letter. Well, I didn't have to, but I wanted to go. Or rather Audley could go for me.

I had to look up Chuuk; I'd never heard of it.

One of the reasons I'd never heard of it was that it's on the other side of the world, and comprises little more than a few sandbars in the Pacific. Walter's face appeared to me scoffing incredulously at my failure to go anywhere in Barcelona: 'you didn't go . . .' 'you didn't see . . .' Why ever he chose Chuuk as the cache for his last communication, one of the reasons was to make me travel.

The entire population of Chuuk could easily fit into a stadium. I studied the map of the main island, Weno, which has one road. With a single glance I know it like the back of my hand. Maybe it's so small that you wouldn't feel awkward going into a bar and asking, 'Anyone know Bruno?'

What is the population of the world? A lot less than Chuuk. There can never be more than a thousand or so, because, practically, there can't really be room for much more than that in your cranial census. Even if your address book is full, how many names does that come to? Two hundred, three hundred? Even if you're a toadying networker, how many? Two thousand, three thousand? But how many do you really get to work on? Four hundred, five hundred? Even if you have a large family, what does that come to? A hundred? Two hundred?

Richard once told me that one of the initial oddities about diving was that while you were on the surface, you could see for miles, but once you submerged, depending on the light and water, you could only see for five, ten, twenty yards, or if it was in English waters, six inches. The ocean comes in small pools; you move from one to the other. The world's like that: you rarely see more than a few hundred people at a time. I doubt if you can have any deep knowledge or emotional intersection with more than a thousand others in a lifetime. The rest are ticket inspectors, passers-by, spear-carriers. Repetitive scenery.

I danced because I loved it, but also because I wanted to be successful at it. Success would ultimately have meant a few dozen figures in dance high command rating me. A few dozen journos loving me. A few dozen of my peers recognising my recognition. A few dozen of my friends and family being proud of me. A few dozen of my enemies piqued by my progress.

Money's great. And it must be exhilarating to go to a country you've never been to before, to a town you've never been to before and have a crowd baying for you. But all in all, I don't believe it can be that significant that a fertiliser salesman in Gabon knows who you are (unless you went to school with the fertiliser salesman or you want to go to bed with him). It all rests on the admiration of a small group.

I feel I've met enough people. It's one of the signs of ageing, like your first crow's foot. It's true of all of us to some extent. Even the superrich and the superfamous, who have stadiums full of admirers to munch on them, have their steady companions. The emotional world will always be a village.

The cake. That's one of the biggest problems. You start off, or at least I did, with the sentiment that the cake is infinite. I wasn't jealous of other talented dancers because I believed there would be enough cake to go round. Good for them. Is all decency predicated on the belief that you will be all right?

If you had it demonstrated to you at the age of five that no one would ever help you and that you would fail in everything that matters to you, would you have the inclination or resolve to help others? As the evidence mounts, that the cake is very small, and that thousands of us are chasing a sliver of happiness, it takes extraordinary strength to retain kindness. Before my hamstring hamstrung my career, a dancer I knew was killed in a car crash. If you had said to me, 'Do you want her to die?' I would have been horrified by such a suggestion. But I'm ashamed to say, somewhere in the recesses, deep down, I had a pulse of satisfaction because there was a little less competition.

When I got back from Barcelona, I had a moment of enormous pleasure. One of the doormen at the Babylon, Curro, who was a keen footballer, had asked me to see if I could find some English team who would want to set up an exchange. I said I'd try. I knew nothing about football, I didn't have a clue about how to even start a project like that. I hadn't been especially friendly with Curro either, we were on little more than hello terms. One morning I considered what to do; I envisaged innumerable phone calls, days of my life wasted in something I had no interest in, for someone I hardly knew. Then it came to me: I wouldn't do it. Perhaps it's obvious, but all my life if I've been asked for help or a favour I've done my best. It's the only time in my life I've let anyone down and it was a real joy.

It's a little depressing to think that helping others doesn't help you one bit. You can spend a lifetime doing favours, but you won't get so much as a glass of water or a five-minute remission on a headcold for it. Maybe it should be like that, but there's no question that the selfish and uncaring have the easiest lives; not necessarily the happiest or most successful, though that often is the case, but certainly the easiest. Sometimes I feel that decency is an elaborate con trick that has been played on me. Or, finally, it's simply a question of style, on the same level as whether you paint your walls magnolia or gamboge.

I look at my watch. Audley should be arriving in Chuuk about now. I'll be with him shortly.

It's a long way to Micronesia. Even if I didn't mind leaving home, I'd hesitate travelling that far. Friends of mine who fly a lot say that after eleven hours or so you hit the wall and accept your fate and even start to enjoy it to the point where you don't want to get off the plane.

Sending Audley to Chuuk instead of going myself is in one way absurd. It would be easier just to walk out the door and do it myself, but I'm not going to do that. The trick is to solve the problem, and if the solution is a little cumbersome, well, I'm sure I'm not the only person who has gone to unusual lengths to solve a simple matter.

You can hate what you become and you can fight what you become, but you can still become it, even if you struggle against it with all the will in the world. Without some luck, we are nothing. I thought about getting help but, put simply, the problem is that I don't think the world is worth it. Outside is just disappointing. No doctor can change that. No argument will alter that. It's like throwing blades of grass against a wall.

Once you've been backstage at a theatre, the theatre is never the same for you. Once you've noticed the crack in the vase, the vase is never the same. Once you've seen a friend do something appalling, the friendship is never the same. That doesn't mean you won't go to the theatre, or keep the vase or the friend. You can choose.

Audley visibles.

'How was your flight?' I ask.

'Dull. Can you believe this? This isn't an airport, it's a

garden shed.' I see what he means. The airport at Chuuk is just a large hangar.

'Thanks for checking in. Everything's working isn't it? Why don't you go to a hotel and have a rest? We can start work later.'

'How do I get to a hotel? There aren't any taxis. This place is so laid-back they don't even rip you off.' It's true even the hangers-on and those waiting for friends or relatives are wearied by the effort of hanging around.

'I'll have a walk and see if I can find something. This is a bugger of a distance to come for a letter.'

'I know. I'm grateful.'

'I understand. Curiosity. That can be very powerful. Very tormenting. Did I ever mention my mate Martin? He worked for a firm of organ-makers. He had to deliver an organ to a church in Ipswich. Ipswich, as you probably know, is a quiet – let's not pull punches – a dull place. He's outside the church, in a district which, even as Ipswich goes, is a quiet, leafy corner, helping to unload the organ, when his right buttock gets a slap, as if someone had hit him with a bat. He wheels around, sees no one standing there with a bat, and then notices he's collapsed. It's the last thing anyone would expect so it takes him a while to work out he's been shot in the arse.

'As being shot goes, it's not too bad. It was a small-calibre, low-velocity round, he hardly loses any blood and he's out of hospital in a few days. There's a scar and he gets a sporadic twinge, but otherwise, physically, no problems. What he can't get over is why was he shot in the arse?

'No one could come up with a plausible motive. He lived in Newcastle and had only agreed to take the job at the last moment because a colleague was ill, so if it had been someone specifically after him, they couldn't have known he would be there. Besides which, no one could think of any reason why anyone would even be annoyed with Martin, let alone want to shoot him; he was that type.

'No one had been shot in Ipswich for twenty years. No gun club or shooting range near the church. Armed crime almost unknown. The only explanation was either that someone had been cleaning their gun and it had misfired or that someone had had a perverse desire to shoot an organ-deliverer in the arse. Only one shot. No more attacks like that again. It drove Martin up the wall. He just wanted to know. He posted ads in the local paper asking the shooter to get in touch.'

'It must have been frustrating.'

'I have an idea, but . . .'

'What?'

'No, no. We're not getting into that one.'

Considering what he's already told me about his past, his reticence is out of character, but doubtless the story will materialise eventually.

'I've got to get sleep,' he says.

This is the great benefit of travelling from home. While Audley has to schlep around to find a hotel, I can have a bath or cook myself supper. Even ten years ago you would have had to be a government to pull off a stunt like this. Now I can sit at home watching my big monitor, while Audley feeds me Chuuk with equipment that's barely bulkier than a camera. With his earpiece, Audley appears to be inconspicuously listening to his personal stereo. The picture and sound quality aren't superb, but I can leave Chuuk any second I want to and be instantly sleeping in my own bed.

Dance

My career in dance came to an end shortly after I got back from Barcelona. I was changing channels on the television from a very comfortable armchair when I heard a tearing sound. It was my left hamstring. That was that.

I then spent a year attempting to get into dance

administration. I sent off hundreds, and I do mean hundreds, of applications. I only got one interview, for a post in Bristol. I was up before dawn to be there on time for the nine o'clock interview, paying the most expensive on-peak fare. Twenty other candidates were waiting when I arrived. We had all been sent a letter telling us to turn up at the same time. Clearly the administration needed some help. Then it was explained the person interviewing us was busy and we had to come back at two. No apology. No coffee. We all returned at two and were herded into a small room with two chairs. No apology.

The post was a non-job with a non-wage. They knew they'd get someone like me who wanted to stay in dance at all costs. After half an hour of fidgeting in this room with no sign of anyone being interviewed, I walked out. There were one or two admiring glances, one or two satisfied smirks. Looking back, I can never work out whether I was right to walk out or not. In one way, it was arrogant – *I* won't be treated like this. I walked out because I could: I wanted the job, I wanted the job a lot, but I didn't need it. Perhaps I didn't deserve the job because I wasn't willing to gobble up shit, perhaps it should have gone to someone who would have done anything to get it. Mind you, judging by what I saw of the organisation, there probably wasn't even a job going.

It was hard giving up dance. I continued to see dance for a while: if it was bad, it annoyed me. If it was good, it annoyed me. So I stopped.

Me

I'm not like other people. Or maybe I am. Am I more sensitive than most? Or is it that everyone feels the same but others get on with it? I stay in because I can. If I couldn't then, inevitably, I wouldn't.

The shopping is a giveaway though. In my days of going out, I could hardly ever find clothes that I liked. London is a big city, but I could go days without seeing one thing I liked. There were lots of things that I would make do with, but clothes that made me want to buy them on the spot were rare, and when I found them I almost felt as though they were a mistake. It was the same with food. Whenever there was a new type of rice, a new sandwich, a new biscuit, a new dip in the shops that I liked, it would disappear in weeks. I began to infer that my purchases were observed and that anything I bought regularly would be promptly discontinued. Almost all of us have the hankering to be famous, to be important, to be admired, to stand out, but the assumption is you have to be different or better to get that. No. The best thing is to be famous, to be cuddled by the public, but to be like everyone else.

I can't fault my parents. But it has to be said that being brought up loved and treated decently is poor preparation for life. We were a family, and although I didn't realise it at the time, that made us freaks.

I look out the window. There are a couple of prostitutes waiting on the corner. They're not obviously prostitutes. They are ugly, badly dressed, foully behaved and most of them have the aura of the dying. But those interested know that and that this street is where to find them. That they have clients is something that both astonishes and appals me. Men are known to be willing to put it in a keyhole, but these women, apart from being their biological target, have nothing to recommend them. The prostitutes who work the hotels in London can be beautiful and sophisticated. The women on the corner have nothing, not even a room to work from; but men turn up regularly to be serviced behind a bush by them. The men aren't pensioners either, unable to get regular access to young flesh. Most of them are young and, compared to the prostitutes, glamorously good-looking.

It's quite shocking to see that men will put it anywhere, and that the bulge in the trousers is really nothing to do with you.

I acknowledge that it's remarkably easy to mess up your life. One moment of carelessness or even no moment of carelessness and you're stuffed. But I have to say I hate these women for the reason that they are pure evil. One morning I was woken up by the doorbell. A woman explained she was 'from the end house' and that she needed money for electricity so she could warm up a bottle for her baby. I looked at my watch. It was four-thirty in the morning. Now if you ring a doorbell at two in the morning, there's a chance the occupants will be up late. If you ring a doorbell at six in the morning, there's a chance the occupants will be up early. Ring a doorbell at four-thirty and you're going to be inflicting misery on someone.

The women's story was straight crackwhore guff. It's four-thirty, the clients have dried up. You say you're from 'the end house'; thus you're not some feckless passer-by but a neighbour, but not a neighbour likely to be known. You don't want money for yourself, but for your baby. You can't ask anybody in your house, you have to come to me. I was 99.9 per cent sure she was lying, but in fact the end house did have a high turnover of transients and no-hopers and I've seen women with infants go completely insane and do stranger things than ring doorbells at four-thirty in the morning. I wanted to be able to return to a sound sleep. I gave her some money, which she said she would immediately repay. She didn't. I never saw her again, so at least I had the satisfaction of being proved right.

Pure evil is not caring about anything but yourself, even if its effects are sometimes as undramatic as merely ruining someone's sleep.

Hotel

I rejoin Audley who has found a hotel. The hotel is so run-down and deserted it mostly resembles a building site. Audley strides up to reception, which is empty. He helloes loudly. There is no response.

'It looks like a dump,' I say.

'But it's the dump by the airport. I need sleep,' says Audley. He hails some more. I'm beginning to realise having this long-distance contact isn't always necessary. Can I train Audley up to call me only when something important is happening? Audley roams round in his search for staff. The hotel is huge, but empty. Even with the poor picture quality I can see formidable amounts of dust.

A small man emerges from a back room. The Chuukese I am to discover have no interest in height.

'I'd like a room,' says Audley. The man does it very well. He thinks it over. 'Do you have a reservation?' he asks. 'No,' says Audley, obviously too tired for sarcasm. The man consults a ledger. 'I can let you have room number seven. How many nights?'

Audley whips out his plastic to pay. 'If you have any valuables,' says the man, 'I suggest you leave them here in reception. And will you want any diving lessons?'

'No. I don't want diving lessons.'

'Give me your bag, sir. I'll have it taken up to your room.' The man sloths into the back room behind the counter. Audley goes up to room seven and fiddles with the lock.

My phone rings. When I get back, Audley's standing in reception.

'What's going on?'

'I don't know.' Audley shouts quite savagely for service. 'I can't get into my room and the receptionist's having a break. You see, this is the problem with countries like this. They can't be bothered. They do bugger-all and then they're upset because they're neck-high in shit.'

Audley vaults the counter and goes into the back room. There's no one there. There's nothing there.

'I don't believe this,' seethes Audley. 'He's had it away with my stuff. He's fucking turned me over.' Audley has lost his passport, his credit card, his ticket, nearly all of his money and his rucksack. All that he has left are the clothes he's in and my equipment. 'Right,' he says. 'I'll be angry later. I'm going to sleep now.' He takes the dusty key for room eight off the rack and makes his way there.

'Shouldn't you talk to the police?' I suggest.

'Talking to the police would be as much use as talking to the candlestick-makers. Cash injection. Mainline me some money. That's what you should do.' The building is devoid of life. Room number eight still has an eight on the door, but only just. Audley jiggles the lock. He starts swearing softly. My phone rings. By the time I get back to the monitor Audley is yelling and kicking the door.

Watching someone trying to open a door is rather boring, but I felt I should be supportive.

'Audley, getting angry won't help.' As soon as I say this, I know it's a mistake. Audley goes nuclear. There's nothing worse than talking sense to men. I switch off the monitor and go and have something to eat. An hour later, I reopen the line. I see Audley is now struggling with the lock on room thirty. Rotation is achieved, and Audley steps into the room. But not for long. The images are confusing at first but I comprehend that Audley has fallen through the floor. He shakes off bits of plaster and floorboard.

'Welcome to room seven,' he says. 'I knew I shouldn't have come. This is why I don't do foreign. I'm on the next plane out of here if I have to hijack it. Goodnight, dear viewers.' Audley pulls the plug.

What I find significant is that no one seems to have Hope any more. One-off hopes exist. You hope the rain will stop, you hope you get that job, you hope you win the lottery, you hope you get to go out with someone attractive. But belief in the future seems to have no future any more. The perfectibility movement appears to have come to a halt.

I look out my window. The argument is a long way off, but loud enough for me to hear the details. Two Albanians have been haggling with a prostitute for a blow job. She wants the price of two sandwiches to service each of them. The Albanians bid the price of two sandwiches for two. An outraged pimp cuts in: 'Do you think she'll do it for that? What do you think she is?'

'A prostitute,' replies one of the Albanians.

'No, I'm not,' says the prostitute. 'I just get paid for having sex.'

The pimp stabs one of the Albanians in the leg. We're all the same. We all get outraged, just by different things. I phone the police but they don't pick up the phone.

I check in periodically. The next day, Audley is back in the hotel reception, presumably looking for something to steal or eat. I inform him I've booked him into a hotel, paid everything from my end. He sounds in a better mood after some sleep.

A large African waddles in. 'I do not want to be ripped off,' he says waving a finger at Audley who is behind the counter. 'I am an important man. You. You cannot rip me off. I want your best room at the best price. No tricks. You cannot rip me off.'

'I trust we can help you, sir,' says Audley in a smiling voice.

'Don't do it, Audley,' I say. He hears, but he doesn't listen. He gives the African a 70 per cent discount on a room, sells him some diving lessons at 40 per cent discount, arranges a blow job at a 10 per cent discount but leaves him one of his two suitcases.

'Why did you do that? His clothes are too big for you and I don't think his passport will work too well.'

'All he has to do is wait for the daily flight tomorrow,' says Audley trotting down the road with the suitcase. 'Now where's this hotel of yours?'

The road is a conglomeration of potholes. Every now and then a four-wheel drive bounces along, heavily laden with Chuukese.

'What's that on the right?' I ask.

It's a statue. A life-size bronze of a man. I don't know anything about statues but I know a cheap statue when I see one. It's very odd to see it in the middle of nowhere, by the roadside.

'What's up?' says Audley. 'You never seen a statue before?'

We go to a bar. Audley chats to a local, Kangichy. Kangichy offers Audley diving lessons in an American accent. Kangichy went to university in the States. Chuuk is not in good condition according to him. The local government is feeble and corrupt. Investment is fitful. 'Investors from outside get upset because the chief concern here is drinking beer and jollification.'

'Sounds like home,' says Audley.

'Then some of the younger ones like me go abroad to study and those of us who come back get annoyed with the state of things because the chief concern here is drinking beer and jollification.'

Kangichy goes on to explain that the chiefs in Chuuk have their own language.

'Sounds like home,' remarks Audley.

'Ask about Bruno, will you?' I urge.

'The drinking's just started.'

Osk, the barman, is from Birmingham. He talks a lot. Initially you think the chatter is just extended repartee, but after a couple of hours you understand there could be no one in the bar, but the chatter would still be there. Unlike many talkaholics, he's quite amusing, though after three hours in the bar I sense we're nearing the end of the cycle.

Osk was a car salesman. Married with a young kid, money was tight. One night he went out drinking with some friends. He took a taxi down to London, bought a ticket for Concorde, flew to New York and had a three-day bender in a hotel, moderate by the prices of New York, but immoderate compared to the salary of an only moderately successful car salesman in Birmingham. 'I think I could have squared it with the wife; you know, twenty years of washing-up. But then I had to have a burger.'

Osk stopped for a burger on the way to the airport. He was served by a charming waitress, waitressing her way through university. Softened by her charm and her predicament, with the last of his plastic he left a tip three hundred times the cost of the burger. 'Even that would have been fine, but I was shafted by the media.' Waiting for his ignominious return home, at the coach station in London, he saw a report on the news about a generous Brit who had given a waitress in New York an unheard-of tip.

'Even then, I could have been in the clear. Why weren't there any wars? Why weren't people starving somewhere? Where had the floods and earthquakes got to? No, there was universal fucking peace and plenty that one day. So the whole of the news, the whole of the news was about a waterskiing giraffe and me. I could have been a mysterious, gallant figure riding off into the sunset. But no, I was put in the frame. "All I know is his name is Osk, he's a car salesman from Birmingham and that his wife is a very lucky woman," she says.

'Now I have to make the toughest decision of my life. Do I go home or not? Will my celebrity status have escaped the attention of my wife and everyone she knows? Because running up a mountain of debt on an insane, ruinous bender is one thing; every woman expects that from her husband, that's part of the contract. Enriching a waitress with fabulous breasts is different territory; very different territory when only two weeks previously you had a flaming row because your wife bought an expensive loaf of bread and you expressed the view that she was letting the side down on the savings front.

'Many married men say "my wife'll kill me", but this translates as day-to-day suffering. Objects will be thrown at them. They'll be sleeping on the couch. They'll have to buy an expensive coat. Their favourite tie will be shredded. At worst they'll get slapped or bitten. But I knew that if my wife had found out about this, she would kill me.

'She's a woman of principle. That's what I like most about her. That's why I married her. I knew she wouldn't get angry. She'd do the calculations. She'd mull over what she'd get for stabbing a drunken, spendthrift husband in a moment of rage. She'd work out her sister could look after the kid for the five to ten years while she was inside doing some courses. She wouldn't be keen to go to jail, she would prefer not to have to kill me, she'd wish things could be different, but she'd kill me.'

'Come on,' says Audley.

'No. I'm deadly serious. When I asked her to marry me, she refused time and time again. Finally she said, "Osk, I'm not like other women." I was alarmed. Had I been having hot transsexual rumpy-pumpy? Did she have some awful medical complaint? Did she need five men at a time to satisfy her? She says, "I can't bear to be disappointed." "No one likes to be disappointed." "No. Osk, you're not listening to me. Listen carefully to what I'm saying: I can't bear to be disappointed. I can't bear it. I wish I could, but I can't. You can annoy me, but if you disappoint me, I'll kill you. I can't apologise enough, Osk. If you cheat or let me down, please, please make sure I don't find out because if I do, I'll kill you. Literally, in the undertaking sense."'

'So you came here?'

'Not at first. First I went to Barcelona. But it was too close to home. And I knew the longer I got away with it, the harder she would be looking for me. She would be paying off my debt, then saving up to hire detectives and contract killers. That's one of the reasons I married her. She's a very stable, industrious woman; I knew she'd be successful and that I wouldn't. I was looking forward to being looked after. I've never had any pride. She has to be loaded by now. There will be people looking for me.'

'How do you know your wife didn't send me?' asks Audley.

'Do you want some diving lessons?'

'No. Do you know how I could find Bruno?'

'Bruno? Bruno Munday. You don't want to have diving lessons with Bruno.'

'You're right, I don't. Do you know where to find him?'

'No one does,' interrupts Kangichy. 'He moves around. But if you're patient, he'll turn up. When he fires his crew.'

'When he fires his crew?'

'He fires them nearly every week. He's been out here for twenty years; he worked his way through the islands. Hiring the Udotese, Dublonese, Umanese. Folk are pretty relaxed around here, they concentrate on the beer and jollification but even they get bored with being kicked off the ship. Especially when he fires people and throws them overboard. Now he gets crews from the Philippines, Malaysia. Some say he's in league with the airlines.'

'Why does he fire them?'

'There are two schools of thought. There's Bruno's school of thought which is that he is the last of the old-fashioned brimstone-and-hellfire skippers who really know how to run things and that crews nowadays are thieving, ignorant, cheeky idlers. Then there's the crew's school of thought which is that Bruno is an evil, dangerous lunatic who shouldn't be in a charge of an aircraft carrier.'

'Aircraft carrier?'

'Yeah. But it's an old, small one.'

'Anyone agree with Bruno?'

'Only Bruno.'

'Where did he get the money to buy an aircraft carrier?'

'His mother bought it for him.'

I catch sight of Audley in the mirror behind the bar. His hair is so short it's like shading. He'd look better if he let it grow (deep down inside me, there's a hairdresser wanting to get out). Although he's rejected all things military, he could easily be mistaken for a stroppy squaddie. His clothes are always the cheapest and easiest-to-wash items, as if he's expecting to spend the night in a ditch.

'What does he do with an aircraft carrier?' Audley delves.

'Diving holidays. But I wouldn't go to him for diving.'

'Why's that?'

'There are two schools of thought. Bruno's, which is that the tourists who come to him are a bunch of whining, worthless, lily-livered reptiles, and the tourists', which is that Bruno is an evil, dangerous lunatic who shouldn't be in charge of an aircraft carrier. Most captains, for example, like to avoid typhoons, which occur frequently in this region. Bruno likes to steam towards them so his guests can have a real weather experience.'

'How do the guests enjoy the real weather experience?'

'They usually break down and beg for their lives, and offer Bruno large sums of money to be taken to the nearest airport. Why are you interested in Bruno?'

'We have a mutual friend. There aren't any other Brunos you can think of, who don't happen to be evil, dangerous lunatics?'

Osk, Kangichy and the other regulars all shake their heads. 'If he invites you to supper you should go,' insists Kangichy. 'His captain's table is legendary.'

Audley recounts his loss of goods at the hotel. One of the drinkers, a tall Brit, picks up on a detail.

'You say this person was very short.'

'He wasn't tall,' replies Audley.

'And then he vanished?'

'He ran off.'

'Did you actually see him run off?'

'No. It's possible he might have walked very fast.'

'Crispin,' says Osk, 'it's not going to happen. Crispin here is looking for invisible pygmies, despite everyone telling him that there aren't any.'

'Not everyone.'

'They must be hard to find,' says Audley. 'Tiny and invisible.'

'You can laugh all you want,' says Crispin with assurance. 'There are stories.'

'I can believe that.'

Audley announces he'll move on to another bar. Osk says he should be able to get word to Bruno; he and the others then warn Audley to be careful. Here in the centre of Weno, things are okay, they say, but it can be risky in the north and the south. Anything could happen out there. In a bar in the north, they assure Audley it's okay around there, but to be careful in the centre and the south. Anything could happen out there. In the south, they tell him it's okay around there, but personally they wouldn't wander around in the centre or the north of the island.

In the last bar, Audley meets a greying, tubby gay who waxes lyrically about New York in the seventies, how the limits of pleasure were breached. 'They might have tried hard in the past, and they had some of the drugs, but they didn't have the technology.' He tells Audley about the Book which was kept under the counter at one of the clubs. A standing offer of enough money to buy half the club would be awarded to anyone who could come up with a new sexual practice. 'They'd come up full of confidence,' he'd say, the last survivor of the charge into euphoria, 'and the barman would just sigh, and point to the relevant paragraph in the book, and they'd slink off back to Iowa with their food blenders.' A generation that pleasured itself to death generates some admiration, and you can't help speculating as to whether you'd be able to beat the Book. An elderly British couple latch on to Audley.

'We're here for the diving. It's incredibly expensive, but worth it.'

'Isn't it?' says Audley

'Have you done the Fujikawa Maru?'

'Of course.'

'We're thinking of staying another week. But it's so expensive, and we're retired. We have to count the pennies. I used to work for Lambeth Council, and everyone assumes if you did . . . you know . . .'

'No.'

'You know.'

'No.'

'Embezzlement? Back-handers? Corruption?'

'Never heard about that.'

'You must have. Lambeth was notorious for its corruption.'

'No.'

'Lambeth was a laughing-stock. Inefficiency. Lunacy. It was in the papers all the time.'

'I didn't see anything.'

'You must have. How could you miss it?'

'I don't know.'

'Anyway, it's very tiresome when someone hears that you worked for Lambeth and they automatically assume you're a bloated thief enjoying tropical holidays in your retirement while little old ladies are in misery in Lambeth.'

'Must be.'

'It's a relief to find someone who understands that not everyone who worked for Lambeth was crooked or dim. Nothing could be further from the truth. If you want, you could have a threesome with the wife and I?'

'Don't hit him, Audley, and keep an eye on your drink,' I say.

Audley makes his excuses and leaves. The barman is confident he can get a message to Bruno. Some homemade greeting cards are for sale on a rack. Even with the poor picture quality I can see the cards have been on sale for some time. Audley wishes me goodnight by reading one: 'You say you're everything. The world says you're nothing.' He replaces the card on the rack and samples another one: 'Depression: the endlessly fascinating hobby that's easy on your pocket.'

Everyone claims they can get hold of Bruno, but nothing happens. Audley sits on the beach. An elderly Chuukese couple are the only other people around; they are doing the grandparent business with a small boy, whom they are gently introducing to the water.

'Why don't you have some diving lessons?' I say to Audley. Down by the water, somehow the horizon is a little disappointing. It's perfectly tropical, the palm trees are there, the beach is clean, if holed by hermit crabs. But it's vaguely disappointing. It's real, I suppose. And it's harder to imagine being on a tropical beach if you're on a tropical beach.

'I'll give you one good reason: I don't want to,' Audley retorts. 'I'm a bad swimmer.'

'That's surprising considering where you grew up,' I said thinking of the Humber and the sea only a short walk away.

'No. I'm a bad swimmer in that I have a lousy style, but I'm also a bad swimmer in that I don't like swimming much. I had a girlfriend once who'd been a competitive swimmer and she was always going on at me to correct my technique. "You've got to trust the water," she said, and I realised that was it. I didn't trust the water. I didn't trust the water one bit. And I never would. It wasn't fooling me. A swimming pool's nothing but a conspiracy of water, just waiting. The water's just waiting to do you. Even in a bathtub, it wants to do you. It's waiting for you to slip up. It acts all innocent, but it's just waiting to do you. And with cold water . . . cold water's the worst, it doesn't matter how good a swimmer you are, how hard you are, how determined you are, cold water kills you in minutes.

'Then look at this,' he said, indicating the Pacific. 'You should try flying over this. You go *hours* without seeing any land. And when you do it's something the size of a football pitch. There are waves the size of houses. And worst of all, it hides things. You can't see what's under it. The sharks and their nasty chums. No way am I going in.'

'Everyone says the wrecks are wonderful.' Chuuk lagoon was famous for its wrecks. The Japanese had made it one of their major naval bases during the Second World War and had been clobbered by the Americans. It was the attraction that brought divers from all over the world.

'Explain that one to me. If you had a bit of rusting metal on land, it'd either be ignored, complained about or carted away. I'm not much of a fan of rusting ammunition or skeletons. It's the sort of attraction that appeals to people who've never been to war. I know how those sailors were shitting themselves. I never want to see another gun as long as I live. Almost anything can kill you. A pillow. A steak. A peanut. A frying-pan. A bit of string. A bra. But a pillow or bra is designed for other things. A gun only has one purpose; it's a truly ghastly statement.'

'What about the fish?'

'A fish's place is on my plate. Happy to see them there anytime.'

'It's not the same.'

'Is the agoraphobic calling the hydrophobic phobic?'

'I'm not agoraphobic.'

'Then why aren't you here?'

'It's a different phobia. I don't think they have a name for it yet.'

The camera follows Audley's line of vision, so we probably see the breasts at the same time. A topless woman is walking along the beach. The breasts are formidable, but as they come closer you can see they are the formidable breasts of a woman whose time is running out and who's using them while she still can. I recognise the breasts before I recognise her. It's Azra, or someone who looks exactly like her, years on.

She smiles at Audley. I know what that smile means. So does Audley.

'How's the diving?' she asks.

Audley visibles.

'We're in business. I've had a call from Captain Bruno himself.' We're both relieved. Audley's been hanging around for over a week and he's had enough.

However, Audley has to hang around some more at the jetty. He's not a natural waiter. After an hour, a tender bounces into view. It speeds up to the jetty with a lack of concern that suggests to me the driver is not the owner. The driver gets out and addresses Audley, 'Nee-tude?'

'Yeah, I want the Omnitude.'

The driver thumbs in the direction of the horizon. 'That way. I'm not going back.' He walks off in a cheery manner.

'Well?' I ask.

'You think I'm going to mess around in the Pacific on my own in that tin can?'

'All right. We can get out another time.'

Audley is silent. He has a slurp of beer. 'This is cash-injection time.'

'How much?'

'A nifty bonus. I'll go out a way, and if I can see the ship, I'll carry on.'

'An aircraft carrier should be hard to miss.'

'Easy for you to say. How many times have you been up before a firing squad?'

'Why do you keep on saying that?'

'Because I have.'

'I doubt if that'll be a problem here. You might drown or get eaten by sharks, but I'm prepared to guarantee you there are no firing squads.'

'They're not always that obvious. If they were, no one would get shot, because they could see them coming.'

'What do you mean?'

'I don't like to talk about it.'

'If you don't want to talk about it then perhaps you shouldn't talk about it at all.'

'It's probably my fault. My father died dozens of times because of me. I used to pull the old funeral stunt when I was doing shitty jobs on building sites or working as an ejectioneer to get a day off. The bosses half suspected that I was making it up, but they'd go, no, no one would do something as black as that to get off a day's work. Maybe that's why I keep on getting the close calls.'

'How many?'

'Yugo was the first. Then I got asked to go to Las Vegas to pick up some dresses. I was a bit edgy about going, but I thought it's Las Vegas, it's not a war.'

'Dresses?'

'A friend of a friend was having a messy divorce. I was sent to pick up some of her belongings. The most perilous aspect of the job should have been cutting my finger on a sequin. Next thing I know I'm in Cambodia, digging my own grave.'

'How did you stray from Las Vegas to Cambodia?'

'No comment.'

'You had to dig a grave?'

'There were four of us, prisoners. They told us to dig our graves, but they said the one who digs hardest will be spared. We were all thinking, of course he will. How stupid do you think we are?'

'So what did you do?'

'Started digging like fuck.'

'You had no choice really.'

'No, you do. You may not like the things you're choosing between, the options might both be so horrific that you don't feel it counts as a choice, but you always have a choice. Instead of digging, I could have used all the fuck-words in the world and been shot straight away. You always have a choice. Always. It's like when you wake up in the morning and you're unemployed; you can get up, wash, shave and trudge around all day being humiliated by arseholes, or you can have a wank and go back to sleep.'

'It's always better to do something.'

'Not in that case. My brother Kold Hard and I were both out of work once. I got up and trudged around all day eating shit. Kold Hard was snoring away when I left and I said to myself, you lazy bastard, I'll have a job by the end of the day. While I was out eating shit, a gorgeous pouting television producer phoned up and asked Kold Hard to go down to London to be interviewed about being unemployed. He was put up in a flash hotel, did the television producer all night, stole a Ferrari, and was given a well-paid job the next day by a concerned viewer. You always have a choice, but you don't always find out whether you make the right choice.'

'Digging was the right choice?'

'Maybe not. Maybe I should have told them to fuck off, because maybe the gun would have jammed then, instead of later on when we had finished digging the graves, and I'd have had the satisfaction of being the hard man.'

'One gun? That's not a firing squad.'

'There were two of them. Kids. No proper training. In the British army, one of the first lessons you get is that you carry

217

your weapon as if you mean to use it. You don't lean on it while you pick your nose, because in the second it takes you to level your weapon you're finished.'

'Did you kill them?'

'I didn't. But, let me put it this way, they didn't get any older. I've never killed anyone. I had a good opportunity once. I was at home, cleaning my shotgun. There had been a lot of burglaries at the time and I was thinking how funny it would be if someone tried to burgle my place now, when the window is pushed open and this guy climbs in. This is how stupid the guy was: I'm sitting there in clear view with a shotgun and he climbs in. It even takes him a few seconds to spot me once he's in the room. Then he gives me this irritated look, as if I've just climbed into his home. I had the gun there and I thought hard about pulling the trigger, but I didn't. And it was nothing to do with morality or respect for life, or that the police would have ended up charging me, because there's no question we'd have all been better off without him.

'I just realised that I'd be crossing a line, and once that line had been crossed, I couldn't go back. I might have been over the moon afterwards about blowing him away, but if I wasn't, there'd be nothing I could do about it. So I made him strip to his underwear and I handcuffed him to the railings outside. It was January, raining and freezing. He was out there for four hours before I talked to the police. I only wanted to leave him out there for an hour, but you know the police never pick up and they only came round the next day.'

'What about the other firing squads?'

'I didn't want to go abroad ever again after the Las Vegas–Cambodia trip. But I was offered a job walking this girl to school. This woman's daughter kept on playing truant so I was hired to walk her to school, to make sure she got at least that far. That looked like a risk-free job, cash in hand. The girl was only eleven and small. The school was round the corner. How much trouble could that be? I ended up in Somalia.'

'How did you get there?'

'You wouldn't believe me. Compared to how I got to Cambodia, it's straightforward, but you still wouldn't believe me.'

Audley takes the tender out to sea.

To his relief, Audley sees the *Omnitude* almost immediately.

'Did you ever meet any of the crazies from Yugo again?' I ask.

'Yes.'

'Roberto?'

'No. Not Roberto. I'd never want to meet him again.'

'Real John?'

'Yes,' he says in an I-don't-want-to-talk-about-it tone. The *Omnitude* doesn't seem to be getting any larger. 'Fuck. How far away is that thing?' The tender slams along for several minutes before Audley volunteers: 'I spent years imagining what I'd do to Real John if I ever caught up with him. He was the one I really hated, because although he obviously wasn't my mate, I felt he had betrayed me. He could have spoken up for me. Lifted a finger. Something. There were all sorts of things you could say against Roberto, but he was straight, and there are basically two types of people, those who can run towards a machine gun that's shooting at them, and those who can't. As someone who can't, I have some admiration for someone who can. Roberto might have been an evil, dangerous lunatic, but he had bottle and he wasn't a bullshitter. Real John was the bottom-feeder.

'I didn't know how to look for him. His surname was supposedly Smith, but that was certainly a lie. I went to

Liverpool a couple of times, but after an hour of looking at the faces in the street I had a splitting headache. So I said to myself: if he turns up, he turns up and then you can kill him. And I was determined to kill him. I wasn't even angry. It was beyond that. It was more like deciding to have pasta for supper. Just one more decision. I thought a lot about how I'd do it, at first. But I thought less and less about it. It was nine years later I was doing ejectioneering at a big wedding for a local celebrity when I saw Real John, working for the caterer's. He didn't recognise me, I'd changed, and anyway I don't think he made much effort to remember me.'

'What did you do?'

'First of all I went to the toilet and had a good cry. Then I calmed down and made my plans to wait till everything was over and settle the score.'

'You didn't kill him?'

'No. I waited till everything was over and the crockery was being packed away. It was perfect. He was all alone round the back loading up a van. I'd got one of their steak knives. I double-checked no one was around and I walked up and said:

'"Hello, Real John. You don't remember me do you?" He gives me the once-over. "No, sorry, mate." "Yugo," I said. "Does that help?" "No. Yugo was a pain in the arse though, eh?" "It's me, Audley." "Good to see you again, Audley, sorry I didn't remember you."'

'He was putting it on.'

'No. He didn't remember me. If he had, he would have been running for his life. He wasn't a big man, he wasn't a hard man and he didn't have a steak knife.'

'What happened?'

'He took the steak knife off me saying, "Thanks. We're always losing those." I was so angry, I fainted. When I came to he'd gone. I could have tracked him down, but there didn't seem any point.'

The *Omnitude* was getting larger.

220

'Do you believe anything changes?' Audley asks.

'What do you mean?'

'Do you think you can break the pattern?'

'What pattern?'

'The pattern. Nothing changes. I used to do a lot of military history when I thought I'd be getting into the army, so I could impress everyone. You can take the thinnest slice of history and it's all there. You know about the shortest war ever?'

'Can't say I do.'

'It was so short it doesn't even have a name. In 1896, the British mullahed the Zanzibaris. It lasted about forty minutes. Some say it was shorter. Almost everyone agrees when it started. Promptly at nine o'clock, because that was when the ultimatum to the Sheikh expired.'

'What was the ultimatum?'

'Does it matter? Perhaps it only lasted forty minutes because they couldn't hear the Arabs screaming surrender under the bombardment. There are a number of elements in this episode that will be familiar to anyone who's been to war. Blockheadism, with a big bag of chips. The Sheikh and his men knew there was a British fleet offshore, so they all gathered in one place, in his palace in a convenient bullseye sort of way.

'The Arab soothsayers had been going round saying that the gunboats would only fire water. There's always room in a war to wave goodbye to reality. Offyourheadism, with a big bag of chips. I don't think anyone knows what happened to the soothsayers, but I'd have a bet they weren't in the palace.

'Only the palace was flattened. None of the adjacent buildings were touched. When the Sheikh's yacht started firing at the British fleet, their fire was so feeble the British commander ignored them for a while, and it was only as they got the range that he sank it. Morals: pros don't get off on killing, and technology wins.

'As the Sheikh's yacht ate water, they hoisted a Union

Jack. Moral: most fighters in a war don't want to be there and can't surrender fast enough. That's why there are so many famous stories of martial valour in military history, because there are so few.'

Audley clambers aboard. He is greeted by Bruno who doesn't look like an evil, dangerous lunatic, but that I assume has always been one of the problems with evil, dangerous lunatics. He doesn't look like a sea-dog either. He looks more like an irritating choirmaster I knew who persistently announced, every eighteen months, the arrival of the Messiah. He has grey curly hair and wears a terrible pullover.

'Where's Tommo?' he asks with a big grin.

'Who?'

'He went to pick you up.'

'Oh, him. He said he was quitting.'

Bruno turns purple. It looks unreal. It's like watching an exotic lizard in some courtship display. From smile to bile in under two seconds. I've never seen anyone turn truly purple. It's distasteful.

'Find him,' he shouts to a crewman. 'Find him and tell him he's fired. Tell him I fired him yesterday. No, tell him he was never hired.' A Malaysian jumps into the tender with what I would describe – even with the patchy picture quality – as a suspicious amount of enthusiasm.

'Do you have the one tender?' asks Audley.

'No. Four. You can pick whichever one you want for diving.' Bruno's face has suddenly deflated, apart from two small blotches.

'Great.'

'And if you want to play tennis, we have the only tennis court for one thousand miles. And the only bowling alley for two thousand.'

The *Omnitude* is in poor condition. Every five minutes or so into the tour, we glimpse members of the crew hidden in shadow who gaze at Audley plaintively as if they want to be shot. We pass by large numbers of packing cases, which are stacked everywhere.

'This must have been quite an investment,' Audley comments.

'I did some good business.'

'I heard your mother bought it for you.' Audley is not doing the diplomat tonight.

'Let me get you a drink,' says Bruno. He opens a can of coke, pours it and passes it over to Audley.

'Do you have anything else?' asks Audley.

'No. Would you like a packet of crisps?'

'Barbecued ostrich flavour? I've never had these before.'

'They stopped making them four years ago. I've got the last few crates.'

Audley's munching ceases.

'So, Bruno, how did you get into the aircraft carrier business?'

'I used to be a bereavement counsellor. Then I managed to accumulate some worth and hey presto. The great bonus about living in a place like this is that you can go years without leaving.'

'Why would you want to do that?'

'I wanted to see what it would be like to go mad.'

'What was it like?'

'Really unpleasant. A real sevenoaks. Really, really unpleasant.'

'So why did you want to do it?'

'Because I wanted to. I once knew someone who wanted to be publicly executed. Haven't you ever wanted to do something other people would find crazy?'

Audley sips his coke.

'And the other great thing about being out here is that you can do anything you want.'

Audley sips his coke.

'You didn't say thank you for your drink. Mortals should be careful. You know the story of the Forever Man?'

'No.'

'Local story. Big Chief died and went to see The Guy in the Sky. "You're very lucky to have me. I'm the most important person you'll ever have in heaven." "You're right," said The Guy in the Sky. "You are the most important person we will ever have here. We should have all of you. Go and get your body." So The Chief goes back, gets his body and knocks on heaven's door. "Here, I am," he says. "Let me in." "No, no, no," says The Guy in the Sky. "We'll only let you in when we have all of you." "But all of me is here," says The Chief. "No, it isn't. You have to get every hair, every bit of skin, every bit of nail, every bit of spit." "But that'll take for ever," says The Chief. "You'd better get started, hadn't you?" says The Guy in the Sky. So the Forever Man has to scour the earth for his dandruff and that makes him very angry. He still wants to get to heaven though, so he only takes it out on the bad. He tests people, and if they fail, he punishes them, habitually by killing them.'

'Thanks for the drink. What's for supper?' Audley asks.

'Would you like another bag of crisps?'

'Don't you have any fish?'

'Wouldn't touch 'em.'

'Why not?'

'Ciguatoxins. The parasites. Let me tell you about the parasites. And then if the parasites don't get you, the pollution. It's unbelievable. I've written to the government about it. Here, I'll show you the letter.' Bruno vanishes for five minutes. I can't tell whether Audley's relieved about this or not. Bruno returns with a sheaf of letters.

'Yeah, I see,' says Audley, after a cursory glance.

'You can't have read them properly.'

'I got the gist.'

'Read the letters properly,' says Bruno purpling.

Audley picks up the letters and lets a few minutes elapse. We have to keep Bruno on-side.

'Yeah, that's what I call prose,' says Audley. 'In fact it's about a letter that I want to talk to you.'

'Which letter did you think was the best?' asks Bruno.

'Uhh. The first one.'

'Are you sensitive, Audley?'

'No.'

'Let me tell you then that you're very stupid. I was nowhere near getting it right in the first letter.'

'I can see you're right. I wanted to ask you about a letter –'

'Read them properly,' says Bruno, producing a gun.

'Here we go,' says Audley.

Bruno has a lot of letters. Letters of complaint he's written to the airlines about their failure to attract more divers of the right type to Chuuk. Letters of complaint he's written to numerous maritime authorities about the small fishing vessels that keep on crashing into the *Omnitude*. Letters of complaint he's written to crisp manufacturers about them withdrawing some of his favourite flavours from the market. Letters of complaint to world leaders bemoaning the effect their policies have had on tourism in the Pacific. Letters of complaint to the postal authorities of several countries about his letters of complaint certainly going astray because he has had no reply to them.

'You better switch off, the power's going to run out soon,' I say. 'I have every confidence in you, Audley. You should tell him that people know where you are.'

'I'm having such fun here, thanks. And to think in England people are going to bed.'

Audley cuts the juice. I get a number for the police in Chuuk and phone them, but they don't pick up the phone. I feel uneasy about leaving him stranded at the mercy of an armed evil, dangerous lunatic, but there's very little I can do, except offer him a major cash injection. In my defence, I do sleep badly.

Audley visibles.

'Hello?'

I can tell by the tone of voice that the situation has improved. I see Bruno is tied up, and even with the poor quality picture I can make out two black eyes. A member of the crew appears to be pissing on him. He zips up, and is replaced by another who takes aim wistfully.

'What happened?'

'I may not be a hard man compared to my father. Or my brother. Or someone like Roberto. I may not be the hard man I'd like to be, but compared with some people, primary-school teachers, flautists, florists, hairdressers and, say, bereavement counsellors, I'm very hard indeed.'

'How did you disarm him?'

'Praise. I told him his use of commas was genius itself, and that I had to read some more of his letters. We were great mates; many cans of coke and packets of crisps were opened. As soon as Bruno put down the gun, I beat the shit out of him. He may be an evil, dangerous lunatic, but he's not a hard evil, dangerous lunatic. That's the great benefit of a place where you can do anything, or maybe the drawback is that anyone can do anything.'

'So any luck with the letter?'

'Not yet. We have a few thousand more crates of crisps and coke to chuck overboard, so maybe Bruno will be helpful yet.'

'I'm sorry,' Audley says. He speaks directly into the camera and I notice he has acquired a deep tan. 'I couldn't find it. I don't think it was there. You must be ringbarked.'

It's disappointing. What could Walter have put in the letter and why did he leave it with Bruno? With Walter the letter could contain anything from frankincense to a photo of his arse.

'You did your best. No one else could have handled it better.' Audley has earned a laudation. 'I don't understand why Walter entrusted the letter to someone so unreliable.'

'I don't think Bruno knew about it. Mind you, talking with Bruno is like pushing water uphill.'

Audley goes back to the bar, because there isn't much else to do. I stick with him, because I have nothing else to do. Chuuk is that sort of make-your-own-entertainment place. Kangichy asks Audley how he got on with Bruno.

'I was tested, as you say here in Chuuk.'

'What do you mean?'

'The story of the Forever Man?'

'What story?' Kangichy denies ever hearing it.

Osk has been recounting his spree again. There's an Australian who, even with the poor picture quality, scares me. He has that look of extreme self-reliance that comes with insanity. He has spent a lot of time in out-of-the-way places such as the Solomon Islands and PNG. That doesn't surprise me. You wouldn't want to look under his floorboards.

'You have to have your doxies and yes-men sorted out before you become successful. Entourage first,' he's saying. He's not joking. There are, however, no doxies or yes-men in his vicinity.

'Stay away from the Australian,' I say.

The invisible-pygmy hunter is there staring morosely into his beer. He is in a bit of a quandary; obviously he hasn't been bagging any invisible pygmies and he wants to go home, but he doesn't want to. At the moment he is an explorer, even if he is considered an idiot by some of his intimates back home; but when he returns he will be officially joining the risible. It's getting immemorable and I am about to switch off, when the Australian suggests everyone tell the story of the worst thing they've ever done. I sense that he's done this before, but of course I want to hear what's coming. I soon change my mind after a couple of abyssal exploits and switch off to go and make a cup of tea.

I switch back on later. There is a Frenchman, who I could have sworn was Vlan. Less hair, more fat, same indefatigable, largely immemorable gassing. He matches Osk's tale of uncurbed spending.

'A homeless guy I was conversating with told me this story. One day he's doorwaying away, with only his urine for company, when a car pulls up and a man throws him a thick envelope. "For you," he says and drives off. The guy is suspicious of the envelope because the homeless are not very popular, and opens it very carefully, expecting it to be dog's business. But no, the envelope contains an astonishing amount of money. It's a year's wages for a manual worker. He could get himself new clothes, a room and food for a year. So what does he do? On a Friday afternoon he takes himself to the most expensive hotel and attacks the minibar. By the time he regains his doorway on the Monday morning, he has shattered room service and two blonde Latvian relief consultants. Now my question is this: was this a *chef-d'oeuvre* of the school of fucking-up, or a well-seized *carpe diem*?'

Opinion was canvassed, and generally the assumption was the doorway jockey had gone too far and should have fifty-fiftied the money between indulgence and prudence. Audley dismissed him as a tosser and the pygmy-hunter insisted it was his right to spend the money as he pleased.

But of course the Frenchman wasn't really interested in anyone else's opinion.

'No, you are all wrong. The answer is we don't know.'

'Wait a minute,' says Audley turning to the Australian. 'You never told us the worst thing you've ever done.'

I'm not surprised to hear that.

'Okay,' says the Australian, 'until tonight the worst thing I've ever done is to get a girl to put a paper bag over her head before I banged her. I don't know about you but attractive women don't do much for me. I prefer real dogs. I have to be in a situation where I'm saying to myself, "Shit, you're not going to bed with that are you?" to really get going. So I was with this total walrus, and she was gagging for it, and so am I, but I wanted to check out how desperate she was so I told her I'd only do the deed if she slipped a paper bag over her head.'

He's lying, he's done far worse things.

'And what about tonight?'

He pulls a gun from his waistband and sticks it in Audley's mouth. 'The worst thing I've ever done is to shoot someone called Audley.'

He waits a second and then pulls the gun out, replaces it and laughs solitarily. I wait for Audley to hit him.

Audley leaves as the Australian shouts, 'Can't you take a joke?'

Audley stumbles out into the night. The picture quality at night is surprisingly good, considering how poor it often is during the day.

'Are you okay?'

'Yes,' he says unconvincingly. There isn't anything I can do, but I'm bound to stay with him.

As Audley makes his way back to the hotel, I glimpse the statue again. Mostly to make conversation I remark:

'Can you see who that statue is supposed to be?'

'Too dark,' he says.

'Never mind,' I say. 'You've done a good day's work. I'll leave you.'

'Yes,' he says. 'I got it right today. It's been a long time since I hit anyone. Last time, I got it badly wrong.'

'What happened?'

'I was in a pub feeling sorry for myself. I was unemployed,

lonely, and I was thinking, about the beautiful girl at school I hadn't asked out. Every school has that absurdly beautiful girl. I spent years trying to ask her out, then one day, she walked home the same way as me. We were alone, all I had to do was ask. So I asked. Or I wanted to. My mouth opened, it stayed open, but there was no voice. I had another go. My mouth opened but nothing came out. I didn't feel nervous, and we chatted away, but my voice vanished when I tried to ask her out. So nothing came of it.

'I was feeling very sorry for myself, and I see this wimp at the bar, some banker in a flash suit, laughing with two girls, and he's looking at me. He keeps on looking at me, obviously thinking, behold the sad loser with his half-pint. I give him the hard stare and he dodges eye-contact. I'm getting angry thinking about the flash shit in the suit with the girls. I get up to go because I won't be enjoying myself, when I see he's looking at me again. And I'm embarrassed to admit I actually said to him, "What are you looking at?" that brilliantly witty line, before filling him in. I gave him a hell of a thumping.'

'A definite overreaction.'

'Especially when he gurgled through the blood, "Audley, is that you?" It was the beautiful girl's younger brother. He was unemployed, he'd borrowed the suit for a job interview, and the two girls were buying him drinks to cheer him up because he'd been dumped by his girlfriend. He'd been looking at me because he thought he recognised me, but wasn't sure. Apparently the beautiful girl had been asking about me only the day before.'

'You'd probably blown your welcome.'

'Not at all. That was the worst part. He was so good-natured about it. "Audley, it could have happened to anyone." His face was one huge clot and the suit was ruined. But I got a supper date with the beautiful girl. "Don't worry, Audley, I'll tell her I was mugged and you saved me," he said. The really bad news was that she was emigrating the next day to Australia. But I thought, one night can be a long way to enough. I'd dreamed about her for years, and the prospect of getting access for one night was quite some consolation for emigration. And you know what it means when a woman invites you around to her place for supper.'

'You don't have to worry about getting home.'

'Yes. But I should have twigged the evening wasn't going to work out when I saw the police helicopters.'

'Police helicopters?'

'I was walking to her place and these police helicopters were buzzing around. It seemed weird because she lived near Sunk Island and it's not an area where you see police cars, let alone helicopters. As I got closer, I could see the helicopters were hovering almost directly above her house. There was a roadblock, and the police told me to piss off because some armed robbers had been cornered. "Of course, officer," I said, before cutting through the fields. I didn't give a toss about any robbers. I didn't give a toss until, when I was a hundred yards from her front door, someone stuck a gun in my mouth, and hustled me into a house.'

'I see what you're saying about pattern.'

'Right. So there I was all night with three armed robbers who had buggered up a raid on a Chinese restaurant. Now, I don't know how it is for women, I don't know whether they can get as focused on a particular part of anatomy but I had spent years, years thinking about this puss. I was so elongated I could hardly walk. It was the toughest night of my life, with the exception of Yugo.'

'Did they surrender to the police?'

'No. They surrendered to me. When it was too late to be of any use, the next day. I was keeping them talking, trying to be matey. I mentioned that the Chinese restaurant they robbed was the reason my brother got his name.'

'Scargill?'

'Not Scargill. Kold Hard. My father had been in the restaurant talking to the manager about auspiciousness and that, just before he was born. We never had any money so my father named him Kold Hard Kash.'

'Did it work?'

'Two-thirds. The truth about men is that money, fame, admiration, stuff like that can be very important. If you have more money than me, if you've discovered a cure for a terrible illness, if millions of women want to sleep with you, if you speak five languages fluently, I might be slightly or even very envious, but that's not what it's really about. Can you beat the shit out of me? That's what it's about. In the heart of most men is the desire to walk into a pub and for everyone to be terrified. Not admiration. Not respect. Terror. That's how Kold Hard Kash is, he walks into a pub, drinkers jump out of the window to get away.

'So I mention to these three muppets that my brother is called Kold Hard Kash. They shit themselves. They apologise in triplicate for twenty minutes straight. They give me the money they've stolen. "Would you like to kick us in the head?" they say. "Please give us a couple of kicks in the head," or "If you want to kneecap us, that'd be fine."'

'What does your brother do to people?'

'Not much. That's what's interesting. He doesn't have to do much. He simply terrifies. I have to be honest, for a long time I wanted to be hard like that, to empty pubs. But I wouldn't want to be Kold Hard.'

The next morning I don't expect to hear from Audley as he's off to the airport. But he visibles.

'I had a look at the statue for you.'

'And?'

'The inscription's sort of rotted away, but I could make out part of a name. Rotger something or other.'

SUNK ISLAND

T HE LAST letter arrived two days after Audley got back.

Dear Oceane,

How was it?

This is a copy of the letter that was waiting for you in Chuuk. It's a wacky place and even if it weren't, as you may or may not know, Bruno is even wackier. The wackiness or his crew might well have got to him before you. So I took out some insurance.

I'd like to think the voyage did you some good. Don't let Bruno see this. Bruno is the most incredible arsehole, but there is a use, I think I've discovered, for arseholes. They can introduce you to interesting people. That's what they are there for. You remember Rutger introduced us?

My guess is you'll need to be shaken up. Were you? Scheming is a slog. Ten years is such a long time to think about. So much can happen in ten years, but also nothing. Looking forward ten years seems an almost unimaginable time, it's almost frightening to think of what could happen in ten years. Allegedly time speeds up as you get older. Could be a breath for you.

You're not going to take this as too vexing, are you? Unfortunately, I can only be me.

Possibly, you'll find this all vexing. Sorry, if you do. There's always the risk when you buy a present for someone that they won't like it. Sorry, if you didn't like it, but I spent a lot of time cooking it up. A tiny typhoon for your tum. Doesn't motive count for something? No? Tell your kids you knew an amusing idiot who liked to play games.

The worst part is looking at those who will live: the collectors of matchboxes, the plankton who never say thank you when you hold a door open for them, drivers who can't park, the insurance employees, the lawyers, the junkies in glowing health. Wherever he is, Rutger will live to be a hundred and five.

It's hard, isn't it, to stop believing that you're better than anyone else? And it's also hard to swallow that you have no power. Wherever power comes from, it doesn't come from us. You know how when you're ill, one minute you are, then ten minutes later you're not, you're better and you spring out of bed. One day you don't get better.

The fear is bad to deal with. The days aren't too bad, your mind can beat it back. Reason and light have strength. At night I wish I didn't have to sleep, because that's when the fear rises up. It's a great, horrific burp from inside. You can do a deal with your mind, but not your heart. I'm so scared, but I'll love you as long as I can. Go for the happiness.

PS Pure evil is Xavier. Xavier Quintero.

Goodbye.

Walter.

Xavier? Who was Xavier? I don't remember any Xavier. I mull it over and start working my way through the cast list, I can't even come up with some nameless faces. I knew most of the bunch at Babylon pretty well, but there was a lot of to and fro, those who worked front of house, the barmen. Maybe it's my faulty memory, but I have no idea who he is.

What happened in Barcelona? Who did what? What did who? You never know, finally. About this world, you never know. Emotions, or the good ones at least, are the only knowledge; probably the only knowledge worth having.

A detective was sitting down at his desk in a South London police station, when a car ploughed through the wall behind him, almost crushing him. The driver of the car, on examination, was dead. It wasn't the crash that had killed him but loss of blood from a bullet wound to the upper leg. It was assumed the driver had been seeking medical assistance when he had lost consciousness and control of the car. The case would have drawn a lot of attention anyway, but because the driver was a well-known local criminal called Totally Innocent, it was ramped up even more. Totally Innocent had changed his name by deed poll, so that in court appearances he could have the amusement of hearing 'Totally Innocent, you are charged with . . .' He swore it tilted the juries in his favour.

The police, along with everyone else, were gleeful over his demise. But, unhappily, since this wasn't a little old lady getting one on the noggin in a mugging but a much-televised fatality of a raping, gun-toting scumbag, they had to do something. The theories proliferated. Turf wars. Contract killings. The police made a series of public appeals for information. The Russians, the Jamaicans, the Colombians, the Albanians and other fashionable luminaries of crime, numerous ex-girlfriends and the police themselves were accused of shooting Totally Innocent. Several other shootings were deemed a by-product of Totally's withdrawal from the scene.

The embarrassment of the authorities grew daily. Journalists crusaded and barracked. A year later, the police received a video taken by a concert pianist the day he started off on a year-long world tour. He had just bought a camera and was casually pointing it down the street to give it a test. He caught a figure getting out of a car fiddling with something and putting it down the back of his trousers. A muffled bang. It was Totally Innocent, shooting himself in the rear with his own gun. The pianist thought nothing of it since people were always getting shot in Brixton. Away on tour, he was surprised to discover the fuss on his return.

The disappointment at the miscarriage of speculation was general.

Everyone was looking in the wrong direction. The one suspect who wasn't taken into consideration was the culprit. If the answer hadn't handed itself in, no one would have detected it.

Now I have an unsolicited answer, or what looks like an answer and I don't know what to do with it. Did Walter save me from something or was he just flexing his speculation muscle?

I'm glad Walter wrote. There have been very few people who've made me feel good. Not just the obvious benefits of one-ification, the pleasures that couldn't wait to happen. I liked his snoring. He had a gentle snore like the sound of a distant train. I've always found distant trains reassuring. I liked buying his favourite foods. I liked hearing him moving around the bathroom. I liked hearing him approaching, he had a special rhythm in his walk. A prospect of same boxed bones.

Audley's the man to talk to about the answer.

Later, I call Audley. I tell him to set up the gear.

'Why not use the phone?'

'I wanted to see how you are.'

Audley has picked up some colour, but he looks wasted. He has an extraordinarily wiry body. So many fingers have gone down so many throats in the dance world for such steeliness.

'Rough flight?'

'That and the habit everyone has of pulling guns on me or trying to shoot me. It's as if I'm getting what I wanted even though I no longer want it. It's as if I took out a subscription to a magazine and now it's impossible to cancel it.'

'I got the last letter.'

'How?'

'Walter sent me a copy.'

'Why didn't he do that in the first place? So what did he say?'

'It's personal stuff.'

'You send me around the world, you mad cow, and you won't even tell me what he said?'

'It's personal, but it was worth it. You know how grateful I am.'

I am. If I hadn't sent Audley, somehow I don't believe the letter would have turned up. The search had to be made. The payment given. But delivery isn't always how you'd expect it. You might say I should have done it myself, but ironically getting someone to do something for you is often more work than doing it yourself.

The doorbell rings. 'Don't go away,' says Audley. He walks out and then slowly walks in backwards, with a gun stuck in his mouth. The gun is held by a short, chubby, baby-faced man. Audley is even more terrified than anyone should be with gun in his mouth.

'Well?' asks Audley's visitor. He has an odd accent.

A low whining sound emerges from Audley.

'Well?' he asks again. I pick up the phone and call the police. They don't answer.

Audley is still whining. The gun is removed.

'I was optimistic you'd know. But you don't. So Audley, my old comrade-in-arms, how are you?' It must be Roberto, I guess; gun or no gun, he terrifies Audley to the bone. Audley is panting harrowingly.

'Audley, you are a deteriorator of merry-making. Where do oyster-breeders meet?'

It's not an everyday question. Audley is having trouble understanding English. 'Audley, sometimes it's fun to be nice to people before you're nasty to them. Sometimes it's fun to be nasty before you're nice to them. Now where do oyster-breeders meet?'

Audley shrugs his shoulders.

'Where do blood-splatter analysts meet?'

'At a blood bank?'

'That's not the answer I'm looking for. How about hairdressers? The answer's the same for all of them.'

Audley doesn't come up with anything. He's wiped. I certainly can't see any connection between oyster-breeders, blood-splatter analysts or hairdressers.

'They all meet at conferences. Every profession has its conference, where they exchange ideas and network. For killers, the conferences are called wars. The war in Croatia was one huge job fair.'

'Just shoot me.'

'Why would I shoot you, Audley? You make me laugh. The years have not been kind to me since Croatia. Shall I tell you what sort of jobs I was offered? You get a call from a foreign country, suggesting you meet at a hotel. Someone says: we hear you solve problems. We'd like you to travel to our country where you can breathe in seven types of hepatitis and solve our problem with so-and-so. So-and-so lives in a fortified compound with enough technology for a moon shoot and a private army. And if anything goes wrong, his private army doesn't kill you, you'll be treated to a hundred years in a jail, a jail regularly voted into the ten worst jails in the world, that's if you aren't tortured to death by the police. Oh, and by the way, we can't help you in any way, and did we mention we want it to look like an accident? They then offer you an honorarium unable to cover the drinks bill at the hotel.'

'So what did you do? Stick a load of soap into his bathtub so he'd slip?' Audley seems to be moving into the hysterical form of terror.

'Hedgehogs.'

'What's a hedgehog?'

'The small insectivorous quadruped, the one with spines.'

'Hedgehogs? How does that work?'

'Trade secret, Audley.'

'Your employers must have been pleased.'

'Not enough to pay the honorarium.'

'You didn't get your money? That doesn't sound like you.'

'You have this problem when your employers live in fortified compounds, with private armies and all that jazz. They don't pay, and they don't appreciate. Killing people, of course, is easy. The challenge is in killing people and getting away with it. As you know, Audley, the drawback of being close enough to shoot someone is that they are close enough to shoot you. There was a job. In St Petersburg, man with a fortified compound, private army. He never went anywhere without body armour. I sat in a room for ten days, with an almost impossible angle on a doorway a kilometre away; I have half a second to hit him as he scuttles to his mine-proof limo and turn his bodyguards into clowns. You make a shot like that, do you get any credit? No, your patrons either think you're lucky or that it's easy and reassess the honorarium. You don't look well, Audley.'

'Sorry, it's quite a mental event seeing you.'

'Disappointment lurks for us all, Audley. My girlfriend went to the hairdresser one day and I couldn't believe how much money she demanded. I asked if she was buying the hairdresser's rather than having a cut. When she came back I couldn't even see any difference, apart from a good combing. I made the mistake of saying so which put me in the dog-kennel for a week. Here I am, I said to myself, gambling my balls for puny honorariums while this turd-bugler makes a fortune in half an hour. I stick a gun in his mouth and tell him never to charge my girlfriend again. Problem solved? No. It's awful but even violence misfires. The hairdresser vanished, my girlfriend was irascible and found an even more expensive hairdresser. Then there's my neighbour. One morning I look out and see him in an ostentatious car. He's a primary-school teacher. I drive a wreck. There are certain things you look to in life, certain certainties, and being better off than primary-school teachers is one of them. You remember our war?'

'Yes.'

'While you and I were gambling our balls for a zero honorarium, this teacher made money. You know Krt?'

'Drug?'

'You monolingual insularity. It's an island, much favoured by holidaymakers. While we were on the front line, this teacher built a shack, which he then sold for big money. I realised I had made the wrong decisions.'

'Mid-life crisis.'

'To business. Four years ago, I was asked to travel to England to a hotel. I didn't like this. I had come to realise those who live in big countries look down on those from small countries. They think we're stupid and love farm animals. The London mouse has no regard for the mouse from Kiskunmajsa.'

'Who did you have to kill?'

'No one. That's what I liked even less. It was a very strange undertaking. They wanted me to bury someone. I was worried that perhaps my command of the English vernacular had failed me, that I had misunderstood. I expressed surprise. I was unaware that England had a shortage of funeral technicians. The patron wanted to bury a friend in an unofficial way. The job smelled bad.'

'But you took it.'

'The honorariums had not been seen for a while. The patron said he wanted to use me because he wanted someone from abroad who could keep quiet about it. There were plenty of willing hands, but confidentiality was important. I didn't believe a word of it, but . . .' Roberto shrugs his shoulders. 'Here I have to thank you.'

'What for?'

'I had to find some remote, quiet place no one would ever disturb. I remember you telling me about Sunk Island, how it was as you phrased it the capital of fuck-all.'

'I don't remember that.'

'You were too busy sneevelling and begging for your life. It is pronounced sneevelling?'

'Yes.'

'One night I find myself next to a huge trench in the middle of the countryside. Two huge container lorries are driven up. The drivers sent away. The patron and I unload a Rolls-Royce and two Mercedes, all armour-plated. One Mercedes goes in first. This is the most dearest model. The car contains two lightly chilled bodyguards, in expensive suits, wearing sunglasses and armed with the most expensive German weapons. Then the Rolls-Royce goes into the trench. The car contains two more lightly chilled body-guards, the patron's friend and three expensively dressed teenage prostitutes covered in jewellery, all lightly chilled. There are fine whiskies, cigars and unadulterated narcotics all over. Then the last Mercedes, two more bodyguards, goes in last. We disempower the cars and fill the trench with a digger. You grasp what is happening here?'

'You're burying a lot of money.'

'Did you ever visit school, Audley? This is a ritual in imitation of the earliest rituals. The big man dies, he takes his household with him. He takes his wealth with him, but that's not what this is about. Any hairdresser can get trinkets. This is galloping your power. I'm dead and behold what I can do.'

'Why?'

'So that you can imagine in a thousand years you will be dug up and everyone will be impressed. No one wants to be forgotten. Or lonely. How do you feel about the future, Audley?'

'Not a great deal.'

'It is interesting. Optimists, I judge, are an endangered species. Being in a burial party like this is also traditionally

243

bad for your health. I was very unhappy when the true nature of the job was clear.'

'Doesn't seem to have done you any harm.'

'But it has. I remember that night very clearly. I remember waking up in a hospital six weeks later. I had had a car crash and been in a coma. Now in my profession you find it hard to believe in fatal or near-fatal accidents. Who knows, maybe it was? But someone certainly tried to decease me on my way home. It was the patron, Mr Sleep, after me. Revenge was a tempting preference, but by this junction in time, I wanted to go home. My girlfriend was rancorous about a leak in the roof.'

'Tell me about it.'

'Now imagine my surprise a few weeks ago when I get a call from Mr Sleep. "Hello, you may remember me, I nearly had you killed." Mr Sleep has a problem. He has no money. He used to live in Folkestone. Can you guess what he did?'

'Smuggling?'

'Correct. He was very poor as a child. He was so poor that when he was arrested the police used to collect money to buy him clothes. But he grew up to run the docks. Not just drugs, weapons, migrants. Everything. He made so much money in the end, he retired. He had more money than he could ever spend. So he retired along with his partner, equally overrich. When his friend died, he did him this bizarre burial favour. It meant nothing to him, because he had an extremity of riches that only a very successful criminal or banker could achieve. Mr Sleep owned two or three streets in Central London; but he has a problem. Can you guess what it is, Audley?'

'Gambling? Women? Stupidity?'

'No. Singing.'

'A karaoke kit doesn't cost much. Or did he build the world's biggest bathroom to sing in?'

'It starts with karaoke and it terminates with an American tour with seventy musicians. Mr Sleep wanted to be a singer.

He hired the best studio, the best musicians, the best producer. The result: total feculence.'

'Sorry?'

'You should use your own language occasionally, Audley. So Mr Sleep hires another studio, another set of musicians, a voice trainer and so on. The session musicians of London never had it so good. He's spent a lot of money by this stage, but we're only talking a quarter of a street. No record company would touch him.'

'Why didn't he buy his own record company?'

'Because he wanted to be celebrated for his talent.'

'Was he?'

'No. He had a complete absence of talent. Tone deaf. No musical formation. He couldn't sing or dance and he was fat and bald, qualities which might be of assistance in comedy, but only there. Unfortunately for Mr Sleep he was a determined man, as you would expect in a rages-to-riches biography. That everything was against him, that didn't worry him. He was convinced that the public would respond to his brand of singing, if only given the chance. He toured Britain first. You don't remember the tour?'

'No.'

'No one does. Apart from Mr Sleep, his many musicians and many roadcrew. They played over twenty venues without selling a single ticket, apart from three Dutch tourists who were under the misapprehension they were getting into a gay club. Sleep and his encampment stayed in the best hotels because Sleep didn't want to look like a cheapskate when he was interviewed by journalists.'

'Who interviewed him?'

'No one. After this tour, with all the sundries, he was down another quarter of a street. Mr Sleep had a long, long think about his singing career. He realised where he was going wrong. He wasn't working hard enough. Better musicians. More musicians. More publicists. More advertising. More lighting. This was the glorious American tour, the highlight of which was fifteen listeners in a thirty-thousand-seat stadium, who were only there as a result of a misbooking. A whole street departs. Mr Sleep then had a heart attack, a heart transplant and a divorce. By the time the doctors and lawyers had feasted on him, he was living in a small flat in an unfashionable part of London. Mr Sleep is confined to a wheelchair and, one day, a teenager pushes him out of it and walks off with the wheelchair. Mr Sleep abuses the thief who returns and pisses on him. Mr Sleep realises he has not only lost his money. What was his mistake, Audley?'

'Spending his money?'

'No, he should have thrown a war. Then everyone would have come. Would you say he was wrong to spend his money?'

'Looks like it.'

'If you are not willing to risk everything for what you want, do you deserve to have it?'

'Why are you here, Roberto?'

'Be patient. Mr Sleep meditates on something I didn't know about the burial. Apart from the finery I saw displayed, there was a small fortune in gold in the boots of the cars. Not enough to buy a street in London, but some big houses, enough to sweeten life in a wheelchair. Mr Sleep would like to dig up the cars, but he can't.'

'Why?'

'Because he can't remember where the cars are. I chose the location, I guided everyone there but he didn't pay too much attention because he never thought he'd need the money. He knows roughly where the site is but he can't dig up every field twenty miles from Hull. So he needs me.'

'Cheeky of him to phone you.'

'No, people find it quite natural that they try to kill you and then ask you for a favour.'

'Why are you telling me all this, Roberto? Whatever it is, I don't want in.'

'Buried treasure? You're not interested in buried treasure?'

'No.'

'But it's the best sort of treasure.'

'My guess is Mr Sleep made another mistake telling you about that.'

'No. His mistake was phoning me. Telling me about the gold was quite sensible; it extended his life for another five minutes. I ask you, Audley, in one corner you have a man who perhaps in his youth was a serious stockist of violence, but is now a fat, half-dead was-been with no money and no reputable back-up, who thinks he can make a double-cross; in the other corner you have me. Who would you say will be head-down in a bathtub full of water?'

'I'm not going to dig it up for you, Roberto. I don't dig.'

'I had been counting on you to be helpful, but you're not.'

'Why not get the gold? Why the visit?'

'I know where the gold is, but I can't find it.'

'Oh yes?'

'I had severe head injuries in the car crash. I've lost a lot of memory. I remember burying the cars, but nothing else for weeks before or after. I have an image of the field, but fields are . . . fields. I can't dig up evey field for twenty miles around Hull either. In short, I know it's buried somewhere here, but I can't remember where. I couldn't remember whether I'd asked you for help. I remember I wanted to.'

'I was probably in Cambodia.'

'But if you had known anything about it, it would have shown. I can read you like a thermometer.'

'Aren't you worried that I'll find the treasure?'

'No, Audley. You would never mess me around. Help me find it and there will be an honorarium. A small one, naturally. I'm planning on sticking around. I've always wanted to open a restaurant, and investigate the ontological difference between galuska and nokedli.'

Even with the poor picture quality I can see Audley is floundering. There is a crucial difference between acceptance and capitulation. We never went abroad as a family, but we did have some daytrips to the seaside. I built a sandcastle which was immediately trodden on by a rampaging boy: what has stayed with me is the perception that he didn't do it deliberately, he was jumping around headlessly in a testo frenzy and his foot split my castle. In some ways the accidentality of it and his unawareness made it worse. I built a smaller castle in safety underneath my father's deckchair. Our happiness is destruction's coffee-break. I have given up, but I don't like to see the same look on Audley's face. You may see someone fall, but you rarely see their fight. When you go for a run in the park and you see sweaty runners staggering towards you, gasping and pale, you don't know whether they've been broken by three minutes' effort or three hours'.

Roberto takes a seat and passes the gun over to Audley.

'Shoot me if you want. No? This is how it should be between two old soldiers, chewing over the past. Truthfully I have suffered much chronological unkindness. I was in jail for a while.'

'Genocide? Hairdresser-bashing?'

'No. Preventing someone from stealing my car stereo. It was in Romania. Sometimes, although I come from a small country, I believe it's right to look down on small countries. I got back to my car to find the window smashed and my stereo being stuck into a bag. I said "hey" as an owner should, but the thief ignored me.'

'If someone doesn't know you.'

'I grabbed the bag. He shouts, "Let go of my bag." So I extended my palm into his nose. I was delighted to see the police, but not so delighted when they charged me with assault. Someone witnesses that I attacked the man with the bag, who only had the bag because it had been dropped by another man, the man who had stolen my stereo. I get six months and I never see the stereo again. After it's too late to be of any utility it is reported to me the policeman is the brother-in-law of the thief and the cousin of the witness.'

Audley is required to make coffee for Roberto, who then complains about Audley's coffee-making skills. Roberto hangs around for an hour because, I suspect, he's bored, because he needs to be appreciated, and because leaving involves a decision about where to go. We all have a need for a listener to whom we don't have to explain ourselves.

'I am not vain, but I do appreciate myself,' confides Roberto. 'What do you think, Audley, are losers losers? Or winners-in-waiting?' Audley makes little conversational impact.

'You are really deteriorating our merry-making, Audley. Rejig your aplomb. Man is elastic. He can be pressed down into nothingness or stretched out into prominence, all by destiny. Give me the most whimpering zero and I could transform him into a monster of big-headedness in hours: money, fame, the guestiest parties, porters of gratification all around you, it is inevitable you will believe you are one of the universe's most valuable assets. I will not drip names, but I knew many successes before they were successful, and they were like the unsuccessful. Some would buy me drinks to have someone to talk to. What is the difference between a pavement-warmer and an international phenomenon? Stretching.'

When Roberto leaves, suggesting they could go and see a film tomorrow night, Audley slumps back in his chair, impaled on gloom. He says nothing for a while, then sighs, 'I can't go on.' I've never seen him like this.

'Why not?'

'The pattern. No matter what I do, I can't beat the pattern. I don't even have to leave home any more. It rolls up on the doorstep.'

'You won't do something rash, Audley?'

'Doubt it. I haven't got the guts. What's worse than being suicidal and too cowardly to do it?'

249

'Come on. You've done your firing squads.'

'What do you know?'

'I understand fate.' I ponder for a moment, because obviously I don't; I've got to come up with something good and then a good answer comes to mind. 'But you only have to escape from prison once, no matter how hard it is. I'll help you.'

Audley smiles sardonically.

'I'll see you this evening,' I say.

Audley says nothing. He has fallen into himself.

'I'll see you this evening, okay?' I repeat, Audley nods eventually, and I switch everything off. I should be finishing a project, but it can wait. In anticipation of a lengthy absence, I water the plants.

I dust off a bag and pack a few things into it. If the trains happen to be working today I should be able to get to Sunk Island by the evening. I can fix a proper supper for Audley. You can always fix supper for yourself, but it's not the same as having someone cook for you. Having supper fixed for you is one of the great blows against terribility. It's like flowers; you can always buy them, but they don't smell as fragrant as flowers bought for you.

Outside, I walk down the driveway which feels more like a driveway than any other I've walked down. I pass a tatty car which has a handwritten notice displayed. *This car has been broken into three times already. There is nothing left worth stealing. Please leave it alone.*

At the bus stop, there is a small queue. A woman with cropped hair. I had my hair as short as that most of the time when I was a dancer because it was more serious. She wears a 'We hate hate' T-shirt. A porky teenager talking into a phone, 'I'm not lazy. I'm just choosy about what I do.' A woman with two four-year-old girls in tow. Children that age are usually pleased, as if they know a wonderful secret, and so pleasing. One girl points at me, and whispers into the other's ear. Nastily, they laugh. I check for some embarrassing irregularity in my appearance, but can find none. The whisperer notices my gaze, stops laughing, and beams me a big, imploring, let's-be-friends smile. The switch is instant and astonishing.

My head is stretched by the light, the space and the sounds of the street. No sign of a bus, but I'm unflustered. The teenager complains loudly into his phone: 'This chaos is poorly organised, know what I mean?'

I would never have left to save myself, I can see that. Never. But I'll leave to save Audley. Audley told me how his father had been depressed in his youth and had gone to the Humber Bridge to jump. When he got there he found someone prepping to take the plunge; Audley's father pulled him back, slapped him around and told him not to be so foolish. I understand that now. The battle is always with yourself, but that doesn't preclude having an ally. We all need our spiritual backs to be scrubbed every now and then.

Home can never be a place, only a person.